XYZT

Mt. Lebanon Public Library
16 Castle Shannon Blvd.

Pittsburgh, PA 15228-2252
412-531-1912
www.mtlebanonlibrary.org

07/2019

KRISTEN ALVANSON
XYZT

URBANOMIC

Published in 2019 by

URBANOMIC MEDIA LTD.
THE OLD LEMONADE FACTORY
WINDSOR QUARRY
FALMOUTH TR11 3EX
UNITED KINGDOM

BRITISH LIBRARY CATALOGUING-IN-PUBLICATION DATA

A full catalogue record of this book is available
from the British Library

ISBN 978-1-9164052-3-3

Official soundtrack: Zombi, *The Zombi Anthology*

Printed and bound in the UK by
TJ International, Padstow

Distributed by the MIT Press,
Cambridge, Massachusetts and London, England

K-Pulp: New Adventures in Theory-Fiction

www.urbanomic.com

For Americans and Iranians alike

بتساوی برای ایرانیان و آمریکایی ها

CONTENTS

WITH ITS UNEVEN paneled walls and low-level droning noise, nearly everyone complained of vertigo when sitting in the small niche hidden off the inner circulation system of MIT's Stata Center. The consensus was that the walls, leaning inward toward the ceiling, created the sensation of an overbearing downward pressure which became more apparent the longer you stayed in the space. Students and faculty alike had therefore collectively deemed the niche problematic, and it usually remained empty.

This was Amir and Kade's meeting place of choice. Not because of the uneasiness induced by its ceiling and uneven walls— it wasn't something that could be used as a means to access new lines of thought, like a ley line, a sinkhole or an item in a computer game's inventory list. It simply offered a rare opportunity for privacy in Gehry's too-public building.

'You really want to proceed?' Amir asked. The ethical issue was not really in question anymore; it was a matter of whether the logistics were in place to move on to the next phase.

Kade cradled his chin in his hands as he leaned across the table, his eyes sunken with sleep deprivation. 'We proceed.'

'You know what this means?'

A figure passed outside the niche. Kade waited for the passerby to clear. 'Yes. Do you?'

'It's for the future.' Amir watched the light on the wall slowly wane before his eyes, eclipsing the freshly painted surface. 'The cheapest route was Boston to JFK to Heathrow to Bahrain to Tehran. There's so much layover time between flights.' He glanced down at the stack of books and papers in front of him.

As the minutes ticked away, the ceiling began its descent.

The buzzing intensified. 'I don't know why you're actually flying over there. Why not just...?'

'You know why. This is earlier than we planned. I want to try from Tehran to New York and back one time before we start. Just to make sure.' The Iranian tugged at the hair at the back of his head. Uncut for the last year, it had become a dark mass of twisted chenille, and for the first time in Amir's life he had been getting compliments from women—a welcome novelty for him. Things were different for Kade: people said he was a mirror image of Rob Lowe in his Brat Pack prime, though he always shrugged off the suggestion. But Amir was an introvert—a trait he blamed on an early interest in chess. As a child, he had sat on both sides of the board for years, playing against himself. A combination of this youthful obsession and the lack of a dating scene in Iran had left him with little ability to respond to American girls' forwardness.

'When do you leave?'

Amir glanced at his watch. 'Should head to the airport in twenty minutes.'

Kade closed his copy of Linebarger's *Psychological Warfare* and took a spiral notepad from his messenger bag.

'If there are no delays, I should be in Tehran in time to spend Nowruz with my family on Thursday. Friday evening Tehran time I'll run the final comms trial to New York, if that works for you. I have the coordinates logged.'

'That works.' Kade wrote a string of numbers on his pad. The sound as he ripped off the sheet faintly reverberated somewhere else in Stata. He gave a sidelong glance at Amir. 'Hey, I saw Estella in the lab yesterday.'

'Did you talk to her?' Amir asked, with suppressed excitement.

'No. Sorry I mentioned it, we shouldn't get sidetracked.' Kade had learned what he needed to know: Amir was still into the girl.

Eager for any additional scrap of information on Estella, but suddenly self-conscious, Amir let the subject drop. 'Okay, carry on.'

'If there's no problem on Friday, then we'll make sure everything is in place on Saturday.'

'Yes, and the timing is perfect. Wednesday is Oil Nationalization Day and Thursday is Nowruz. Most of Iran will still be closed Saturday for celebrations, including government offices… safer for us.'

'Sunday is Easter here too. Okay then. I'll send a notification through the master account that Saturday is a go. Do we have enough contacts in place?'

'One Host in each of the fifty states and thirty provinces, plus an extra twenty spread throughout Tehran, Esfahan and Shiraz. That makes fifty in each country,' Amir said.

'What about DC?'

'Irrelevant, don't you think?'

'I guess.'

'And all the details and coordinates are on the server?'

'All there.' Amir moved closer to his friend. 'Let's talk location. I'm going to set up at the underpass near the Bazaar. The place with the gold shops I told you about. A lot of people around there. What about you?'

'Madison Square Garden, as planned. How about supplies?'

'The sensors have been in Iran a couple months now. There are plenty there for me to use. The hardware made it to Tehran through DHL a week ago.' Amir continued with his inventory: 'Laptop, touchpad, satellite phone, recon. GPS, connectors, backup, everything. If they ask at Khomeini, I'll tell them I'm going hiking in Dizin. I have the docs encrypted, but they're on the server too.'

He paused. 'I was talking to Zubair about satellite phones.

He thinks they're listening pretty closely. Remember that.'

'Code words then?'

Amir laughed. 'Ha, wouldn't you like that? No, just be vague...and brief.'

Kade pulled out his Pentel and doodled the word CODE in his notepad, surrounded by radio towers, and then stylized bolts of lightning from each tower.

Amir shifted in his seat and started to unfasten his watch. 'Do you have both of yours?'

Taking his own watch off and pulling a second from his bag, Kade placed both on the table next to Amir's. All four double-faced digital watches were synchronized to the second for EDT and IRST.

'I'll take the supplies for New York with me. I'll be there Friday when you arrive,' said Kade. 'Oh, make sure to buy the headscarves, preferably in black.'

A vision of Estella wearing a black headscarf flashed into Amir's mind as he glanced up. Odd, since he knew she would never wear a veil. He shook his head to get rid of the image. Then he thought of the black box, unsure why he had left it. Some kind of insurance policy? But Kade could be trusted. They had been working on this operation for over a year now. He was just keen to get things moving.

'Amir?'

'Sorry, the ceiling is fucking with me again. Are we forgetting anything?'

'We can do the final prep in New York. The townhouse on Sutton Place.' Kade stood and zipped up his orange Columbia. 'Be careful on your trip. Everything's in place. Don't deviate. All right?'

Amir nodded as he checked to make sure he had all his stuff. At the doorway they shook hands, hesitated, then embraced like soldiers before the battle.

'Will you be out for the Saint Patrick's pub crawl tonight?' Amir asked.

'Too much to do.' Kade had to take care of something before they started, and he had to do it alone.

'Only happens once a year. It would do you some good.'

'I just don't have the time,' Kade said, with all the sincerity he could muster.

Amir smiled at his friend and started to take off down the inner circulation system, but suddenly halted and grabbed Kade by the arm before he could leave. 'I forgot to tell you, we have a time problem. Iran is changing over to daylight savings on Friday. Tehran will be eight and a half hours ahead of New York.'

'Right.' Kade took out his notepad again and flipped back through it. 'The US switched over on March 9. Why the different dates?'

'Iran is Iran. You shouldn't try to figure it out.'

GHAMSAR: ROSE ESSENCE

Suddenly I find myself in another room, a good deal larger. A kitchen, but there are no stoves. A few women and men busy working. Along the wall a series of plastic tanks six feet wide, each placed under a faucet protruding from the wall, from which small drips seep into the containers. One man stirs one of the tanks with a wooden stick as long as he is tall. Scent of Glade Jubilant Rose. The others are standing around a table mixing something in industrial-sized bowls.

'I think I'm lost,' I say.

'Took a wrong turn?' The man stirs faster.

'Yes, sorry to interrupt. Can you tell me the way back to the tea house?'

'Of course. Have a seat.' He points to an empty wooden stool next to the table. 'Can you do us a favor before you go?'

'I can do that.'

'Try our *Faloodeh* before we serve it to the customers?'

'Sure. What is it I'll be trying?'

He tells me it's like a Persian kind of sorbet, but it sounds better than it looks. While they scoop a heap of the white slush into my bowl, he adds that the base is frozen starch noodles. They dose it with rose water from the liter-size bottle sitting on the table. The tanks along the wall are filled with rose essence, which is being extracted from large piles of petals outside. The essence has been fermenting for months, he says.

I taste the sorbet. Cold shock as the freeze drips down my throat. I wait to let the palate respond.

Instead, illumination! I see a Persian miniature like the one my uncle brought back from the Orient years ago...although this is no dusty painting from centuries past. No, this is something more convoluted, bristling and teeming with life. I swallow another spoonful. The miniature fills out in front of me. There is no visual space that is not covered with elaborate patterning, vibrant figures in wild dress, animals, plants. I can no longer call it a miniature: it is life-size. I take another spoonful. Cold churning in my stomach, scene moving before my eyes.

Strangely, the image preserves its flatness as life builds around the core of the main scenes, radiating from the center. Figures in turbans and robes doing all sorts of things I cannot fully grasp. Things happening. The more I eat, the more I see.

In the center, a man in a long-sleeved red smock that covers his whole body. He is wearing knee-high leather boots. I know because he leans back on a pillow and extends his booted leg towards a woman. She is fully clothed and looks away from him while caressing the leather. Meanwhile he looks in the opposite direction, grabbing the arm of another woman and pulling her towards the party. They all lounge beneath a wall painted baby blue with gold ornamental patterns. The boot-caressing woman glances down to a lanky man walking near a bush bursting with rust-colored flowers. On both of his shoulders he carries covered food platters, the curves of the steel domes rubbing against his beard. Above him, a cleric in a flowing umber gown with a turban and ancient white beard reads from a scroll in his hand, gradually unfurling it as he speaks.

Below him to the left, a beautiful pink tent with Arabic lettering scrawled on the side is held up by an orange pole. The flaps open just enough for me to see a man in a brown shirt with a royal blue apron stirring a pot on the ground, smaller than the tanks of rose essence. Two women are with him, one in cherry red, the other in orange. Orange lady is holding a piece of meat on a stick from which she takes dainty bites. Cherry lady cradles a long loaf of bread, singing to it. Outside the tent, rocks line the ground and petite flowers push up from the yellowish dirt.

Nearby a horse drinks from silver water. Another blue horse loiters behind the pink tent with his friend, the camel. A tiny man saddles the camel and mounts it; he wears a green suit with red sleeves, and has a bluish-white beard and pointed hat. Off he goes, seated in a saddle of the same blue as the cook's apron.

As he rides away, the tip of his hat points toward an elderly woman carrying an oversized suitcase made of animal hide with the help of a man who pulls as the old woman pushes. The man becomes lost behind black and white pattern stripes that separate the vignettes before my eyes.

Above this, a bedroom, a seduction scene. She's wearing a silk robe that looks more Chinese than Persian. He gazes up at her in admiration. Another woman's torso—a torso, nothing else—is slatted sideways, hanging between the side of the roof, a red-white-blue patterned rectangle, and the corner of a Persian rug which is guarded by its owner from above.

Further from the center, the stories become less straightforward. Less straightforward! Two women with head coverings share a mysterious round item, passing it back and forth. A man in blue carries firewood on his back, held there with strings. He must have come down from the high rocks, past the orange tree. Two men, each with only one eye, crawl through a cave. A musician tries to sell a silver container with stones embedded on the top to a man with a rearing horse. A mountain rises up in the distance, its snowy white peaks slowly thawing. Below, a girl dressed as a boar collects firewood in the forest. Flying through the scene, a chunky albino demon with horns waves a staff in its hand. A couple of men barter over a bulbous copper vessel big enough to fit a person inside. The buyer wears a small purse embellished with gold embroidery hanging from a chain. A zoned-out figure who looks like some kind of prince stands holding a long pipe that touches the ground—the way he is holding it, at first it looks like a golf club. A glorious indigo blue peacock with a thousand or more eye-spots glimmers in the sun. A yellow scorpion rides on the shoulder of some great brown beast.

Birds hide in trees holding private conferences. A nomadic tent spins through a colorful starry night. A see-through square, next to the long rectangle filled with a navy blue floral pattern, next to a bigger see-through rectangle...all taking up visual space at the edge of the story. Will they be populated some-time in the future? I wait, nothing changes. I start to become overwhelmed by the effort of keeping track of the scene, all the details. Rose ice going to my head. A shifty camel looking east. On the other side, another one, just as shifty, looking west. Two women doing something.

AT HIS SPOT by an escalator in Madison Square Garden—potential Tests would pass on their way to Penn Station, the subway, or the lower-level arcade all day—Kade stood behind the small folding table he'd bought at Staples for the occasion. Brushing aside the temporary embarrassment of looking like an unlicensed street vendor and trying for once to be organized, he had neatly arranged twelve bracelets on the table to his left, and on the right a flat-screen touchpad to log the names and GPS locations of the Hosts and to monitor bracelet charge and activity.

Folded into neat squares, the black headscarves were piled in an open cardboard box beneath the table. Kade had attached an electric blue cord to the messenger bag containing the bracelets and secured it to his left ankle with a bike lock.

Amir glanced along the street running parallel to the north entrance of Tehran's Bazaar. It was a busy road, and the city had installed barriers so that pedestrians couldn't dart out into the traffic—common practice just about everywhere in Iran. Here, pedestrians had to use the underpass to get to the other side of the street, unless they wanted to walk a few blocks out of their way to cross at the traffic light—something few Iranians ever bother to do. Amir scanned the scene. Everything was going to happen simultaneously, and he wanted to get into position ahead of time. Tehrani naps lasted from just after lunch until about 4. By 4:30 most retail workers were heading back to open their shops, and around 5, places started to reopen their doors for business. Like the Mexican siesta, this sleep during the hottest part of the day was also practiced in the winter out of habit.

But over the last few years, as the economy had worsened, naps had become more of a luxury for Tehranis. Amir noted that the bazaar was not as chaotic as usual. Saturdays being regular workdays in Iran, he assumed it was slow this afternoon because of the holidays.

In the dank armpit-smelling underpass, small shops selling gold jewelry lined both sides of the tunnel. Amir would have plenty of time to attach the sensors along the escalator. The devices required descent to function, and Kade and Amir had found that escalators were ideal because they kept the Test in steady descent, as opposed to the choppy motion of walking down a slope or stairs.

The sensors were lined up in zigzag formation, at unequal distances, closer together as they descended. Kade and Amir had committed the correct ratios to memory. Hardly microscopic but small enough to pass unnoticed, the minuscule contraptions were inconspicuous round metal disks with small holes in the center and sticky tape on the back.

Few people were passing through as Amir started to work, but by the time he had finished, most of the stores had opened and foot traffic had picked up. He pulled out the GPS to check the first set of coordinates.

Back on street level, the *Farvardin* sun and wind hit his face. He squinted over at the bazaar entrance on the other side of the road, with the blanket shop to the left, and on the right a spice stand that had been there for years, the round barrels out front always causing congestion at the bazaar's entrance as customers lined up for their black cumin and saffron.

Pulling out an aluminum foil pack, Amir took a couple of Iranian pills, washing them down with the last of his bottled water. He was sure he'd caught his cold in the Bahrain airport.

On the ground he had laid out a woven cloth like those used

by the local street vendors to display their wares, thinking that he might want to sit down when he wasn't dealing with the Tests. Maybe he'd even have a chance to come up with a way to ask out Estella. As he waited for the satellite call to connect, he turned on the touchpad to check it was charged and online.

Kade's voice crackled in his ear, broken up with static and sounding remote, as if the signal had to cross a space greater than the physical distance between the US and Iran.

'Hello, Kade?'

'It's me. Are you in position?' Kade yelled.

'Ready to start, how about you?'

'I'm set up in the area to the right of the escalator near MSG. I've been here for an hour already, what took you so...' His voice faded.

'Kade? Maybe we should hang up. The orbit is worse than I thought. I wish we could have gone with LEO.' Amir waited for his friend's response, but there was only feedback on the line. He enunciated into the bristling static: 'I'm starting.'

CHEROKEE: A RIDE

They tramped briskly along the farm's driveway. For kilometers in every direction, all that could be seen was flat, snow-blanketed farmland, an unwalled icebox. *So these are the farms of America.* Faint whiff of manure. How it permeated up through the crusted layers of white he wasn't sure. It reminded Mohammad of the smell of city gardens at night. *Suddenly dropped into this cold place...escorted around by people I do not know...it is just what he said would happen, but this is...unfathomable.*

Turning to examine the unfamiliar features of his guest, Steve asked, 'Where you from, Mohammad?'

'Originally, Sari, in Mazandaran Province near the Caspian Sea.' Mohammad ran his tongue over his teeth, wishing away the taste of sloppy joe meat.

'My brother's been to Ohio,' the young farmhand replied.

When they got to the towering tractor, Mohammad was hoping that he wouldn't actually have to drive it as his Hosts had suggested. Tractors reminded him of bulldozers, and bulldozers reminded him of the story his uncle had told him of how he had volunteered to help out in the rescue following the Gilan earthquake in 1990. As he was trying to clear the rubble with a bulldozer, something had stuck in the blades—the head of a child, its eyes still blinking.

He had heard them calling the green monster 'John Dear', but now saw it written as *John Deere* in yellow on the flank of the mighty vehicle, which stood almost four meters high. He wasn't sure he could even get his foot onto the step to the cockpit.

'Up we go.' Steve jumped onto the tractor's platform. He wiped his hand on his dirt-covered snowsuit and opened the door. 'You might not get another chance to drive one of these.'

By the time Mohammad had climbed inside, Steve had already started the engine and the heater was blowing out warm air.

He moved over so the Test could take the controls.

'Put her in drive.'

Slowly Mohammad shifted and warily put his foot on the gas. The giant wheels with their deep traction grooves reluctantly turned and the machine lurched forth in the direction of the snowy plain toward which the hand was pointing.

DASHT-E LUT: FIRE GIRL

Hot sensation. Heat on your face. You squint and see dust swirling. The ground goes up, the sky down. Hell as orange as Heaven. Burnt cadmium grains meet waves of shifting dunes. All hot. All iron-oxide orange.

You pull off your jacket and throw it down. You rip open your shirt. Your skin burns more. You try to retrieve your jacket but it has melted into the clumps of rock. Red fingers, red bones. Grasp your shirt to close it again. The heat decreases. The sand grains are now barred from hitting your chest, but they do not stop there. They move toward your head, getting stuck in your nose, your mouth, your eyes.

Visibility is not good. It's best not to look far. As far as you can see, nothing but orange dust. Look down or look low. You try to move your feet and become aware of the soles burning, noisome toasted wheat odor. The heat comes faster. Swift here. All is swift.

Noise of the storm—the roar of an overworked furnace, then hissing gusts of wind. Orange-out. Suffocating sky. Sauna stench one second, campfire smoke the next. All hot. Hued flame. Rippling sand dunes like rows of weather-shifted trim. Your teeth hurt. You hadn't realized there is a place on earth that looks like the craters of Mars. Abiotic. Incalescence, you think it cruel on your already charred body. Crueler still the speed.

You forgot about Iran before you arrived. Fall to the ground. One moment you think, *What kind of person am I?* The next, you have forgotten who you are.

Jinn's blue light pierces through the color with a force that only true complementaries can deploy. Her light is cool blue, but hot to the touch. Jinns are smokeless fire.

A person's body can call a Jinn. You did not know you had called her.

She makes no mistakes, punctures the orange in one straight shot. Jinn appears before you, first as glowing absence defined by orange dust, then visible in quasi-human form.

You ask, 'Where are we?'

'Hottest place on Earth.'

She taps the center of your back, cracking the bones in your body in one smooth motion. Next, she deactivates the constraints of the time and space in which you move.

Blue squaring around you, as if looking out from inside a bottle of Bombay Sapphire. You close your eyes. When they re-open, you are on the back of Jinn. The body before you is solid. You hold tight.

Jinn shoots up like a rocket, kicking up sand mounds and stirring up the air. Elements collide—aggravated, they turn to deeper hues while pluming below you. The heat is still there, digging into your flesh, but the destruction it wreaks is further accelerated.

Jinn's burst of speed creates an arc in the sky, curve of the Gateway Arch. You and Jinn touch down six hundred leinters from where you were, although in your state you are unable to gauge distance. As soon as Jinn hits ground, she springs up again. Over and over Jinn jumps with you clinging to her back. So fast is Jinn that her bounds leave trails of blue afterglow, like a row of arched plates on a dinosaur's back. Jump-curving out of the waves of heat. At each touchdown, the temperature decreases. Trail after trail out of the desert.

Jinn has been jumping for over a jarct but you can't tell exactly how long. Below you can see the plateau—flat, hardened soil full of cracks. Here, Jinn's touchdowns hit the ground harder than they did in the dunes.

Over time, the landscape changes once more, from desert to rolling mountains. Air becomes breathable again. The heat, while still scorching, is bearable.

The speed of the jumps has increased. You close your eyes.

The wind feels cooler, soothing the skin like aloe vera. No longer able to hold on, your arms fall to your sides, yet something keeps you attached to Jinn.

Jinn slows down near Sabalan, and you open your eyes. A valley between the snow-covered mountains. She tells you, without speaking, that when the snow of Sabalan melts, then the end of time is near. Further along, umber-toned formations jut from the ground, winding, gracefully weaving towards the sky, their curved rocky peaks stationary yet in apparent motion. Hundreds upon hundreds of cone-shaped rock structures emerging from the earth, all over the incline of the hill, each rock two or three stories high and, she says, ten leinters wide at the base.

Suddenly it becomes clear to you—the tinge and indentations of the rocks: honeycomb. *Land of the Beehive.*

You soon make out that the rocks are dwellings, with doors and windows carved out of the stone, paths and wooden rafters weaving around. Jinn's landing is precise: a small clearing between two abodes. The larger of the two has smoke coming through its cutout chimney.

A quick, inexplicable motion, and you are lying on the ground. The surface of the path has been cleared, although snow remains at the edges. You are so numb that what must be frigid earth doesn't make you cringe, although you are conscious enough to realize that your body can't withstand any amount of freeze for long—especially after being burned by the desert.

'Brought you to an algid place.' Jinn does not seem winded after the journey.

'I would have died without your help in the desert.'

'True, humans can't survive in Dasht-e Lut, but I have done nothing for you... although I can do, before I leave you with the hive.' Jinn helps you sit up. 'Can tell you what I see, if you like.'

'What are my injuries?'

'Not that kind of seeing. You need to warm up and drink the mineral water, and you will survive.'

She pauses to look up the paths leading to the higher dwellings, then leans down next to your ear. 'What I see...' She surveys the area again. 'You will lose your faith.' After saying it, she shakes your shoulders in rounded motions, and bones crack as your body realigns.

'What do you mean?' It's a lot of work getting the words out.

She stands, takes a deep breath, and blows blue toward the door of the closest house.

What are you? You shiver.

The wooden door and metal window on the second floor shake as if they are being blown out by a hurricane. She nods in your direction, then leaps up so fast you can't make out an afterglow.

Slowly, the door opens.

SHIRAZ: FEAST

Brian entered a seating area with sofas and chairs similar to Victorian furniture—gold-embellished upholstery and wood crafted into graceful curves, everything overly lavish. Nearby, an oversized TV fed the room images from its position on the table. Ornate, highly lacquered oriental panels hung on the walls. Texture upon texture, rugs of varying styles and colors covered the already carpeted floors. Carved screens, wooden elephants with ivory tusks and elaborate glass oil lamps filled the room. A massive copper bowl that sat on the center coffee table had finely carved patterns on its sides and was full of fresh fruits, piled high. Candy dishes on every side table. Food simmering in the kitchen, not far away.

Still dazed, Brian was led over to one of the chairs, his coat and vomit-stained scarf whisked away. Members of the family joined him, and Mrs. Fakhar brought over a silver tray that held tiny silver teacups with clear glasses placed inside, and a sugar bowl. 'Chai?' she asked.

Brian took a teacup and placed it on the closest wooden table. 'Thank you.'

'What do you think about Mister Bush?' they asked first. But Brian had no time to answer. Mr. Fakhar handed him a plate, along with a fork and knife that were barely half the size of normal utensils, then presented him with a tray of fresh fruits. He took a mini banana.

'We are hopeful that your election will go well, as we aren't too crazy about Mister Bush. Who do you hope for, Hillary or Obama?' the Fakhar's daughter Zari asked. Zari pointed to the television. 'We are following it. Our satellite dish has many American channels. Personally, I'm for Hillary, but everyone else is for Obama.' She grinned.

Brian couldn't help but stare. Surprisingly, he was not turned off by the roundness of her face. He rather liked it, for when she grinned it was filled entirely, like the Cheshire Cat's.

As soon as he had finished sipping his chai, Ali Reza, the Fakhars' adult son, rose and picked up a metal bowl full of thin cucumbers. Brian took one apprehensively and added it to his plate. Ali Reza then went around the room again with a tiny metal container. Brian watched the others add a small amount of a white substance to their plates. Mr. Fakhar took his knife and cut the skin off the cucumber, the green shavings falling onto his plate—then dipped it into the white stuff before taking a bite. Next came crust-like pastries, which Zari called baklava, but they didn't look or taste like any baklava he had eaten in the past. It seemed to Brian as though every member of the family was taking turns getting up to bring him food.

Continuing with the political talk, they turned to their own election next year and how they would get rid of Ahmadinejad once and for all. Feeling physically better and less embarrassed that he had been ill upon his arrival (no one had mentioned the episode), Brian found himself more able to focus on the conversation.

'You know, we just celebrated the first day of Nowruz on *Panjshanbeh*, I mean Thursday. Nowruz always begins on the first day of spring,' said Zari.

'That's your New Year's Day, right? How do you celebrate it?' Brian asked.

Zari smiled. 'Nowruz is not just a one-day event for us. Long preparations lead up to it, it begins a month before, and the celebration continues for days after. When the first seeds have sprouted...around this time everyone cleans their house real good. Spotless. Items are purchased for Nowruz: food, new clothes, and we get new coins and bills from the bank.'

'We also prepare the Nowruz table with all sorts of things. Come see, we have it out in the hallway,' said Ali Reza. His pants swished as he walked toward the hall. On the low table a number of items were arranged, including candies, a Quran, a mirror, decorated eggs, some grass and a bowl of water with a goldfish. 'In Shiraz we also include a poetry book from Hafez, see it there? These are all the *Haft Sīn* things, you see? Everything represents good for the new year.'

'Cool.'

'Indeed. Nowruz is rather cool. The tradition is very old. A worship of the sacred order of the sun. Years ago it was even more elaborate. Some say Persepolis was constructed for celebrating the holiday. What do you think of Persepolis?' Ali Reza asked.

Brian shrugged. 'I don't know.'

'It's only the grandest ancient site in the world, dating from 550 to 330BC, how could you not know? Much of the stonework remains today. Some say it was built as a symbol of the empire, for majestic atmosphere,' Ali Reza recounted with nationalistic pride. 'Not far from Shiraz, but there's not enough time to take you.'

'Sight of Spring! Purple. My favorite color!' Zari announced, pointing out the violet-colored eggs. 'I love the grass too. It's prickly to the touch.' She gestured for the American to touch it.

Brian thought it was the same green carpet that juice bars always have—wheatgrass, perhaps. 'What do you do with these?'

'Ah, on the eve of Nowruz, dinner is prepared, and everything is moved to a tablecloth in the living room. We will have it like that tonight. New Year happens each year at a different time depending on the moment of the spring equinox. When it arrives, we celebrate by putting new coins in a dish and making a wish for good luck, then we exchange gifts and call our relatives on our mobiles.'

'We watch the celebrations happening on satellite. Not the traditional one in Mashhad on Iranian television, but broadcasts from Los Angeles,' Zari said. 'In the days following, almost everything is closed, so we go from house to house visiting family and friends.'

Ali Reza looked enthusiastically at his guest. 'What about you?'

Brian wondered how the two could be siblings, for he was tall and thin, as if all the air had been sucked out of his face, while his sister, although not fat by any standard, was so much rounder. 'Ours is celebrated on December 31st. It's pretty simple. Everyone gets drunk on champagne at a party, or they stay home and watch the ball drop in Times Square on TV, counting down the last minutes of the year. If you live in New York, you can go to Times Square and stand outside to watch it. I always thought you'd have to be crazy to do that because you'd have to get there hours before, and it's in the freezing cold of winter. I leave it for the tourists. Midnight hits and you blow horns and kiss the nearest person to you and drink some more.'

'I saw something like that in a movie,' said Zari excitedly.

Ali Reza led the Test back to the living room, where the center tables had been moved aside and replaced with a long plastic tablecloth covering the floor. Mr. and Mrs. Fakhar were carrying heaped platters of food from the kitchen and placing them on the ground. Plates, glasses, forks, spoons and tissue boxes were also dropped onto the plastic.

Brian took a seat, crossing his legs as his Hosts were doing so that he could sit close to the cloth. Then the feast began.

Stell. Concerned we weren't ready but Kade has pushed things forward. Displacement worse than we imagined. In case I don't come back, remember what I entrusted you with.

Delete this.
Sorry A

AND THAT, thought Estella, *makes no sense at all.* No surprise, since much of what Amir said didn't exactly compute. Classic eccentric genius type would be the generous reading. But Kade? She didn't know they were that close. *Confirmed, Kade's pushy and arrogant, but what is Amir talking about?* She dropped the message in the trash and emptied it immediatcly, as if to disappear it more quickly from her brain.

Estella had been watching *Mythbusters* reruns in her studio when this latest specimen of Amir's awkward communication style had come through. The two of them had some overlapping interests and spent a lot of time together in the Computer Science and AI lab. Of course Estella thought Amir was truly brilliant, as did everyone else. But she had soon realized what was going on with the shy Iranian, as he was always 'accidentally' crossing her path outside the lab too. Sure, she counted herself as a fellow geek, but he just wasn't her type. So she had got used to him always being around and tried to be as nice as she could, while controlling carefully for any appearance of a signal on her part. Estella would see the innocent creature daily at her favorite teashop, along the paths that connected the various sites of the institution, or occasionally at Taco Bell—one of her few guilty pleasures. Some days Amir seemed more aware of her schedule than she was herself. But these emails, and now the cryptic references to Kade? It had begun to seem like there was something else at stake, but it was never clear. Either way, the best policy was not to get involved.

ASHEVILLE: OZ

'Awww, Mom, do we have to watch that?' Noah batted his arms in protest, his brother joining in from their usual spot on the family room floor.

'Azita and her mom have requested it, and so you guys are going to watch it,' came the firm reply from the open-plan kitchen. 'What have we discussed about being good hosts?'

'Can't we watch a new movie? No one watches that anymore.'

'Noah, get on Video on Demand and find it. *The Wizard of Oz* is a classic. It was one of my favorite films when I was a little girl.'

'See what I mean? It's ancient.'

'Not funny. Get it ready before the pizza gets here, or I'll send some flying monkeys your way.'

Azita sat silently on the rug near the boys, looking intently at the copy of *American Fairy Tales* she had pulled from the Pottery Barn baskets, a book the boys had discarded long ago.

When Domino's arrived the boys carried the three extra-large boxes into the family room, ceremoniously opened the lids, and passed a paper plate to their visitor. She loaded up a lukewarm slice from the nearest box and sat looking at it while Noah started the movie on the flat screen.

'What's wrong, Azita? Don't like Memphis BBQ Chicken? There's Philly Cheesesteak too, and Honolulu Hawaiian,' Noah's mom said solicitously.

'I think my daughter needs some ketchup,' Azita's mom said.

'Ketchup? What for?'

'For the pizza.'

Noah's mom went to the refrigerator, took out the plastic Heinz bottle and carried it over. 'Here you go, honey.'

The boys and their mom watched as the mysterious girl with the dark eyes squirted a large dollop of ketchup on top of her pizza slice, then bit into it.

'Give me the bottle, I want to try that!' Noah said.
'Cool! Me too!' said his brother.

YAZD: POWER OUT

The first thing to hit him, more disturbing than the scent of burning wood and the coolness of the brisk desert night air that he sensed afterwards, was the total darkness. He noticed indistinct noises some way off in the distance as he allowed his left hand to run along the cool, grainy surface next to him, like rough sandpaper punctuated every so often by what felt like embedded haystalks. Greisen decided he would feel his way along the wall, but he had no idea where he was, or which way might lead to the Soroushes' place. Blood pumping through his veins, still queasy from his unconventional mode of arrival, he proceeded along the path in front of him.

A flash of light ahead. Moments later, another fleeting spark that lit the path for an instant. 'Who's there?' Greisen called out, too fearful to move.

A faint voice responded from the gloom. 'What are you? Another tourist?'

'No. I'm here to visit the Soroushes. Can you tell me where they live?'

For a while, silence. Then, slightly louder, 'Come over here, but make it quick.' The beam of light lurched over again to reveal the path ahead. Greisen edged toward the source. When he came close enough, it tilted up to illuminate both his own face and that of the man who held the flashlight. About the same height as Greisen, the figure was of a scrawnier build, with a short haircut and newly grown beard. For a moment the flashlight made his eyes glow red, before he turned it back on the ground. As Greisen's own eyes readjusted, the waves of nausea swept over him again, and his pulse increased. The stranger was wearing a khaki vest covered with pockets like a fisherman's, and a coil of rope hung from his shoulder.

'Could you direct me to the Soroushes' place?' Greisen repeated in his politest tone.

'I'm not from around here myself,' the stranger answered, in fluent English. 'I don't know the Soroushes. But if you help me, then I can help you.'

'Where are we exactly?'

'From my calculations, on one of the side paths off Fazel Street in the Old City.'

'What old city, exactly?'

'Yazd!'

At least he had arrived in the correct city. Given the situation, Greisen figured he should agree to help. 'What do you need me to do?'

'You see these doors?' The flashlight beam now played over a decrepit wooden double door, its surface broken up by splinters and knots. Garbage had accumulated along the bottom edge where it met the floor.

'Yes,' answered Greisen, who hadn't noticed the doors before the light had hit them.

'I need to get them open, and I've been trying alone.' He switched the light off halfway through the sentence.

'Are you breaking into the place?' Greisen asked, his voice tapering off into the darkness as his apprehension grew.

'No one has lived here for at least half a century, and there is no known living owner. So it's not really breaking in,' the stranger said matter-of-factly.

The darkness was becoming as relentlessly suffocating to Greisen as the noonday sun to a desert traveler—and this guy had a flashlight. 'Are you sure this is the place you want to go in?'

'I'm sure. It's the only entrance along the alleyway, and my map suggests that it faces east.'

'You have a map?

'Yes.'

A map sounded promising. 'Okay, what do we do?'

'We have to bust the doors down.'

Greisen remained silent.

'It's not so bad. If we both use our bodies to push, the doors should give way. Look how old they are.' He turned the flashlight back on and indicated a gap at the bottom of the door where the wood was already splintered and crumbling with age. Setting the rope and backpack down, he moved closer, motioning with the light for Greisen to take up a position alongside him. Obediently, the American placed his hands above the oversized metal handle and below the round metal pegs and leaned in.

'One, two, three...'

After ten minutes of hard work the doors burst open to reveal a gloomy vestibule. With no delay at all the guy was inside, canvassing the walls with his flashlight while Greisen hung back at the refuse line that separated inside from outside.

'I've helped you get it open, now can you help me?'

'That wasn't it,' the guy snapped back. 'I still need your help down in the *qanat*. Get inside so I can close the doors before anyone sees us.'

'I'm not going in there.'

'Suit yourself.' He began to close the doors from the inside.

'Wait,' Greisen said, reluctantly stepping in. 'Why is it pitch black here?'

'Power outage. Haven't you ever been in one?' He closed the doors and rolled two bulky rocks over to hold them in place.

'Yeah, I've been in one. 2003 was the longest, but it was never this dark.'

'Actually, that's because no one is living in this part of the Fazel neighborhood. But many streets in the Old City don't have adequate lighting, even when the power is on. Haven't you heard about the power problems in this country? You never know when the lights are going to go out.'

'Haven't heard,' Greisen said.

'We are going through a bad drought. They say droughts this bad only come once every fifty years, and it's going to get even worse this summer. The city has already set up a system of power rationing. They shut off the power for up to four hours a day to conserve energy when we don't get enough rain for the hydro-electric reservoir.'

'Four hours a day?'

'Sometimes during business hours, so nothing gets done! No one believes that Iran is developing nuclear plants just to improve the energy infrastructure, but now you're here, you can see what it's like.'

'I hadn't thought of it that way,' Greisen admitted.

'No one on the outside does.'

'What's your name? I'm Greisen.'

'Javad. Listen, we need to get down to the *qanat* and find the grate inside it.'

'What's down there?'

'I located this map in the archival library at my school...' Javad paused. 'I've come to check out something important in there.'

'Don't these kinds of things usually involve teams of researchers? And aren't they done during the day?'

Javad shrugged off Greisen's suspicious tone. 'No one else knows. It's just me.' He aimed the flashlight into the corridor, and motioned to Greisen to move ahead. The low ceiling was covered in cobwebs, and streams of termite mud tubes extended down the walls. The short passageway led to an open courtyard with longer sides lined with carved wooden doors and stained glass windows in various stages of decomposition.

When the flashlight scanned the opposite side it revealed an open living room positioned a few feet higher than the court-yard, like a theater stage elevated above an orchestra pit. Thousands of small mirrors were embedded into the walls and ceilings of the room. Once grand, it was now crumbling and largely empty of furniture. Rising up from the flat roof above the twenty-foot-high ceiling there loomed a bulky, rectangular chimney.

As the light scanned the abandoned domestic space, the mirrors divided the beam and transmitted it up into the night in all directions, hundreds of mini-spotlights broadcasting that something was going on down there. Once Javad noticed what was happening, he switched it off and the dark descended once more.

'What is this place?' Greisen asked.

'It's an old Yazd house from the Qajar Era, about 220 years old, built by a wealthy Persian trading family. Yazd was on the Silk Road, you know.'

Greisen fancied himself as something of a spice connoisseur, and he had heard of the Silk Road. 'What happened to the family?'

'From what I've been able to find out, the house changed ownership a hundred years ago when the last of that family died. There is no documentation of what has happened to the new owners, and no records of any ancestors of the Salehi family. They just disappeared.'

For a moment, Greisen thought he may have heard wrong back at Madison Square Garden—maybe it was the Salehi family he was supposed to visit. No, he was sure it was Soroush, because he remembered thinking their name sounded like 'swoosh', which reminded him of Nike.

'We need to get down to the *qanat*,' Javad repeated.

'What is that thing you keep talking about?' Greisen asked,

curious as to what could have brought someone here voluntarily.

'The *qanat*,' Javad enunciated the word deliberately for the foreigner. 'The underground water system.'

'You mean it runs under this house?'

'Well, actually, it is the main water-carrying channel, which originates from the water source outside the city. Once the water makes its way into the city, the *karizes* distribute it to houses. Did you see that structure on the roof above the main salon?' Javad asked.

'You mean the chimney?'

'It's a wind tower with openings in it that pull air in and out. It works together with the *qanats* below ground, which circulate the air through the tower and into the house to cool it. These systems have been around for over a thousand years.'

'How do you know all of this?'

'My grandfather was a *muqanni*. When I was a boy, he would take me down in the *qanat*.' He swept the light across both sides of the grand salon at ground level. 'If there is a wind tower, chances are that a *kariz* is not far off. Let's see if we can find some stairs down.'

The doors to the cellar entrance swung open easily, a sour smell emanating from below as they parted. At the bottom of the steep staircase a trench was cut into the floor from one side of the room to the other.

'This is it. The *kariz*!' Javad cried excitedly. 'You see, the water would normally be flowing through the trench, but it's dry. The sides are still open. No one has patched them up. Good, very good. I can get in there.'

Greisen shook his head. 'You're gonna go through that hole? It's not wide enough.'

'Actually, I've seen smaller channels. That's why my grandfather would take me along on his repair trips. Sometimes he would send me in when he couldn't fit.'

'That's insane.'

'A little. The job is dangerous, I was never to tell anyone I went with him...' Javad grinned as he got down in the trench, the memories evidently starting to flow. 'Actually, this is going to be payback for all the work I did.'

First he pulled two candles from his backpack, lit them and set them in holders on the floor. Then he switched off the flashlight. Next he took out a piece of paper and studied it closely by the glow of the candles. After a minute, he lifted his head toward Greisen. 'Exactly what I see on the map. We are in the right place. I'm going in, I need to get to the grated entrance, about eight meters from here.'

'So you want me to wait here?'

'I will attach myself to the rope. Hold it in case I need help getting back.'

'How long will it take you?'

'Oh, not long, I should think.' Javad picked up the rope and looped it around so that it would unwind as he moved along. He attached the other end to Greisen's waist and quickly tied an intricate knot. Greisen sat on the floor with his feet dangling down into the trench. He was prepared to wait, even though he realized the chances of his spending any time with the Soroush family were rapidly diminishing. Although he was still a little uneasy, this adventure with Javad seemed a more exciting prospect anyhow.

Javad pulled a gas detector from his pocket and took a reading, then put it through a hook on his vest and velcroed it in place. Down on his knees, flashlight on, he set off crawling. A minute or so passed. Greisen leaned over and peered inside. All he could see was a silhouette and faint traces of light. He alternated between sitting upright and crouching in front of the hole, where he tried desperately to get a glimpse of what was happening eight meters down the line.

The rope stopped moving. *Javad must have made it to the grate.* He could make out light flickering below, and the sound of rattling metal echoed back down the channel toward him.

The candles projected patterns onto the walls and polluted the space with a burning crayon smell. Greisen kept looking back over his shoulder, haunted by a distinct impression that someone could sneak down there at any moment and ambush them. Not only that, the ground itself felt strange. It was obviously solid material, yet it felt like there may have been flowing water or empty space beneath the soil. In Manhattan he had once lived in an apartment that was built over the subway. Even though he had never felt the building shake, he had always felt that it was hollow below. This made him nervous, and he eventually moved out. Here he felt ungrounded in the same way.

More vigorous rattling. Javad's voice came echoing back through the narrow conduit: 'I need you to come. Can't get the grate open.'

'I don't want to go in. I don't like confined spaces.'

'Come with the rope. There is no water in here. Gas level is low. I'll light the way for you.'

Greisen positioned himself in front of the hole and reluctantly clambered in, moving along the narrow channel fairly easily despite the claustrophobia.

'That was quick,' Javad said when Greisen reached him at the other end of the passage. 'Check this out.' He showed Greisen what was keeping the grate shut: a rusted oblong lock with a rounded latch and engraved script on it. 'It has a talisman. These spell locks used to be popular. Can't make out much of the writing, but I don't think it is religious.'

'How are you going to get it open?'

'Set of keys in my backpack.'

Greisen held the flashlight in place while, with much effort, Javad maneuvered himself around to locate the keys. A thick wire bent into an uneven circle held the bunch together. They were nothing like the small, flat keys Greisen was accustomed to; these were handmade and predominantly cylindrical. Some of the tips were shaped like empty metal pipes in various thicknesses, others spiraled like screws.

Javad took the first and lined it up with the hole on the right side of the lock. It didn't fit, but he was able to gauge the lock's size, and soon found one that did.

'You're good at this.'

'I have some experience.' Javad smiled as he pulled the grate open.

They gazed into the space beyond, even smaller than the channel they were in but very short, and connecting to a larger room at the other end. Greisen wondered how they could fit through. Yet he had no doubt that the two of them were going further in.

A faint swishing sound drifted up from the tunnel beyond, stopped, and then started again, this time louder.

'What is that?'

'Impossible to know,' Javad said. 'There are things down here that don't correspond with things up there.'

'What kind of things?'

'Like I said, impossible to…' The noise resumed once more. 'Things down here that would put our old Persian bedtime stories to shame. Are you coming, then?'

'Uh, I guess.'

Javad undid the rope from his waist and tied it to the metal loop where the lock had been.

Once through, they surveyed the larger room. Five tunnels,

high enough to stand in, led off in different directions. 'I think we should try this one first,' Javad said, pointing to the tunnel straight ahead. 'What do you think?'

'Okay,' Greisen shrugged his assent, not knowing how he was supposed to know. 'But what are we looking for?'

'You'll see. Judging by the map, we're almost there!'

As Javad hurried forward, the rope abruptly jerked him back and he stumbled. The slack had run out. He untied it and let it drop to the dirt floor, and they proceeded along the remainder of the winding tunnel more swiftly.

'Over there.' Greisen pointed toward a passage that led off the main tunnel just ahead of them, opening out into a larger space. 'The swirling sound. Something's in there.'

Javad turned off the flashlight. 'This is what I'm talking about. Be ready.' A faint amber glow seeped out from the entranceway. Silently, he moved toward the source of the noise, Greisen following behind, unnerved and reluctant.

As they rounded the corner and Greisen's eyes adjusted, he was astonished to find himself in a room piled high with mounds of sparkling gold. A flowing fountain stood at the center, atop which a flaming torch threw its ruddy light onto the mass of coins, which reflected it back at every possible angle.

'This is it. Pre-Islamic coins that have never been recovered.' As Javad cased the room, he walked near to the center and gazed up. 'How peculiar. This is like the vertical shaft of a *qanat*. It must go up two hundred and fifty meters. Unbelievable! But what could it be for? I can't see the top.'

Suddenly, from one of the adjacent passageways the swishing and swirling sound started up again. Before he could react, a bewildered Greisen saw Javad drop to his knees as an eight-foot-tall animal with markings—black fleur-de-lis brandings—all over its short albino skin-fur swaggered into the room. Greisen's hair stood on end. The creature's head was the thickness and shape of a bull's, with small horns, yet it had a catlike nose, whiskers and mouth. Its oversized eyes, with obsidian-black pupils, spat out blazing streams of fire. Solid and muscular, the thing stood on two legs like a man. In its hand—halfway between human hand and feline paw—it bore a golden staff, the top an elaborate sphere of twisted bone carvings, the handle bejeweled with emeralds, rubies, sapphires and white stones, the bottom tapering into a long, disconcerting point.

Greisen fainted to the floor, but awoke almost immediately to the creature's contemptuous gaze.

Javad, still kneeling, turned to him. 'It's a deav!'

'A what?'

'A demon!'

'The brandings?' Greisen asked as he got up.

'They are his, his livid patches, his camouflage uniform,' Javad said, trying to steady the American as they both returned to their feet.

The pale deav moved closer and let out a cry-roar that shook the ground, the most horrifying sound Greisen had ever heard. The shriek continued as the deav leapt into the air, streaming past the torch in the center of the room and shooting up into the endless shaft.

As the thing disappeared, Javad screamed out, 'He's flying.'

'What do we do?'

But before anything more could be said, the deav descended back into the room and took his place in front of them. He held steady for a moment, then boomed, 'What do you want?'

Neither Javad nor Greisen opened their mouths. They stood frozen, unable to do or say anything, not even realizing that the demon was speaking both English and Farsi at the same time.

'What do you want here?' repeated the deav.

Javad was first to build up enough courage to speak. 'We came for the treasure.'

'You want my fortune?' The flames around the deav's eyes brightened with sparks of white fire.

'We didn't know it was yours,' said Greisen, thinking he could reason with the creature.

'It is,' snorted the towering fiend.

'Very sorry. We will leave and not bother you again.' Javad grabbed Greisen by the arm and started to pull him toward the exit.

'Not so fast,' replied the deav. 'Look around. You can see I have more treasure than I need. Take as much as you can carry. But there will be consequences.'

They glanced at each other and then back at the deav. Javad eyed the demon dubiously. 'What kind of consequences?'

'Well, they wouldn't be consequences if you knew what they were ahead of time, would they?' The deav crossed his massive arms and fell silent.

Greisen wasn't sure this statement made any sense at all.

'Bad consequences?' Javad tilted his head toward the deav.

'Don't waste my time, human. Decide now,' the deav roared, his body momentarily propelled up into the air only to drop back down, the gigantic feet smacking onto the ground ungracefully.

'Let's do it,' whispered Javad to his cohort. 'Each one of those coins is worth maybe a million dollars.'

'A million dollars?' repeated Greisen incredulously.

'They're very old, and very rare.'

'But what about the consequences?'

The deav paced up and down, obviously growing impatient.

'The consequences won't be that bad, I shouldn't think,' said Javad.

'I don't know.'

'Around here, if you find something, you take it.'

'But what about him?' Greisen asked, with a sidelong glance at the deav, who was glaring at them disdainfully.

Javad said in a whisper, 'It may not even be his!'

'I don't know...I guess.'

The deav's ears were good. He had heard enough, and without their needing to give him the answer, he gestured toward the gold, tapping his foot impatiently. 'Take what you can, then.'

Javad emptied out his backpack and started to fill the bag with gold from the nearest pile as if his life depended on it.

'What are you waiting for? Grab as much as you can.'

Greisen reluctantly shuffled over to another pile and, in turn, began filling his pants and jacket pockets. When the two had as much as they could carry, including some coins stuffed into their socks and underwear, their eyes found the deav, who was standing in front of a mirror on the other side of the room, patting down his skin-fur and adjusting the gold and emerald collar he had placed around his neck.

The creature turned toward them. 'Are you finished?'

'Yes. Can we go now?' asked Greisen awkwardly.

'Wait just a minute. The consequence.' There was a long pause, the two of them shuffling about before the deav like schoolchildren waiting to be disciplined. The deav let them wait for a few moments before announcing: 'You shall never see again, so that you will never come here again.'

Javad's mouth fell open. Greisen's body shook uncontrollably.

'Please don't blind us,' begged Javad. 'We won't come back. He doesn't even live in Iran, and I will move to, to...Beirut!'

'Too late. I will take both of your eyes.' The deav raised his staff and pointed it at them.

'Oh, please no,' Greisen cried. 'Not our eyes! How will we get out of this maze? We'll be forced to stay with you here forever.'

The deav thought for a moment. He didn't want them hanging around, but he did want their eyes. 'I will take one eye from each of you. Together you will have two, enough to make your way out.'

Ignoring the screams, this time the deav did not delay, but lifted his great staff aloft, took the sharp tip and spiked Javad's right eye, twisting the eyeball out and greedily sliding it off the pointed tip. Then he turned to Greisen and jabbed his left eye with the point of the staff. Pleased at their screams of agony, the deav took out a cobalt box from the satchel around his waist and placed the eyes neatly inside. He squinted at the bloodied heads before him; he could not make out the surface of their faces. Standing there side by side, to the deav, whose hearing was far better than his vision, they looked like one human, their heads fused together into a blob of crimson with one black hole for an eye on the left and one on the right.

There the two of them stood side by side, unable to move, blood pooling on the lapels of their shirts.

Satisfied, the deav retrieved the eyes from the box just as quickly as he had put them in. He punctured each with a safety pin and attached one to the skin near his left eye and one near his right, in the hope that his vision would improve for the rest of the day. He took an evil eye trinket from his satchel and, with another a safety pin, attached it to the back of his neck. Walking over to the flashlight on the floor, he picked it up and, lifting himself off the ground, began to fly toward one of the tunnels, creating a wind behind him that snuffed out the flaming torch on top of the fountain.

After a few moments' silence, Greisen finally let out a tremendous scream of pain.

'Better to have one eye than to live in poverty,' said Javad. They grabbed each other's hands and, without a word, started back. At first they walked along together in darkness, then over time they came to crawl. The further they went, the less sure they became of their direction, yet still they clawed their way along the endless tunnels.

By the time they felt the edge of the path drop off in front of them, the skin on their hands was bloodied and torn. They swiped and flapped their arms into the empty space, but there was nothing there.

'We'll have to jump,' Javad said.

'But we don't know how far down it is,' replied Greisen, petrified.

Confused and too tired to turn back now, together they allowed their bodies to tumble over the edge, freefalling into the void. As they hit the bottom, water broke their fall. They splashed around to get their bearings, but it was no use. The swift current pulled them through the speculum and down the *qanat*, sweeping them away once and for all.

PERTH AMBOY: FRESH KILLS

Over lunch in Anthony's unpretentious kitchen in Perth Amboy, New Jersey, Darya boasted of how Iran was such an old place and how Persian history was full of myths, bedtime stories and folktales detailing the land's creatures, gods, demons and their ilk. Anthony countered that the United States has its own folktales, and asked those gathered around the table if they might like to hear one that came to mind.

'I heard this when I was back in Staten Island visiting my sister. I grew up on the Island and she's still livin' there. She was tellin' the story to her kids, their friends and me after I'd mentioned Fresh Kills. If you really wanna hear it...my sister's so smart, this is how she said it goes...

'This was back in the late '90s, before there was all that talk about the environment, but some people were already wise to it. So this elementary school teacher on the Island, she was a bit of a greenie, decided her class field trip for the year would be to the Fresh Kills landfill, which wasn't too far from their school. Of course the trip was approved, the principal was happy enough, because it didn't cost any more than the bus to get them all there.

'On a beautiful sunny day, they boarded the charter bus, which carried twenty-six children plus the teacher, a student teacher and the driver to the site.

'The students were excited like they always were on field trip days—usually just because it meant they could get off the school premises. But on this trip they were going someplace they had never been. In fact, most of the students had never heard of Fresh Kills before their classroom lessons the week before.

'The teacher had gone through all of the approval processes necessary for the class to visit the site "for educational purposes,"

and so they were greeted by a Fresh Kills employee and ushered on foot to one of the mounds, a fair distance from where
they had parked. Massive in size, the mound extended as far
as the eye could see, all the way to the horizon. Seagulls were
everywhere.'

Anthony paused. 'When my sister got to this part, I remembered the seagulls on the Island growing up. Poopin' on me on
my way to school. I asked her why mommy didn't walk us to
school when we were younger. My sister wanted to get on with
the story...fuckin'...she was looking at me all worried and wondering what I was gonna say. The kids were listening. I didn't say
it, but I had to wipe that shit off me every time.

'My sister said sometimes the birds melded with the sky, other times they mixed with this flowing mass of "things" on the
ground, spread out like a piecework quilt containing every gra-
dation of every color—although the main color would have to
be black, because of all the garbage bags. The movement of the
gulls diving down, hopping through the trash piles, and rising
up again made it seem as if the mass of garbage itself was slow-
ing shifting and churning. Even with the sun's glow warming
the mound, it appeared moist in the lower layers, a soft mass
with garbage juice bubbling up under the surface, belching out
choice notes of the five boroughs' foulest odors.

'She waved her hand in front of her face, like she was right
there smellin' it.

'The kids were to treat the visit as an exploration, and so they
did. One boy brought a compass, a girl binoculars. They fanned
out in small groups over the garbage heap. The schoolteacher,
lost in her own thoughts, went her own way, as did the student
teacher and the bus driver.

'After some time had passed, it was difficult to know exactly
how long, the teacher remembered to check on her pupils, by

which time only a few remained in view. *Where'd they go?* She was worried that they wouldn't get back in time for their noon lunch, which was to be a picnic on another part of the Fresh Kills complex.

'The seagulls had increased in number and were squawking and cackling non-stop. With the sun in her eyes, the school teacher squinted to try and make out the children in the distance, but the light must have been playing tricks on her. It seemed like a child was there one moment and gone the next. This happened again and again. Tramping over the mound, she attempted to find the highest spot to get a better view, but with every footstep she sank back down to where she started.

'To the teacher's horror, eventually even those deceptive, fleeting glimpses of small distant figures became less frequent and then stopped altogether, and she was left standing alone, unsure of what to do. Feeling that she was about to faint, she pulled out a bottle of water, drained the last of it, and added it to the pile.

'Panicking, she spotted a small man not far from her to the right. He was stooped over inspecting garbage, and had one of the black plastic sacks in his hand. Convinced he could help, she screamed persistently in his direction until, eventually, he fixed his eyes on her and she coaxed him over.

'My sister, she's a good storyteller; I can't do it like that. But this bit right here, she starts to get a little confused.'

The listeners prodded him on, encouraging him, reassuring him that he was doing a good job.

'So, the teacher introduced herself and asked the stooping man if he could help her.

'"Ah'm the Garbage Picker-Upper for this here pile," he declared, ignoring her question.

'"What do you mean?"

"'Ah means, ah gets anythin' that don't belong here and ah removes it."

Here Anthony started to really get into it. Scanning the faces of his audience and noting their encouraging nods, he continued....

"'I see. Can you help me? I need help."

"'How long d'ye think ah bin here?" the strange old guy asked, narrowing his beady eyes.

"'Do you mean today, or how long have you been working here?" the teacher replied, hoping she had understood some of what he had said.

"'Since springtime o' 1985," he stated in a matter-of-fact tone.

"'Listen, this is serious, all of my children have disappeared, how can I find them?"

"'What d'ye see of 'em?"

"'They just disappeared right in front of my eyes."

'The man removed his grubby baseball cap and wiped the sweat from his forehead. "Eh...must be..."'

'The teacher said, "Pardon?"

"'Yep, it's Manetuwak alright, ah'm sure of it. He don't like the off'rins. He thinks t'aint a gift but jus' plain ol' garbage! When Manetuwak gets all o-fendied, he becomes troublesome."

'The teacher stood there staring at the old-timer, speechless, then after a moment asked him to better explain, as she had no idea what he was talking about.

"'See, this here land bin Raritan land. And that's how them old tales go." He paused for a moment, then continued, "Ye can't jus' keep on offerin' the keeper o' the game garbage and not expect revolt."

"'A myth's just a myth," the teacher said, impatiently.

"'Ah've seen things here, y'know, an' ah do b'lieve it's only gon' get worser."

'This garbage guy is crazy hard to do,' Anthony groaned, but continued on without taking a breath.

'"Ah've bin here long enough to hear the tales, plus ah've done seen things with mah own eyes, bein' here on the ground."

'"So where have the children gone?" the teacher asked, exasperated by this point.

'The garbage picker-upper hesitated. "Mah guess is they done sunk down below yon pile."

'"Oh god. No. That's absurd. Can't be. When will they come back?"

'"No way to tell. If the masked bein' done revealed hisself to them littl'uns, he may just be showin' 'em somethin' or puttin' the fright'ners on 'em. They'll come back up all in good time."

'"You can't be serious." She was really beginning to get spooked now.

'"Now, supposin' 'tis Manetuwak, they may be gone forever. No way to tell."

'"Please, I give in, where are they? Where do you have all the kids, where's my student teacher hiding?"

'"Ain't at all surprisin' this happened." The old timer shook his head and became absorbed in sorting some refuse on the ground.

'After waiting and searching for hours, the schoolteacher, along with the Fresh Kills representative and the police, proceeded back to the parking area without any children. There, by the school bus, sat one lonely boy from the class. Beside herself, the teacher ran to the boy and shook him violently, demanding to know where he had been and where the others were. The boy ashamedly admitted that he had stayed behind because he didn't want to go to the mound.

'The teacher asked why, but, taken aback by her panicked demeanor, the boy wouldn't say another word. Only after much cajoling did he respond: "My mom says we shouldn't walk over other people's trash."

'And that was the story. I did a bad job for you, forget about it.'

Darya and the others shook their heads and asked if that was all, or if there was more to the story. What happened to the other children? Anthony said that was it. In early 2001, Fresh Kills had closed. At the time, the landfill was a heaping garbage pile standing more than eighty feet higher than the Statue of Liberty. It reopened briefly later that year following 9/11, when it was used as an emergency sorting ground for rubble from Ground Zero. Anthony remembered the news, how it had been reported that they were transporting the debris over there from NYC. Some of the others at the table nodded. Human remains, that was what the sorters were looking for.

MASHHAD: COOKING AMERICANS

As they rode along in the taxi cab, Annette became increasingly uncomfortable. Sweat ran down her back and pooled under her bra. She had to get the ski jacket off.

'What are you doing?' Fatima asked, noticing her struggling.

'It's too hot. I've got to get out of this thing!'

'You can't take it off, your arms won't be covered,' Fatima said, knowing full well the American would be arrested if she didn't cover up. The Test had to wear a *chador* or a jacket in public. A lighter weight *manteau* wouldn't work—there wasn't one big enough to fit her in all Iran. 'Keep it on, it's the law.'

Law-abiding citizen as she was, Annette zipped the jacket back up. But she wasn't happy, and from here on out she huffed and puffed.

The taxi stopped in front of a bustling square. Annette pulled at the black scarf under her brimmed hat, assuming she couldn't take that off either. Fatima helped her adjust it, her guest's discomfort making her conscious of the restrictions. She paid the driver 1,500 tomans.

She spoke slowly to the Americans. 'I'm going to take you through Bazaar-e Reza, which is the fastest way to get to the restaurant. If you see anything and want, please be my guest.'

Annette perked up a little. 'Did you hear that Benny? We can do a bit of shopping on our way. Let's look out for some souvenirs.' She walked towards the entrance of the mall, a flat-fronted building of beige brick and blue tiles. Large paintings of two men—icons of some sort with black hats and white beards—greeted them from the top corners of the entrance.

Fatima, their soft-spoken Host, a pretty girl in her early twenties, had offered to take Annette and Benjamin to a restaurant located near the Bazaar. She said it had the best food in Mashhad.

They were more than excited to go for supper at the best restaurant in town. Even though it wasn't yet lunchtime in New York, the Minnesotans weren't going to turn down a complimentary meal.

The pedestrian traffic at the left archway became exceedingly dense, more so the closer they got, with people thronging through the too-small entrance. Fatima elbowed her way into the mass while Annette and Benjamin tried to stay in her wake. Women covered in black sheets brushed against Annette. She could feel the fabric slide over her hands. It reminded her of pushing rayon under the needle on her sewing machine, how it glided through so effortlessly.

Fatima noticed Iranians glancing at the large woman in the shocking crimson jacket as they hurried along. She thought to herself that they must be wondering about the foreigner's excessive weight.

Once inside, the steady stream of jostling bodies continued. Men pushing large carts full of products forced the crowd to maneuver around them and each other in the passageway. Suddenly, a loud waspish droning approached them fast from behind. Fatima didn't have to look back—she knew the sound, and alerted her guests to clear the way. The moment the motorcycle passed, the path was as dense as it had been before.

Annette stopped to catch her breath. 'They allow motorcycles in here?'

'Usually the shop owners themselves.'

They moved on, passing storefronts on both sides of the arcade. Annette scrutinized them one after another. Spices were arranged in hefty copper dishes on a multi-level shelf display covered in paisley fabric. She couldn't be sure of any of the spices based on texture and pigment alone, for there were foreign colors present—cranberry reds, maroons, dirt browns, sage blues and olive oranges that weren't part of her kitchen reper-toire. Benjamin could tell Annette was going to want to pur-chase at least one item from the Spiceman, knowing full well that she wouldn't use anything she bought when she got back home.

'What are these?' Annette pointed to a bowl of small red ber-ries. 'Are they dried cranberries?'

The Spiceman took his eyes off his other customers. 'Barber-ries, good for cooking in rice.'

'Can I have a small bag of them, please? How much are they?'

'1,000 tomans a quarter kilo.'

'I only have dollars. How much in dollars?' she huffed.

'For the lady in red, you can have it for two dollars.'

Fatima eyed the Spiceman.

'Sold.' Annette reached for her wallet and the man measured the barberries into a plastic bag and handed it over.

Fatima led them deeper and deeper into the elongated build-ing, which seemed to go on endlessly. Annette asked, 'How big is the bazaar?'

'Over eight hundred meters long.'

'Sure isn't Target.'

Different materials—sometimes brick, sometimes thick ce-ment, and sometimes makeshift fabrics such as pink plastic or heavy canvas—separated out stores and sections. Artificial flow-er stands, belt and buckle shops, bead stalls.

'Benny, don'tcha know, it's a good thing we wore our tennis shoes,' Annette said over the loud pop music blasting from tin-ny speakers, as she leaned against the wall of a knock-off shop and rotated her foot.

Benny inspected the fake 'Timmy Hilfiger' polo shirts. 'The music sure is loud.'

'It's Mansour! He's from Mashhad, but lives in Los Angeles

now,' Fatima blurted out, immediately embarrassed at showing her enthusiasm for the heartthrob.

They walked through a warren of pathways off the main arcades, passing leather saddle and antiques shops. Peddlers were selling nuts, figs and dates along the paths. As Fatima paused to take a call on her mobile, Benjamin glanced down a dimly lit alleyway. Boxes lined the walls, along with metal pots. At the end, he could see a man waving and motioning for him to come closer. 'Can we go down there?' he asked.

'Why would you go down there?' Annette asked, wiping the sweat from her forehead.

The alleyway didn't seem to be in the bazaar's main building. Benjamin saw the man still beckoning him in, so he started down the path, with the women right behind.

A strong bodybuilder type and a much smaller man greeted them. Even though their physiques were so different, they had similar facial features, as if they could be brothers.

'*Salaam*!' they said, and Fatima returned the greeting.

Annette was astonished by the array of metal goods on display. Every inch of the store seemed to be crammed with metal products. The most amazing were the extra large pots stacked up to the ceiling, massive vessels lined up row after row along the walls—the really big ones, Annette figured, were over four feet in height.

'What are these for?' she asked, pointing to the grand pots.

The man replied in Farsi.

'He says that they are pots used for cooking Americans!' Fatima giggled.

They all laughed except for Annette and Benjamin. Benjamin watched as one of the men closed the door and bolted the lock. The men continued to laugh so hard that their bellies jiggled. Fatima fell silent, looking at her guests from beneath dark lashes, an unreadable expression on her face.

The bodybuilder pulled one of the grandest pots from the stacks. Biceps bulging, he brought it down to the floor in one motion. The noise of the metal hitting the concrete reverberated everywhere, echoing off other pots and bouncing off the metal racks and door.

'How you think this one would work?' he asked in his imperfect English.

'They certainly are big enough,' Benjamin replied, warily playing along.

'You never know what may be cooking inside a pot so big! You haven't heard stories at home? We Iranians have a reputation around the world, you know.' The strongman scratched his five o'clock shadow, glaring at the pot.

'I've never heard any stories.' Annette moved up alongside her husband.

'I guess they don't teach you these things, do they? You have to learn it on your own. Now, what you think about this fine pot?' He ran his finger along the lip of the copper.

'The pot sure is lovely, but we wouldn't be able to take it back with us,' Annette said. 'Fatima, maybe we should be going round about now. I'm getting real hungry.'

'Oh yes, we're all so hungry around here! Dinner should be cooking right about now!' the strongman belted out. The two men laughed some more.

Annette looked at her husband, hoping he would do something, but he just stood there nervously fingering his blue tote.

The strongman walked over to Benjamin and put his muscled arm around his shoulder. 'What about you? How is that pot looking?'

Crushed under the weight of the man's arm, Benjamin cringed, 'Looks nice.'

'Perhaps you should better look closer before you come to some conclusions.'

'Oh, I can tell from here, it's nifty.'

'Why don't you go on over?' He gave Benjamin a nudge and, reluctantly, the Test walked over to the antique copper pot.

'Go on, feel it,' the thin man said with a smile.

Benjamin touched the rim of the pot just as the strongman had done. 'Okey Dokey. Real smooth.'

'Now have a look at the fine craftsmanship inside. Go on.'

'I can see the pot has been forged nicely.'

'What do you know about forging?'

'Nothing really.'

'Go on, get inside.'

'Hey, hold on here...that's not necessary.' Benjamin shook his head, grinning uneasily, and took a step back from the huge vessel.

But it was too late—the strong man was on his way over. 'I insist, get in and have a look. Otherwise, maybe your wife might want to take a look herself.' He lifted his finger towards Annette.

Benjamin glanced over at Annette and back at the pot, then carefully lifted his haunch up over the rim and placed one leg inside. Holding the edge, he brought his other leg into the pot. 'Let me take a look, eh.' He peered down into the depths of the pot.

Fatima looked on, covering her mouth to hide her giggles.

'You've got to get down in it to see it better.'

Benjamin kneeled down in the pot and pretended to inspect the metal.

'There you go,' the skinny man said, stretching his arms and moving closer to the pot.

'Now see what like it would be with lid on.' The strong man walked over to the cover pile.

'Benny doesn't need to do that. He can see enough already.' But Annette's self-contained sauna was reaching boiling point and her thinking wasn't at its best. She looked over imploringly to Fatima, who avoided her gaze. Before she could say anything more, the strongman was carrying over a matching cover. Annette no longer wanted to play along with the joke. Again she looked to her Host for assistance, but Fatima was hiccupping between nonstop peals of laughter.

'Drop your head, Mister Benny, so I can put on the lid.'

Non-confrontational to a fault, Benjamin could do nothing but follow the big man's suggestion. He ducked down, and the cover was on.

Everything went black. Inside, the pot gave off a suffocating smell of metal. But Benny could still make out the waves of laughter coming from Fatima outside.

Annette's face took on an unpleasant cast, like an aged grandma version of the snowsuited mutant child in *The Brood*.

The men started up a conversation in Farsi with Fatima who had now finally regained her composure. But Annette was fuming. *Is Benny getting enough air? What are these crazy foreigners gonna do next?*

The Iranians continued their banter. Fatima made a call from her phone.

Annette wanted to take a stand but the words wouldn't come, as if her midwestern manners were making a last ditch bid to handle the situation politely.

Minutes ticked away before a tentative knocking came from under the pot cover.

Tap, Tap, Tap...Tap, Tap, Tap...

The men turned toward the pot. Fatima ended her call.

The muscleman sauntered over and lifted the cover. His eyes bore down on Benjamin. 'Well, how did it feel, Mister Benny?'

Benjamin seemed confused, yet he was able to pop up and out quite quickly. 'Very dark and smelly.'

'I'm sure.' The Iranians burst into a chorus of laughs that resounded off all the surrounding metal, the room a swirl of echoed laughter that didn't subside.

The smaller brother tried to focus on Benny as he wiped tears from his eyes. 'So you would buy this pot?'

'We really don't need it, ya know.' Benjamin moved closer to his wife, who was nodding.

'We know you cannot purchase it, how you would get it home? Of course...we are just teasing you.'

'What do you cook in them, then?' Annette asked, still uneasy.

'Apart from Americans...?' There was a long pause for yet more laugher, but eventually the big man composed himself and continued.

'Sir, these pots we mostly use for cooking *Halim* for large groups. In old days it was more common, now we mainly use them in the month of Muharram, when we mourn Imam Hussein. In Muharram, male performers come to the streets at night to perform a mourning parade. There are places for the performers and people watching to get warm, and sometimes they are cooking food in these pots for the crowd.'

'Oh, that would be something to see,' Benjamin said.

The strongman unlocked the door.

'One thing,' said the smaller man. 'We should like to present you a gift from our store.' He walked over to a group of metal pieces hanging from the ceiling and with a long pole took down a copper set made up of tiny items. A small version of the grand pot, a tiny tea kettle, a miniature serving tray and a ladle, all attached together by a copper chain.

'A replica set!' said Fatima, 'you can hang it on the wall for decoration.'

The tiny pans reminded Annette of an oversized charm bracelet. She was surprised that after what had occurred they were going to give her something, and immediately went into a long monologue about how she had never received such an adorable gift. She even momentarily forgot about how hot she was. They passed the item to her, and she passed it to Benjamin, who dropped it into the tote.

As they headed back through the alleyway, Fatima told her guests that the section they were walking through sold supplies related to Muharram. They stopped in front of a stall selling chains and fabric banners in black and green. Benjamin picked up a set of chains.

'Body lashers!' Fatima cried. Seeing the shock return to her guests' faces, she suppressed a smile. 'The performers do lash themselves, but it's all symbolic.'

Annette looked back towards the pot store.

'No need to worry about them, they are my uncles,' Fatima said, giggling again. 'The restaurant is just around the corner.'

'Is the water safe to drink here? I sure am thirsty. If not, maybe they have some pop.'

'The water is fine. But I don't think they have pop.'

No one else had seemed to notice Amir's absence from their morning seminar. He always grabbed a seat next to Estella wherever she happened to be. This morning his place had remained empty.

In the early evening she was ordering chicken salad and a chamomile at her regular takeout place, having spent the day trying to pretend to herself that she didn't miss Amir's constant presence around her. It didn't help settle her nerves that, as she waited for her order, she felt the presence of a male body moving up suddenly behind her, and was almost certain that when she had turned, the man's hand had swiftly pulled back from the bag that was slung carelessly over her shoulder. A twenty-something wearing a black trench over this year's Gap offerings, he seemed innocuous enough, except that his long pointed fake leather shoes didn't look like they had come from a Cambridge boutique.

Somehow the unsettling incident became connected in her mind with Amir's absence. And when she turned into her street and the same guy was still behind her, she became increasingly tense as she rummaged around for the key to open her building's front door. When he just passed straight by, not even looking back, she attempted a self-deprecating laugh, cursing her own creeping paranoia.

Holed up in her studio, Estella scrolled through her iPod, stopping at *The Zombi Anthology* and hitting play. She was annoyed with herself when, after dinner, her mind returned to Amir, thinking idly back to his email, wondering about his sudden absence, about Kade, and about why she even seemed to care so much.

Then she remembered the black box.

OLD GREENWICH: PIRATE OR PRINCESS

Fireworks, a silver-sequined star wand, and a black skull-and-crossbones flapping in the sea breeze. The smiling faces of children. Diamond shapes in the Starry Night, waves crested hard on the dark, shape-shifting rocks. The agitated midnight blue spanning an endless abyss. A storm, a torrential downpour, a gale lashing the deck from all directions.

I had to keep calm after XYZTing, or I could have fallen in. How could he have sent me right onto a dock? Could have ended up in the water. Not exactly a smooth ride. Not sure what happened exactly. I was on my way to the bazaar.... Anyhow, once I saw the house that the dock belonged to, I forgot about all that. An impressive waterside property. The breeze brisk, carrying the scent of Lux soap with it. I walked around the side of the house. Overgrown plants spread out across the path that led around to the front.

An engine was churning. A truck, someone was on the move. It was a Humvee, a black one. An odd sight on the perfect driveway, this vehicle that belongs in a combat zone. I guess I'd seen somewhere that they are driving them now in North America, and this one did look like more of a fancy version than a combat ride. 'Souped-up', someone had called them online. I moved in front of the Humvee so the driver could see me from behind the tinted windows.

Waving. 'Hello.'

I waited for the driver to respond. A not-so-intimidating guy got out, in his late twenties like me, I guessed. 'What are you doing on my property?'

'I'm from Iran,' I said. Which, to be sure, did not really add up to a satisfactory explanation.

He looked me up and down, and didn't seem impressed by my frail appearance. I know I still don't look healthy for someone my age, but I haven't been ill at all in the past few years.

He pulled out an iPhone. I'd seen the model online. 'Right, is it today? I didn't realize it was today.' He started touching the phone. I was close enough to see that he was looking at the calendar.

'I just found out about it myself,' I replied. As he scrolled and swiped, I glanced at the home's yellow front door and the spiraled pine trees growing in planters at each side.

'Man, sorry, I'm usually pretty organized. I totally missed that you were coming.' He seemed genuinely apologetic.

'No problem.'

'Listen, you wouldn't mind coming with me to the office, would you? I have some urgent things to do.' He was dressed in a simple jacket, dark grey pants and casual shoes. I wondered what he did for a living.

'No problem.' I really didn't care what we did. I was just interested in the whole experiment and being in the United States.

He walked over to the passenger door—it's the same in Iran, drivers drive on the left side and passengers ride on the right—and opened it for me. *Definitely not combat-ready*, I thought, checking out the luxury features, the leather, the stereo.

The Host was definitely late twenties, healthier-looking than me of course, his hair light brown, parted to the side, a cowlick spread across his forehead. Still, something seemed amiss—maybe his ears.

'Do you live here?' I asked.

'Oh yeah, this is my place.'

'And your family?'

'Single. Haven't had time to find a wife yet.' He laughed.

'It's a big house for one person.'

'Man, I know. But I only had to put one percent down, so why not?'

'It's very nice on the water.'

'Yeah, views of Greenwich Point and the lighthouse. You can even see the North Shore of Long Island. It's pretty exceptional, if I do say so myself.' He put the vehicle in reverse and backed into the circular part of the driveway, turned around and drove to the end of the property, then pressed a button on his key-chain. The high metal gate started to open.

'I'm Firooze,' I said as I let my head sink back into the puffy headrest.

'Carver.'

I was confused. 'I was supposed to meet a person named Ray.'

'Yeah, that's me, but they know me around here as Carver.'

We drove along some winding tree-lined roads, passing more grand houses along the way. 'What do you think of the new Hummer? The H2 SUT is a 6.2-liter V8. Puts out a total of 393 horsepower.' He took his eyes off the road to check my reaction.

'Really something. I haven't been in one. They used jeeps when I did my military service back in Iran.'

'You sign up for that?'

'No, it's mandatory.'

'Hey, you hungry? I'm supposed to buy you lunch.'

I hadn't eaten since morning, and then only a bit of bread and *Bahar-e Narenj* tea. The faint taste of sour orange still lingered. 'Yes, I am.' Iranians are always hungry.

'What do you feel up for? We can pick it up and take it to the office.' He slammed on the brakes a little too hard as he slowed for a traffic light.

'How about McDonald's?'

'McDonald's? You eat that stuff?'

'No, I have never tried it. That's why I suggested it.'

'Never had Mickey D's? How's that possible?'

'No McDonald's in Iran. I heard there was one that opened for two days in the nineties and then closed down. But I don't know if it was a real one.' The Hummer's aircon blew streams of warm air at my face.

'No shit. There is actually a place in the world without McDonald's.'

'So you can see my interest in trying it, at least once?'

'Now I do. Let's get you hooked up, then you let me know what you think of it.'

He U-turned at the first opportunity and within a few minutes he was swerving into a McDonald's.

And there they were: two golden arches forming a giant 'M' on the yellow and red sign at the front, next to a flagpole flying the stars and stripes. The building, its unusually angled brown roof more noticeable than the squat brick structure it sat on, was surrounded by a parking lot. All of the spots were taken, so Carver pulled around the back, stopped at the drive-thru menu, and opened his window.

'May I take your order?' crackled a barely audible voice through the speaker.

'Give us a second,' Carver blurted loudly to the box, and turned to me. 'What will you have?'

'A hamburger and fries?'

'Yeah, but what kind? He pointed towards the sign, which from my angle was unreadable. 'Want me to order you up?'

'Please.'

'Go ahead, sir.' The box must have been listening.

'One Big Mac Meal, large. One caesar salad with grilled chicken and a large coffee.'

'What do you want to drink with the meal?' the box responded.

Carver turned back to me.

I saw the Coca-Cola logo on the sign. 'Coca-Cola. And what about a Happy Meal?' I didn't want to have to tell him how I enjoyed looking online at the collectible toys, but I couldn't let the opportunity pass me by.

'Oh, and one Happy Meal.' Carver shouted.

'Hamburger or McNuggets?'

'McNuggets,' I yelled across the car.

'Pirate or princess?'

'Pirate,' I replied, without really knowing why.

The squawkbox continued relentlessly. 'Any desserts for you today? A chocolate sundae or an apple pie?'

'Sure, hook us up, one of each. That's all.'

Long pause. 'That will be...please drive...' The voice breaking up again.

Carver drove the Hummer round the corner up to the window and put it in park, and we sat with it running for two minutes according to the digital clock in front of me. Then the window slid open and bags of food were passed to Carver, who passed them over to me. He pulled his wallet from his pants, took out a credit card and handed it over.

'Let me pay for the lunch,' I said. I knew I only had tomans, but thought I should offer anyway. It is always polite to do *taarof*.

'No, it's going on the card, no worries.' He shrugged.

The food had a strong smell that diffused through the hot brown paper of the bags. I organized them on the oversized armrest between our seats.

'See that store there?' he said, looking ahead.

'Dunkin' Donuts?'

'No, next to it.' It was a car dealership with fancy sports models gleaming inside perfectly polished windows.

'M-hm.'

'I'm gonna get my Ferrari from there when my bonus comes through. April 15, baby.'

'Really? But what about the Hummer?'

'I'll keep it too.' He stroked the steering wheel and put his foot on the gas pedal more than was needed to get out onto the main road. As we zoomed by the dealership, he scanned the cars on display. 'So stoked.'

'What do you do for a living?' I didn't think it was too much to ask, given that we were on our way to his place of business.

'I'm in finance.' His chin might have risen up minutely, though it could have been from the unevenness in the road.

'What area of finance?'

'I'm with a firm here in Greenwich that specializes in equity.'

'In Iran, they have just begun with online trading. It is starting to work. Day traders in Tehran can make millions in a flash. The market is volatile, even more than here.'

My Host seemed interested for a moment, then continued, 'I came here to head up a special team. We work on mortgage-backed security rebundling. Take mortgages here in the US and package them together into investment vehicles, mainly for Asian investors.'

'Sounds exciting.'

'Oh yeah. It is. Exceeded all goals the three years I've been here. Sky's the limit, my friend, sky's the limit.' He pulled off the main road into an office complex and parked in a spot marked *Carver* near the main doors.

On a mission, my VIP Host picked up half of the food bags and left the others for me to carry. As we entered the building he directed me toward the elevator bank, and we rode up to the third floor.

Once in the lobby, a scanned ID card run over the scanner on the wall was all it took and the glass doors made a click.

He let me through first.

'Why don't we set up in the conference room?'

The dimly lit reception room was empty, but when we made our way into the main office space, many of the low-walled cubicles were occupied. Most of the employees were guys around our age. I spotted one girl with long dark hair—rather sexy, like gorgeous American teens online. She caught my attention because she was talking loudly into her headset and standing instead of sitting on her high tech swivel.

At the conference room door Carver brandished his ID again and, as the click sounded, grabbed the silver handle and yanked it hard, as if he knew the door would stick.

He flipped a switch, and the artificial white ceiling lit up the windowless room. With no air circulation, the grease-and-cardboard aroma of the McDonald's instantly took over. The boardroom-style grey laminate table took up nearly all of the space, and was the only item of furniture except for a small cart in the corner that held a phone.

Carver set the bags of food down and started to rummage through. When he had extracted his order he said, 'This should keep you busy for a while. Let me know if you need anything,' then disappeared through the door before I could reply. Seemed like his business really was urgent.

I started to take the items out, looking at the packaging carefully, setting out the Big Mac box, the Happy Meal box, the french fries, some of which fell out on the table, and the ketchup packets. I popped the straws through the lids of the Coca-Colas then lifted out the chocolate sundae, which seemed to already be half-melted; the plastic container felt like it could break open at any moment. Next I pulled out the apple pie in its printed cardboard sleeve. With it came a flyer promoting a charity drive for the New Haven Ronald McDonald House.

Ronald McDonald was featured, but not the other characters. When I had been looking at the toys and other old McDonald's items on eBay not long ago, it had been mentioned that the other characters had been retired.

Separating the golden arch handles on the Disney Parks Pirate & Princess Happy Meal box, I peered inside: Chicken McNuggets and BBQ dipping sauce, a small bag of french fries and the toy—a plastic replica of the broken compass from *Pirates of the Caribbean*. Not bad.

When I had all of the food lined up on the table, I sat down. Everything still warm and perpetually emanating that distinct smell—something like heated oil and *ghormeh sabzi* mixed together.

I determined that I would start with the Big Mac. First, I picked it open to have a look. Iranians like to eat, and even though this burger had two meat patties and three buns, it most likely wouldn't be enough for your average Iranian consumer, man or woman. Lettuce, lightly melted cheese and a chunky pink sauce, but no lunchmeat slices like at home. A couple of pickles wedged in, too.

I bit into it. Lettuce shreds fell to the table. Bun in my mouth. Taste of burger. Tang from the sauce. The sesame seeds on the bun popped. The Big Mac flavors mixed on my tongue.

Clearing my mouth with Coca-Cola from the large cup, I squeezed some ketchup onto a paper napkin and, one after another, dipped and shoveled in clusters of fries. More Big Mac, more Coca-Cola. I noticed I had picked up the pace and was eating faster. Ripped open the McNuggets box and the sauce pack and got a nugget into my mouth as fast as I could. Steaming burst of chicken-soup-flavored rubber, the coating crisp with coarse sandpaper texture, barbeque sauce dominating all the other tastes.

I dumped the smaller portion of fries onto the pile and opened another ketchup pack. Salt rush to the head, dizziness coming and going. *Am I that hungry? Is it really that good?* Meanwhile the sundae was turning to liquid, the chocolate sauce on top sinking down into the ice cream like dirt mixing with fresh snow on the pavement then melting down the *jou*. Even though I hadn't finished the other items, I figured I'd better test it before it liquified completely. Scent of synthetic vanilla in my nose. Stings where the salt left holes in my tongue. Rip open the apple pie package—some type of crust-covered pastry, the hard sugar shell slimy on the inside. Applesauce and cinnamon burned my lips and dripped down onto the discarded shreds of lettuce.

No sound came from beyond the white door.

The feast had made me sluggish and sleepy. Tugging the toy compass out of its plastic wrap, I opened the top to try it out. The needle really worked. You could use this for prayers. The mess of boxes and wrappers moved before my eyes as though it were alive. Leaned my head on the table to rest. Chairs seemed to have shifted. Whole room a white-out fluorescent blur.

A gale lashing the deck from all directions. The Black Pearl was engulfed in it. Thunder. Lightning.

Will Turner scanned the water, making out a distressed ship in the distance, nearly broken in half and sinking, a glowing, putrefied mess, defeated by the storm. He turned toward the deck. 'That's the Flying Dutchman?' he asked. 'She doesn't look like much.' He rolled his eyes and shrugged.

Captain Jack Sparrow played with his braided goatee. 'Neither do you. Do not underestimate her.' He gave Gibbs a calculated look and elbowed him.

'Must've run afoul of the reef,' said Gibbs.

Jack looked at Will. 'So what's your plan, then?'

'I row over, search the ship until I find your bloody key.'

'And if there are crewmen?' Jack slurred.

'I cut down anyone in my path.' Will moved towards the rowboat.

'I like it. Simple, easy to remember,' Jack said.

Thunder roared, lightning blazed through the rigging, and enormous waves rocked the boat. All over the deck crewmembers lost their footing, slipped and fell; Jack and Gibbs grabbed the rail and hung on.

Strange objects began to fall from the sky. 'What are these?' Jack shouted.

Gibbs picked one up and inspected it. 'They look like crab claws.'

Jack contracted his nostrils at the smell. 'That they are, Gibbs.'

When the rain finally abated, they found that the crab claws were not the only flotsam the storm had left behind. Sprawled out on the deck in front of them, apparently deposited there by the ferocious waves that had crashed over the bow, were a number of folk who did not belong to the crew.

Jack blinked hard and shook his head to make sure the rum wasn't to blame for what he saw: a redheaded man in a yellow jumpsuit with red and white striped sleeves and socks, chunky boots, and a big 'M' inscribed over his heart, accompanied by a number of equally odd-looking colleagues.

'Is the circus in town?' Jack asked the motley crew.

Ronald McDonald slowly stood up, steadying his bright red boots on the deck, testing to see if they were going to slip. 'Allow me to make the introductions. I'm Ronald, and these are my friends Captain Crook, Grimace, Hamburglar and Officer Big Mac.' They greeted the whole Black Pearl crew, who had joined them on deck, curious to know what was afoot.

Suspicious, Jack eyeballed Ronald and then Captain Crook. 'What do you want here? How did you find us?' he demanded, arms crossed.

Ronald McDonald, still smiling, could not answer the questions, for he did not know what had happened.

'Oh, I get it,' Jack said, drawing his sword. 'You've come to take over the Black Pearl.'

'No, that's not what we're up to,' Captain Crook replied.

Jack sauntered unsteadily over to the new arrivals. 'There's only room for one Captain on this ship,' he growled, striking the leather strap of the bag draped over his chest.

'I wouldn't dream of taking over your ship. I have my own back in McDonaldland.' Captain Crook glanced up at the unsightly sails above him, then down at the decrepit planks underfoot. 'Beautiful as the ship is and all,' he added tactfully.

'Then would someone please tell us what you are doing here?' put in Will Turner. It had started to rain again. He brushed the water from his forehead and waited for an answer. Grimace, the oversized purple creature, lost his balance and rolled over onto his side. His short arms and feet dangled helplessly from his body, but he still looked jubilant.

Ronald saw that the McDonaldland Crew had gotten themselves into another 'situation.' He walked toward Captain Jack Sparrow with his arms open in a friendly gesture. 'You see, we are on a quest for goodwill. We come seeking alms for the Ronald McDonald House.'

Jack slowly resheathed his sword.

'You're looking for treasure,' Gibbs said, eyeing them suspiciously. 'It's all over your faces.'

'I suppose you could say we are looking for hope. And isn't that one of life's greatest treasures?' said Ronald with a simpering smile.

'In this case, we're not in the business of stealing treasure. We're trying to give it back, in fact,' Jack said. The crew concurred.

Hamburglar got up from where he had been sitting. He crunched toward Jack through piles of crab claws, and made some kind of garbled attempt at speech.

'Don't understand.' Jack played with the beads in his unkempt dreadlocks.

'He said maybe you still have something to contribute,' Captain Crook translated.

'Sorry, I don't think anything's left.' Jack Sparrow paused to think. 'We traded that cursed, I mean *magic*, saw. Harder to keep on a boat than an oversized elephant. What did we trade that for again?'

'Rum.' Gibbs grinned.

'M-hm, rum. What about that, that psychedelic saffron? Traded it...' Jack stared blankly at Gibbs.

'More rum.' Gibbs rubbed his hands together.

The crew fidgeted.

'We had an undead monkey that we would have gladly donated to your cause. But you're too late, we just bartered it off for...for...'

Jack Sparrow glanced over in the direction of the Flying Dutchman, which was sinking progressively deeper beneath the waves.

Hamburglar spoke again, twirling his cape and pointing around the ship as he spouted his agitated hyper-gibberish.

'Hamburglar wants to know whether you have any hamburgers on board,' translated Captain Crook.

'Hamburgers?' Gibbs repeated the word slowly. The crew scratched their heads. 'Afraid we don't know what you're looking for, matey.'

Regardless, Hamburglar began to dart around the ship in search of meat.

The sky turned into a kaleidoscope of Deee-Liteful swirling coloration: primary cartoon tones, then black and white strobe-lighting, spinning off into distorted bull's-eyes.

'Allow me to be of assistance.' Officer Big Mac came forward. 'You see my face?' His oversized Big-Mac-shaped head with its round white staring eyes stood out against the backdrop of the vibrant, pulsing sky.

The crew nodded.

'A hamburger is like this,' he explained, pointing at himself, 'although I'm a little waterlogged at present, and I have an extra layer. A hamburger is just a simple burger and bun, but you get the idea.' Officer Big Mac framed his face with his hands.

'Do you eat it, or be it a treasure?' inquired Gibbs, perplexed.

'Well you eat it, of course.'

Jack had just unsheathed his sword again when he noticed Hamburglar rummaging through a wooden box not far from where he was standing. His sword tip stopped just short of the burglar's chest. 'Don't really like masked bandits snooping around my ship. We don't have any of these hamburgers you speak of. So to look for what we don't have but you want is pointless. Unless you were to look for it in a place where it is, which is not here. Since it is not here where you need to look, you are wasting your time.'

'Good point,' Ronald said, shaking his head at Hamburglar. 'I'm sorry to have barged in like this. We should be on our way.' He did his best to round up the gang ready for departure.

The children in the sky, all dressed in pirate and princess outfits, started to sing: *It's time, it's time. It's time to go now. It's time, it's time. It's time to go now friends...* over the electronic beat supplied by the DJ who had apparently set up above the now becalmed surface of the ocean, far off on the horizon.

'Sorry we couldn't help.' Jack Sparrow rubbed his left eye. 'You've caught us at a bad time. Will has some business to take care of.'

'Thank you all the same. We enjoyed visiting your ship,

Captain,' Ronald said calmly.

Will looked out toward where the Flying Dutchman had been, but it was no longer in sight.

The sound of cannonfire in the distance.

'Douse the lamps.' Jack Sparrow whispered.

The white lights above the ship began to falter. Things were becoming fuzzy, hazy. I was down in the hold, the conference room lights flickering. A stifled voice coming from far away. Rain pelting against me. The lights flickered again. I opened my eyes, then closed them again.

TEHRAN: ENGHELAB STREET

We were walking along Enghelab Street. He was showing me all the bookstores. I shifted my Dolce & Gabbanas onto my head as the sun had relented. A few of the stores we went into had English titles and I browsed through, but the selection was poor. There was always a large assortment of Farsi books, however. Many had bright covers and bold graphics. He explained that most of these books had been translated into Farsi illegally, meaning that no royalties were paid to the author or publisher outside of Iran. Iran has no copyright laws, he said. The price of the books ranged from one to six dollars. There was a lot of activity on the street around us; we had to push our way into some of the stores. I moved slowly because my feet were already hurting in those high heels. I had not planned to be walking this much. Added to that, the two of us seemed to attract attention everywhere we went, to the point where I almost felt like apologizing to my Host for the stares.

A food cart was parked between two of the stores. Metal skewers on the top of it stuck straight up into the air. Thick, burgundy-red chunks were stacked at the bottom of the skewers, each the size of a hockey puck. I asked my Host what they were, but he couldn't give me the English translation. The man working the cart said they were beetroots. He checked out the rings on my fingers and the patterns on my nails, which I had just had done. I think he liked them. True, they were perfect, no chips yet. My Host asked me if I wanted to try one of the red things and I said no, I was already full.

I realized I had not seen a single black face yet.

'There aren't many Africans that visit Iran,' he said. 'They usually go to the pilgrimage to Mecca. But they hardly ever come to Iran.'

'Why?'

He smiled. 'Well, not many foreign individuals come to live here by choice. Why are you asking? Go to the south of Iran and you will see people with skin as dark as yours.'

I wanted to ask more questions, but he ushered me quickly through the crowds. We walked into a small arcade, its walls more closely matching the grey marbled floors than their original white. Yet more bookstores. We did not go into any of them. Instead, he led me to the end of the arcade and down a curving staircase with double-size high steps. Toward the bottom my heel caught on a chip in the marble and I nearly tripped. We arrived on the lower level, where there was just one single store, glowing with sallow fluorescence, full of old books piled up on rickety shelves. No one around except the cashier, a small girl wearing a black veil who acknowledged us when we entered. We walked the shelves. He told me this was his favorite bookshop in Tehran, but to me the smell of mildew and decay was off-putting.

At the back of the store a series of thick volumes, too big to be encyclopedias, were lined up on top of grimy Persian rugs. Pointing out one of the old leather-bound volumes, I asked him what they were. He told me they were the book of *Vendidad*.

Kneeling on a rug, I flipped through one of the ancient tomes—its pages crumbling in my fingers—and stopped randomly on a page. I asked him what it said. He crouched down on the floor next to me, looking over a few pages before he said anything.

'First you should understand *Vendidad*. It is a multi-volume book covering all the known demons and how to confound them. Very old. Written a long time ago by the Zoroastrians.' He was breathing a little too heavily. 'This page talks about Druj-Nasu, which according to *Vendidad* is an avatar of Druj in the form of a fly.'

To be honest I wasn't that interested, but he continued, translating the page I had opened.

'*The Druj-Nasu comes and rushes upon from the regions of the North in the shape of a raging fly, with knees and tail sticking out, droning without end, and like unto the foulest Khrafstras.*' A person must be careful, he continued, when exposing himself to the north wind, especially while in the mountains, for Druj-Nasu could come forth and take possession of them.

The next sections of *Vendidad* detailed how to get rid of Druj-Nasu once it was inside a person. The process my Host described was very involved. Once the Druj-Nasu was pulled out of a person, it would burrow into the person in another place, find another hole. For example, if Druj-Nasu was pulled out of their left ear, then Druj-Nasu would move into their right ear. If Druj-Nasu was pulled out of their right ear, then Druj-Nasu would go somewhere else such as under their right armpit. Therefore, the whole act of ridding a person of Druj-Nasu involved a long and tedious cleansing of the entire body, outside and inside. If Druj-Nasu refused to leave, the person would have to be isolated in a sealed-off space indefinitely.

'I tell you, I've seen enough flies in my day, especially on Coney Island. I just swat 'em and they're gone.'

15238: ON THE MANNER OF SAWING

Drag the garden shears through the house and on to the leather canapé. Your arm should be leaning on the coffee table with the hand and wrist off the table.

This thing must be removed. Why did you put it on your right hand anyway? Can't cut with your left. Why did you do it? With Homeira left behind at home?

Snip the shears in awkward chopping motions to try and cut the bracelet off. Try again. It's impossible. What kind of unholy alloy is this thing made of?

Why is no one home? No, you are all alone. Someone was supposed to be here waiting. An overbearing, heavy presence here, but you hear nothing, just pure quiet. A contaminated absence.

Check the time. 2204. Soon enough, back in Tehran, Homeira will wonder where you are, what's taking you so long. What should you do? A whole life together with dear Homeira, all that you've been through. Tehran has been cruel indeed. How could it be that your love for your country has turned to such hate? No, you must stay here, whatever it takes.

Do it. The bracelet will just slide off.

What? No. That's insanity.

You are a doctor. You can do it. You have seen it done hundreds of times when you were an intern during the war.

I don't do this kind of surgery.

You can still perform such an operation, can't you?

No. No. I'm not going to do that.

You don't need your right hand to do your medical work. You aren't a surgeon, are you?

Technically, no.

Then what are you waiting for? Do it for Homeira and your family. They can come to America. You will finally succeed in getting out of Iran. You have to get out of Iran.

No, I won't.

This is the only way you can leave. You know you have to do it.

A sound outside. What was that? 'Hello?'

Get up and see. Is somebody coming?

To the mansion's entry doors. Spot the alarm box on the wall.

Don't open the door or the alarm might go off. Don't risk it.

Sit on the rug here. Look up and see what you can get in America. Look at the chandelier. Look at the winding staircase. Look at the grand piano in the entryway.

It's not about what you can get, what you can buy. It's about something else.

What, specifically?

Take a look outside.

Go up the staircase to the floor above and peer out of the windows. Up here the atmosphere is yet more unfamiliar: stale American air. A fulgent midday sun. Look down into the yard. There are no other houses around. Seems more like a park than a residence.

Listen. Listen to what you can get. No discord.

You should go back downstairs and sit this out. Turn the television on. It will all turn out fine.

What kind of knife do you need to do the job right?

Stop it. Stop thinking it any more. Sit down on the cushy leather canapé. Pull the side lever up for the leg rest. Wait.

This house is wrong, not quite right. As though no one lives here. There are no photos anywhere. What kind of place is Pittsburgh? What is the meaning of Pittsburgh? A burgh founded by Pitt?

What is that over the brick fireplace?

A coat of arms and a sword.

Would the sword work for a disarticulation? Let's see how it works.

The weapon slides easily from its scabbard with a screeching metal sound. Blade somewhat dull.

You need a saw if you're going to do it right. Yes, a saw.

The saw is in the garage. You don't want to go to the garage again do you? Just stay here and wait for the excursion to be over. It will be over soon.

No time to waste. Get to the garage now.

Garage has a vacant air about it. A mixed stench of oil and peanuts.

Tools. There are two handsaws, one with a bow and one loose. But here is an electric 10-amp reciprocating saw. These tools look brand new.

Using the left hand, you had better saw through the bone instead of using a knife.

Take the saw inside.

All right. You know what you have to do.

Go to the kitchen. Set the saw on the counter. It just doesn't seem right to do it here. Use the other kitchen you found, down in the cellar.

Do you really want to do this? Homeira will be so distressed.

This is for her and our family. Desperate situations require desperate measures.

The situation is hopeless at home.

True.

What else do you need, now? Knives. Look for a curved knife in the drawers. This one looks brand new. The package says it's a grapefruit knife. A useful incision blade. Take all the knives from the butcher-block holder on the counter.

Find a tray. The pots are so small here. Need some good-sized pots for sterilization. Need a sponge for cleaning.

You don't need to clean the pans. They look like they've never been used.

For the body, not the pans.

Upstairs for some towels. Check for drugs. You'll need pain-killers. Bandages, gauze and cotton balls, alcohol.

What do you need cotton balls for?

You don't know, but you might need them.

Rummage through the cabinets in the main hall bathroom. Lots of women's products and perfumes here. A hairdryer. Looking, looking...yes, an old curling iron. You can use this. Sewing supplies—needles, black thread, high-quality surgical steel scissors, and a good utility knife, almost like a scalpel. 'X-Acto'. You can use these.

Head down to the first floor. Go to the bar and find the strongest drink. Jack Daniels Black Label—this will work.

Get two glasses from kitchen.

There's a pad of paper and pen sitting on the desk in the kitchen. You should write something, no matter if your English is not good. They were expecting a guest.

Head down the stairs.

In the cellar kitchen, organize the supplies on the countertop. Run water into the pots.

Oh, don't do this. You're going to lose your hand. And what are you going to do then?

Stop it.

Inspect medical supplies. Take four Codeine pills. Shouldn't pass out.

The water is taking a long time to boil, longer than in Iran. Is it the electric burners? The altitude?

Plug in the curling iron and run the cord from the outlet to the table. Leave it on high.

All the supplies are in place. Thread is boiling, needles boiling. You've got to get going on this.

Fill glass with water and place it on the table. Pour whiskey in other glass.

Press antibacterial soap dispenser for soap. Wash hands.

Check the saw. Turn it on. Cyclical sound. Has multiple speeds. High sounds faster and more earsplitting. Saw kicks back in the hand at the higher speed. It will work, will cut the bone, but will you actually be able to direct the cut as you want with your worthless left hand? Turn the thing off.

Must do it. Do it now. Now's the time.

Now's the time.

Take up your position. This is going to be difficult.

Doctor Namdar, apply the tourniquet. Place it over the artery as high as possible on the right arm. Tie the ligature tight.

Done.

Have to be strong. Cannot struggle once the first cut is made. Remember.

Why did you put the bracelet on the right hand? Bend right arm, position it at 90 degrees. Will help you hold it steady, but will also allow the flexor and extensor muscles to be at equal relaxation during amputation. Remember...since there is no injury around the wrist now, it should be enough to touch the thread of the membrane with the knife, which will give enough covering for a good stump. Shouldn't have to pinch the skin and dissect it back. Difficult with only one working hand. About a centimeter of skin will be enough.

Doctor, before you can saw you need to make your circular incision around the wrist. Do it now with the small knife. Cut perpendicularly through the skin covering the extensor muscles.

You feel it on the skin, the pull of the flesh. Cutting, cutting. The tool doesn't come along as fast as it should. Flesh is clumpy.

Don't want to die. What is it? Pain. Pain felt. You feel pain. Sweep it. Sweep it. Started at the bottom of your thumb, now running along the inside of your wrist. Suiciders go here, go lower, they go lower. Cutting. Cutting. Feeling both the cutting and receiving simultaneously. In chorus. Feraliminal Lycanthropy from the inside.... The pain is here now. Light from above, blinding you. Keep receiving blade. You keep receiving the blade. You continue to receive the pain. Procession of blood along the line. Life line. Move, pull left. Steady. The cut is running, running maroon. Running shiraz-red. Blinding light from the right, smell of boiled water. You pull further to the left. The blade lags behind. Don't want to die. Life line. Line line line, move it along. Keep going. Must be quick, but it drags so. Through the integuments right down to the muscles.

Resist the shaking. Remove knife. Bring the knife to the front of your hand and continue. Push elbow to the table hard. Don't want to die. Don't want to, one more sweeping motion all the way, pull the tool to the left, pull it, pull it. Pull it like a swordsman pulls his blade, like fencers, en garde. Pull it to where the first incision was made. Back to the no way back beginning.

The circular incision has been made, Doctor Namdar.

Leaking blood ring running down the cylindrical black-haired flesh tower.

Painkillers are not working.

Cut through the integuments first, and then the muscles. Divide the loose muscles. Here is a muscle, and it must be cut with the knife. Another muscle. Pull the flesh. Inaccurate left hand. Muscle.

Can't do it. Can't divide another. You can't go on.

You must.

Oh, the pain. Alternate pulling flesh up with left arm, then while flesh is still up, before it falls, divide the muscle. Carve it double-time. Move around the wrist in this fashion. Drag up and cut fast. Not too much flesh here. Pain. Repeat along the lower side of the cut. Wipe off blood sapping out. Pull flesh down. Blood out. Score. Blood out. Score. All the way around the wound. Hurry.

Now for those muscles attached to the bone, use the X-Acto. Cut completely through the deep muscular attachments, Doctor.

X-Acto. Rip the blade away from you. More blood coming. The ripping is more the feeling of your left hand doing the work than that of the pain from inside. Can't tell what is inside or out here. Clumps of tingling, pushing, pulsing down your right arm and then up your shoulder. Hurry.

Everything is cut to the bone.

Apply the retractor by placing the exposed part of the bone in the towel slit and drawing the ends of the towel upward. The retractor should keep the entire surface of the wound out of the way of the saw.

Nearly impossible to do with one hand. Not going to be adequate. Will have to proceed.

A circular division of the periosteum is made. It is here that the saw should be placed.

Turn on the saw.

Hold the tool with the teeth away from the body so as to saw out and away. Hold steady. Line the saw up with the circular division.

Cut a groove first. Pushing the vibrating teeth in...a sensation of déjà vu, as if you're not doing it but have already done it. A tickling as the saw hits the bone while the tremors and pulsations resonate through the body. Legs flinch. Toes recoil in the shoe. You feel wet.

The movements of the saw should not be short and rapid. Every stroke should be long, bold and regular without too much pressure.

Again draw the saw across the bone with a backward sweep. Rumors of movement inside the body. The saw vibrates in the left hand; vibration travels up your arm and takes over you from the outside. Pain at the place of the bone cut.

Must increase the force as the groove gets bigger. Moving the instrument back and forth, grinding the bone. Backward sweeps are less wild, more controllable. Saw to the left, saw to the right. Saw in your head. Don't look up. Don't look away. Cut some more. Blade hits the bone in repetitive gestures. Each time, chrome-sparked bone shards fly past your eyes like schools of whitebait.

Each movement forwards with the saw is an assault on the entire body. Each movement backwards is a fleeting breath of relief. Then back to the chewing of the blade. Homeira, when will you be here? Urine stench. Blood from the sides. A good size pile of bone fragments on the table, press elbow down. Press it down! Don't turn saw off or you'll never start again.

Two-thirds of the bone is cut through. Pressure and force must be decreased so the bone does not break. Yes, it feels very brittle.

Gentle sawing. Two or three more gentle movements backwards will complete it.

Hand falls to the table, taking an ungainly dive into the pile of bone fragments stacked like fossilized finds of the earth around the elbow still rooted to the spot. Tower of silence. Defleshed by the flesher. The bracelet comes after, rolling off the counter and landing in the blood pool below.

Turn the saw off.

Set bracelet on the table.

Inspect. No splintering. No broken bone.

Reach over and pick up one of the empty pots from the far side of the table. Claw it over. Quickly place the discarded hand inside and cover the top with a towel. You can't even look at it.

After the removal of the limb, the arteries are to be tied.

Have to burn the blood vessels. Much more painful, but the only option. Stop the hemorrhaging. Pick up curling iron. Scorch each blood vessel with the iron until it is burned. Pain. Sizzling with each scorch.

The tourniquet should be slackened. Clean the wound well while checking for any concealed vessels that might be blocked up by coagulated blood.

Smell of scorched kebab and used bedpan.

Can you make it before passing out? Place the skin and muscles over the bone so that the wound looks like a line across the stump.

The dressing shouldn't compress. Lightly wrap.

Finished.

Grab the whiskey. Lift yourself up. Move the body to the fur lounge chair in the home theatre room. Get on and let the stump rest on a pillow.

Glass to the mouth. One last thing to do.

Forgive me.

Woodhouse taste.

* * *

Dear Host Family

I am Dr Namdar. I am in the underground of your home. You were not here when I came here. I had to perform emergency disarticulation. Not avoidable this mess. I will pay you for anything I use to perform the much needed operation. I tried to clean the mess as much as possible. Please come to my aid when you get home. My wife, she is Homeira, should there be complications.

Sincerely
Dr Namdar

IT WAS SIX months ago, give or take, when Amir had asked Estella to take the hard drive. He might have to 'go away', he'd told her, and she'd figured it had something to do with Iran, since he was always complaining about visas and problems back home. Admittedly she didn't really know anything about Iran or the Middle East apart from what she had seen on TV, but Amir wasn't the kind to get mixed up with anything political, and most likely the hard drive was full of the code libraries he'd worked on—which he would be keeping out of pride rather than for potential profit. Kade hadn't been wrong when he'd said Amir was all brains and no business sense.

Estella had obliged, taking the heavy black slab and dropping it into her Vera Bradley. When she'd got home that day the bag had been dumped on the floor of her closet and forgotten, and Amir had never mentioned it again.

The closet was too small, and she had to dig out the floral bag, which had already made its way to the back and was buried under a mound of clothes and shoes. She reluctantly extracted the drive and placed it on her dresser, but then ignored it and got to work at her desk.

When she finally crawled into bed she felt the presence of the featureless black box in the room, emanating waves of anticipative anxiety.

BAVANAT:
WINTER WIND OH MY DYING SISTER

This really takes the cake. I never thought he was serious. XYZT, what does that even mean anyway? Where am I? I can't believe I actually agreed to do this. Three hours here and I'm going to miss my deadline for Howard. Shit. He won't have what he needs for this afternoon.

Oh, fuck it. They owe me this. Not one weekend off for the last six months. I can work on it here and have it ready when I get back. Blackberry's charged.

Let me see if I can get a signal on the cell. Out of range. Can I really be in Iran?

This place is freezing. What a stunning landscape though. Somewhere rural, in the middle of an earthen-clay field, surrounded by trees with heavy trunks and naked, winding branches.

Tire tracks ingrained in the road lead up to a makeshift shack of sorts twenty feet in front of me. What should I do?

The air smells clean, sky unsmogged, the kind you don't see in New York anymore, or anywhere in the US. Everything's so still and quiet. An intense breeze sneaks up on me, getting in my ears, messing up my hair. I pull my gloves on. Walking toward the structure, I hear livestock. A truck and an old car are parked to the right of the single-story brick and cement building, a crudely constructed cuboid. As I get closer I notice that there are two pens, one on each side of the center door. One holds goats, the other sheep, separated out by wood strips and barbed wire. Smells like the animal buildings at the Dutchess County Fair.

I'd better put on the scarf the guy gave me back at Penn Station. I wrap it around my head like a handkerchief, tying a small knot under my chin. Feels too small.

Sound of hollow tin when I knock at the door. No answer, I rap louder. It creaks open a few inches. Fingertips slowly wrap around the door edge. I wait. The crack opens wider. He peers at me from behind the door, then finally opens it and welcomes me. Slowly, and just as apprehensively, I greet him and step in. He says he is Bahman and that it is nice to have me visit. Two women and three little ones appear behind him. I tell them my name is Catherine and that I am from New York, and I extend my hand to shake theirs. No one reciprocates. This is turning uncomfortable already. I pull my hand back and it lands awkwardly at my side. I remember something or other from my corporate etiquette courses about shaking hands with other cultures. This must be one of those occasions, although up until now I've only encountered religious Jewish men in Brooklyn who didn't want to shake my hand.

The women's bodies are draped with cotton fabric coverings. White background filled with various subtle-toned floral patterns—brown and black flowers or navy and grey flowers—petite fleurs. The old kind of cotton material used in the early twentieth century to make clothing and quilts, gunnysack fabric or fabric from flour sacks—I forget what my mother called it. Bahman says something to one of the women, and she glides into a side room, returning with a piece of patterned fabric, folded as carefully as an American flag, and, pleat by pleat, opens it out so that it nearly touches the floor. Another flowered body veil.

I'm not really comfortable with this, but I let the woman and her helper bring the fabric up over my head. They carefully remove my black handkerchief from under the flower covering so that none of my hair is exposed in the process. Spending longer than necessary, the women arrange and re-arrange the fabric on my body, touching me curiously, feeling me all over. Back home I would never let anyone I don't know touch me this way, but strangely I don't mind here, as they seem sincere in their concern for me. They drape the edge of the veil perfectly around my face and stroke out the creases evenly so that the fabric flows nicely towards the ground. This is obviously the women's way of becoming friendly with me, accepting me into their home, so I thank them for helping me.

The fabric hangs over my coat and pulls at the top of my head. They nod in agreement that the veil is on correctly. I look down at my shoes and see that the hem stops above my ankle rather than flowing all the way to the floor as it does on them. I notice that they don't have any shoes on, and see a pile of sandals next to the door. I take off my shoes. Another Asian custom, I think, glad that it's a Saturday and I'm wearing business-casual. My feet already feel cold, even in these cable-knit socks.

They direct me through the low-ceilinged hall into an open space to the left that I realize must scrvc as the living room. Although the room contains no furniture, cushions are lined up along the cement wall on top of tribal patterned rugs. I sit down near a heater, an odd contraption—the unit extends out from the wall and has a flame like one of those false gas fireplaces or the window of a vintage Easy-Bake Oven. A duct pipe protrudes from behind it, curving into a round hole in the cement. Faint whiffs of gas. Bahman tells me it is cold in Bavanat during the winter. No shit.

As he walks away, I lift my butt off the pillow and pull the veil out from under me, which takes some pressure off my head. Given the frigid conditions, I don't mind the extra layer enveloping me. He brings over a cheap electric heater that looks like it could set the place on fire if left unattended. When he turns it on, the red-lined coils delight me with their artificial warmth.

Bahman tells me that they are preparing some chai to warm me up, and moments later the pair of women arrive in the room.

They set a tray down in front of me. The woman in gray and blue flowers pours and then opens a tin to reveal sugar cubes. Not like the store-bought sugar cubes I get at Food Emporium; these look as if they have been hand-carved from a massive chunk. I take one and plop it in my tea. I don't normally take sugar, but figure it will give me some extra energy to get through this—whatever *this* is. Bahman takes a lump and places it directly into his mouth, then drinks some tea. The other woman makes herself comfortable, sitting next to me—or maybe just close to the heater. The two of them peer at me in the veil, then take their own veils and pull them tight so that they cover what they have on underneath, holding the fabric closed with one hand and drinking tea with the other. Bent on making an effort to follow traditions, when I think no one is looking I close the front of mine to reveal less as well. Soon I discover that I am totally unskilled at sitting down while wearing the flower-garb—I hadn't pulled it around me properly. To fix this, I would need to get up and try again, holding the sides as I go down, but the heater feels too good to stand up again.

I ask Bahman what he does in this town, and he tells me he owns a portion of a walnut orchard. Walnuts from Bavanat, he says, are known to be of excellent flavor and quality. Usually Europeans visit from Germany and sometimes England. There are also Chinese who come to Bavanat because the weather and landscape are very beautiful and mild in the summer.

'We don't get many Americans here,' he says, still sucking on his sugar lump.

'Why not?'

'Visas are too hard for them to get, but if they do, they have to come with a chaperone. Means they have to pay for a personal guide to escort them around. They can never be left alone.'

We can't be left alone? 'Why?'

He shrugs. 'What is your work?'

'I'm a speechwriter. I'm actually working on a speech for our CEO today. He's at a conference and needs one whipped up. I'm good at it, you know.'

'What kinds of topics are the speeches on?'

'All sorts related to the business really. This one for today, it's on the economic climate globally. The CEO wants to emphasize how Europe is, like, going down. He wants to position us as an American company, as a stronger choice than our competitors in Europe. He says Europe is dying out, that no one there is reproducing, and that soon enough it will be one big graveyard, whereas China and other places have positive growth rates. He wants to emphasize that the US is still in the running too, and that we aren't going to become a ghost town, statistically or economically.'

'Oh,' he says, pensively. 'That sounds very odd.'

'I have to take these sometimes wild ideas, things I don't nec-essarily agree with, and tailor them into a speech that sounds presentable and believable and, in the end, satisfies the CEO and the board.'

'What does your husband think of you working?'

'It's never been up for discussion.'

Bahman turns his head from side to side, contemplating. One of the women asks him a question. He nods and she gets up. 'My wife, Shirin, would like you to try some cookies. She wants you to know she is a cookie baker.'

'Could she understand from our conversation that we were talking about occupations?'

'Yes.'

'Then why doesn't she talk to me?'

'She is shy and doesn't want to be rude.'

Shirin returns with a plate full of cookies. I try one, then another.

'The cookie is known as *Shirini Keshmeshi*. It's made with saffron and raisins, but Shirin adds walnuts to hers. No one else in Iran makes these cookies with walnuts.'

The children hang back on the other side of the room, quietly studying their foreign guest. I glance over at the TV with its deep black body sitting on top of a cheap stand. Even turned off, it looms over us. Balancing on the top of the TV is a plastic flower arrangement. The walls hold a few pictures and a carving of a gold symbol surrounded by Arabic letters.

'We grow the walnuts here, you see. Would you like to visit our orchard before we have dinner?'

'Can I use the restroom before we go?' Bahman and Shirin stare at me. They don't understand. 'The bathroom,' I say.

'You mean the toilet.'

Shirin brings me to the bathroom. She points out the plastic slippers outside the door and suggests that I put them on. They are too big, a man's size, but they are the only pair so I put them on. I turn the door handle and clip-clop in, nearly falling out of the slippers as I try to hold the veil around my body so that no fabric gets caught as I close the door. Fuck. The bidet in the floor emits a queer and repellent odor, although it is too cold for any real reek to build up. Opposite is a new pedestal sink similar to the one in my powder room. A showerhead protrudes from the tiled wall, and I notice a drain in the center of the floor. I now realize why Shirin had me put on the slippers.

Finished, I get organized—put my coat on and try to replace the veil as the women had done. I look at myself in the mirror with the veil around my face, close the veil at my chest, look from different angles at this foreign figure covered in fabric. Then I take a second look and it's me again. Closing the door behind me, I kick the slippers back into their place along the wall.

Outside, the piercing cold hits my face and hands once again.

Our movement causes the goats to become unruly in the pen. Bahman is at my side and the two women are behind us. We come to a dirt road running perpendicular to the field in front of their home. To the right a road twists around various brick and cement walls about four feet high. Some of the walls have branches evenly covering the top, like thatched roofs. The road seems incredibly bumpy, nearly impassable for a car. The air stinks of fire.

The walnut forest comes into view as we turn off the main road. The trees become denser and, even though they are bare of leaves, the winding branches create an enclosed canopy stretching up as far as I can see. Dead branches lie all over the ground, and my footing is unsteady. When Bahman comes across a lone walnut, he picks it up and shows me the huge shell. He cracks it open on a branch and offers me the wrinkled kernel. I've never tasted a walnut like this, so crisp, as if it had been seal-packed for freshness. He tells me that Iran has many fine nuts, grown in various locations depending on the terrain's climate. Here it is walnuts, but elsewhere it is pistachios, peanuts, hazelnuts or almonds. He tells me Iran is 'a very nutty country,' which makes me laugh.

With each minute that passes there is less contrast between the limbs of the walnut trees and the sky as it draws in.

My Host says that we need to get somewhere before it gets too late, so we pick up our pace through the forest. The women are talking and giggling, and I am concentrating on keeping my veil from slipping off my head. Good thing it doesn't touch the ground as theirs do, or I'd have to worry about tripping as well. Bahman leads us up a steep hill.

A vast landscape opens up before my eyes. A hefty mountain of sorts, a hillside of barren gray matter, and to our right a series of smaller hills made of more neutral stones and rocks, although some of them have small tundra shrubs and trees sprinkled here and there. At the bottom, huddled into the lowest recesses of the valley, there appears to be a village, if you can call it that—little more than a few houses. Beyond the village, rolling land with various crops, some bodies of water, and lots of brown acreage.

The sky holds its own against the land it faintly highlights below. Narrowing my eyes, I notice that there is more on the hill than just rocks. The immense gray area is covered with odd-sized stone tombs scattered all the way down the hill, each one just large enough to hold a body. The eeriest resting place I've ever seen. Some coffins stick halfway out of the ground, while others are fully exposed to the elements. Many have ornate carvings, yet some are quite plain, and others seem to be marked with natural stones placed in patterns, like primitive burial sites.

Bahman tells me they are going to pray now. I say no problem. He says that they pray five times a day, and that this is their sunset prayer. I can tell the sun is about to disappear, which means the little warmth I feel will soon be extinguished. I sit down on a big rock while Bahman takes out three prayer rugs, one burgundy, the other two mauve. Either they are very faded or their colors are paling in the light of the waning sun. Shirin and what I take to be her best friend, judging by the tone of their never-ending conversation, line up immediately behind Bahman and get on the rugs. Slowly, over time, and without making the slightest sound, they change position, from sitting to kneeling to a full prayer position with their chests almost touching the rugs. I watch the sun disappear, and breathe in the chilly air. Up here on the hill the wind is strong, and I hold my veil—now a shield—tightly around me. After five frozen minutes they get up. While they roll up the rugs, Bahman asks me if I pray. I tell him I'm an atheist.

'I see,' he replies.

I'm happy that we are heading back, although we aren't walking back through the forest; he is taking us straight down the steep hill. At the bottom, I can barely make out a path to what I think is the main road. *If I can just get down the hill without slipping*, I think to myself. Darkness descends with us. Although the base of the hill doesn't look that far away, my flat-soled loafers tell me otherwise.

I am up front, and Bahman is helping Shirin behind me. I'm trying to move as fast as I can to get down. Brought to me by the wind, signals that sound like the feedback of an amplifier combined with dripping water ring in my ears. These unfamiliar noises intensify as the gale grows fiercer. I look back at my Hosts. They don't seem to notice anything and make their descent without any apparent difficulty. The force finds its way up into the back of my cotton shield and is now inside with me. A sudden gust comes from below and pushes me back so hard that I cannot hold my footing. I fall upward, my back hitting the slope, slide down the gravel, and come to a stop. Moments later Bahman is kneeling at my side, asking if I am all right. Thrown off and surprised that I could be bowled over by the wind, I nod and pull myself up.

'It's the north wind, Druj!' he shouts over its fierce howl. 'She is...' He searches for the right words. He yells a string of words in Farsi then stares at me with wide eyes, his face full of alarm. Struggling, he manages to lift his finger to where the path meets the foot of the valley and motions for me to carry on. Even though I am desperate to get back to the house and warm up, I find it difficult to continue battling against the wind, down the slope. I want to give up, to give in to it.

We're nearly to the bottom, the vortex has settled, and we are able to take the path toward the road. Ahead a great fire burns by the side of the road, its flames dancing behind the silhouettes of six veiled women. We push our way toward the blaze. The women notice I am a foreigner and make a place for me. No words are spoken. I take off my gloves to warm my hands. Burning heat on the exposed part of my face. They look at me, I look at them, and we begin to warm up.

I hear a buzzing around my head, and wonder how a fly can be alive in this weather. It rests on my cheek. I try to bat it away but it comes back, resting on my veil then moving to my skin, then back onto the veil. When it swoops around my feet, I try to stamp it out. But moments later it is back on my cheek, making me itch.

The women watch me deal with the fly. Some are wearing floral veils like my own. Others are wearing dark fabric that is absorbed into the dusk, making their faces stand out as my own had in the bathroom mirror.

At last, we are warmer. The fly has gone or has disappeared into a fold. Bahman returns from the other side of the road where he had been talking with a group of men, and we proceed back to the house.

Inside they take me to a small concrete block room at the back of the house with no windows. Bahman holds the heavy metal door open for me and motions for me to have a seat on the carpeted floor. It is cooler here than in their living room, even though there is a working heater. I would have preferred the living room, but I am the guest here. Bahman excuses himself, closing the door. I hear something slide and click outside the door. Animals chew the fat on the other side of the blocks.

I start to warm up. While they are preparing dinner, I take out my Blackberry. First I check my old notes: *Colossus: The Price of America's Empire*. Ferguson declares he is fundamentally in favor of empire. The reality, however, is that the US is no longer 'the Empire'. This book was published what, like four years ago, and I'm still saying the same thing.

Just as I'm about to start adding to my notes, one of the cinder blocks slides back silently from the wall, to reveal Shirin peering apprehensively through the hole. She hands me two pieces of paper. I gaze uncomprehendingly at the Farsi script. She tells me one is the cookie recipe, the other a page from the book of *Vendidad*, then quickly pushes the concrete block back into place.

OCEAN DRIVE: VICE CITY

He sipped his Bloody Mary from the outside café overlooking Ocean Drive, having picked the waitress's suggestion over his Host's because, as Dennis Hopper said, 'Heineken, fuck that shit!' Palms, clear sky, and the beach right across the street: a replica of the layout in *Grand Theft Auto: Vice City*. He'd also seen the location in TV shows based in the city—*Dexter* was his favorite.

Two women in bikinis passed him on the Miami Beach sidewalk, their skin glimmering in the sun, towels in their totes and iPods in their hands, just like the movie stars he had jerked off to on Oil Nationalization Day. He had watched three films that day, DVDs bought on the black market—a.k.a. his shady friend Reza who had been born the same year as him and lived down the street. Reza, who claimed he was a 'writer', had quit university to lounge around his bedroom all day ripping DVDs for customers. Since nearly all Western films are banned or heavily sensored in Iran, it was a profitable business, and the ripper was able to travel to the United Arab Emirates and Malaysia for his product.

He had watched the films on his desktop computer, alone in his room. Oil Nationalization Day was notable because he had jerked off not once but three times. The films were full of sex. It happened like that: his friend would get films in batches. Thirty films with titles that started with N, or all the big Hollywood films from 2001, or every film made by a certain director. Sometimes it felt like he became a connoisseur of a genre whether he wanted to or not, like the time Reza sold him all of the Pink Panther movies at once and he watched them all in one day, because there was nothing else to do.

The girls were now way down the sidewalk, his eyes still

locked on their swaying derrières, but as they receded into the distance, even though there was no aliasing, he realized that what he was experiencing there on the street felt less real than it had at home in Iran. Maybe because games scrap the whole landscape except for the most essential components—not the details, but those kinds of things the brain doesn't overlook, those that inscribe the character of the environment in the mind. Color, the outlines of buildings, the textures of facades, the geometry of roads and the invisible lines that bring skyline, beach, asphalt, palms, buildings, and passers-by together without your even consciously noticing them. You could drive through an actual city and never notice how the place looks and feels at a specific turn or junction, but in video games you never miss it, and it sticks in the mind forever.

He remembered how, back home, Esmail had been offline for a few months. When he had checked up on his friend, he said he had been on vacation.

He asked Esmail where he'd gone.

'Miami,' was the response, which sounded implausible given Esmail's situation, so he had asked again. Eventually his friend admitted, 'We've been playing *Vice City* for three months straight.'

Americans have their cruises, Iranians their virtual vacations.

NOMADIC FABRIC
(POST-DASHTANISTAN)

We had just come from outside, where they'd shown me their goats—about sixty of them, they'd said. Besides the goats and the tent, for as far as I could see in every direction, the desert held nothing. No cars. I was happy to be getting under cover. The sun's rays were too much for me. I felt especially suscepti-ble. It was the wrong day to be doing this. The tent was held up by wooden sticks and covered in dark panels, woven from the hair of their goats, they'd said. I smelled blood coming. The sun, I couldn't get away from it. In New York you never have to see the sun unless you want to. But here, even inside the tent, the fireball glared through the tiny interstices where the panels came together. They had tried to calm me after I arrived but these pitiless beams, like lasers, too strong to look at for long, made me feel weak again. The air was getting cold but the wom-en wore only long-sleeved tops; two had fabric shawls that did not match their full and flowing skirts. Each woman's skirt was unique—some were patterned and some solid, but all had four rows of decorative piping in gold or silver along the bottom edge. My skirt was so plain in comparison. None of their scarves matched their tops or skirts, and none of the women matched each other. If there was any rule at all, it seemed to be that no one pattern should complement any other.

The women—and there were only women—had strong facial features, and all wore their dark hair the same way. Regardless of which generation they were from, it was parted in the center and flowed down their backs beneath their scarves. Their eye-brows were thick and unplucked, unlike mine. I loved the deep red tattooed markings on their fingers. I always wanted a tattoo.

It wasn't time. I tried to take my mind off it. Layered rugs carpeted the tent floor, for warmth rather than for aesthetics, since they were in the most contrasting patterns and clashing colors. The blood was coming. Flakes of ash floated through the cracks in between the rugs and up my skirt.

Even without the many women crowded into it, the tent was already tight. Towering up from the floor, a rusty portable gas tank with an electric lantern on top took center stage. The walls were lined by piles upon piles of black plastic bags, with blankets, pillows and soft foldable mattresses stacked neatly on top. A few padlocked metal trunks ranging from two to four feet long occupied the space. Either bright green or hot pink with flowers painted on the sides, the trunks reminded me of pimped-out low-rider cars. The women pointed out a loom that they said they wove carpets on. They could disassemble it easily and take it along whenever they moved. I wondered how the nomads managed to carry all of this with them.

The women began bringing the plastic bags over to me. Slowly, they opened them, being careful not to damage the plastic. My underwear was now wet, I was sure it was blood. I stood still as they lifted fabric out, one bolt at a time, some in small folded groups. Nomadic fabric, they said.

Predominantly sequin-encrusted, some fabrics were old and hand-stitched, while others were brand new, their sequins configured in intricate patterns by machines. Old or new, it did not seem to matter to them: each time they pulled out a fabric, they *ahh*ed just the same.

I gazed at the patterns, the flow coming, as if from afar, heavier now. The colors, the stitching. Burgundy net, burgundy sequins sewn with silver thread into small diamond shapes of ten sequins each, and these spread out between rows of scallops. A heavy gold thread sewn into round circles with lilac sequins in their centers; large, rounded half-crescents of gold and lilac...

streams of lilac lacing, hand-stitched over a long crescent shape.

While they continued to pull, it secretly tugged at me inside and I cramped up more. I sat down uncomfortably on the rug and they pushed white fabric organza towards me, covered in petal-shaped designs made up of white stitched thread and silver *sikkah*. As I ran my hand over it, the hole-punched light beams produced a chromatic spectrum on the silver disks—red, blue, green, yellow, purple—dancing around the tent.

Rosy-pink flower buds sequined up. Squid-like tentacles of thick, metallic spun thread in gold, crimson and midnight blue surrounding flattened, flower-shaped petals—five, I counted, per head. Like my overfilled closet when I haven't organized it for a few months, there was so much fabric that the floor had disappeared. Iridescent coffee sequins stitched over black, accents in silver metallic thread and black, a petal flower center set into a round eye, felt heart shapes loosely stitched on, dangling when unfolded.

I held my stomach, hoping they would not see. So help me, it was starting to drip down my leg. Cold on the skin. Flashing by my eyes, sun shining through the holes, the endless twirling of the women. The blood flowing. I tried to stay focused. They brought more fabric covered with purple cylindrical beads over appliquéd gold flowers. Acid green sequins rounded into what they called dogon scales, repeating row after row, the bottom of the curves featuring gold sequins stitched on with green thread.

I figured I just wouldn't say anything, hoping that, if worst came to worst, it would be absorbed into the dark patterns below. I ran my hand discreetly under my skirt along the coarse rug and pulled out my fingers. Glistening crimson. I had to say something. I wiped my hand on my skirt. The woman leaned towards me when I motioned for her come closer. Embarrassed, no longer strong, I lifted myself off the ground a bit for her to see.

She called over another woman who spoke English. The others continued the pulling. I apologized. She looked at me kindly and murmured, 'Ahh, what happens when day and night collide'. I was not sure whether she was telling or asking. She pulled a handful of green olives from out of nowhere and dropped them into my palm, then waited for me to eat. Then she then went on as if nothing had happened. So I did the same.

When there was no more room on the floor, the women draped fabrics over themselves as piece upon piece continued to materialize. They layered material over me. Each woman looked like a starry map, outlines of celestial spheres forming on the pleated ceiling of the tent. The women melded with the fabrics and at the same time were merging together, a collective fabrication. The same feeling came over me as with cramps at work. Unable to focus. Slight errors. Nodding in and out. I tried to maintain my presentability. Folding of movements, creasing of time.

Time...I looked up—no light through the crevices. The only light beams coming at me now were from the sequins. *Maybe the night*, it occurred to me. The intimacy of the collective. Light and airiness. No, the feeling of mass.

Mass, and me within it, moving. Unpredictable the directions that would be taken next. Their, our, undulating shape began to push against the tent, ascending, a force heaving back and forth from east to west and south to north. The shape pushing around me, pulling me, expanding me to the boundaries of the tent.

Shifting back and forth, agitating push push right up and down and bouncing up up we pushed...up we went as we seemed to make headway, up into the swirling fabrics. Moved up light up and ride down. A glide, a glide but a shift forward, jarring shift to the left then the other way. Up, up. Agitate, left convulsion smooth smooth smooth fabric spread out.

Smooth on one layer and layer upon layer upon layer. Pushing toward the ruckus of the stars. Sequins sparkling. Reaching toward delight. Rayons layering up and smooth celestial spheres forming over the expanding, the never-ending. Out to the west, out to the east. North and south storming the firmament.

A bird called. Plain as day, cawing in my ear, two calls. A monarch, vibrant orange and black, passed before my eyes. Then a buttercup moth.

Before me, the stark desert night was permeated with stars so close to each other that they seemed to mark continuous paths. Hundreds of millions of coral-backed disc-shaped beads of unknown patterns cloaking the sky. Passion fruit, tangerine and coral flashed before my eyes. A flower with single-stitched gold thread haphazardly placed in a mass of precious red. Blue ten-sequin structures repeated ad infinitum.

The constellations I knew were highlighted, built on and over purple cylindrical beads over appliquéd purple and gold flowers. Gingery pearls circulating. Secrets shared with the stars. Flowers laid out over blue and silver sequin patterning. A grand circular design, aqua sequins making up bowed shapes, two together opposite one another in the center, next row four, the row after six...all over the horizon underlay. Orange. The boldness of orange laid out brazenly. Orange on top of all colors, no discretion. Then a host of red sequins mixed with dainty flowers made of gold stitching creating an open-ended spider web. Chartreuse in many shapes and sizes getting caught inside. Chartreuse stars, blobs, donuts, flower shapes. Near-chartreuse stitching weaving its way in and out through the night. Reflective facets built on a single line, stems running vertically in fuchsia, flowers made out of scores of geometrical shapes. Star buds, star beads, small sequins dropping from the sky. Diamantés constructed meticulously in the shape of hearts with stitching from the other side interjecting and running through them, spearing haphazard sequins across the entire panorama. The richness of deep, nearly emerald paillettes forming in swaying rows, these rows creating broader curves, occupying large swathes of the night, the outer edges stitched in chocolate brown. Ruckus of the stars. They, we, are the night.

It was so bright that I closed my eyes for just a second. When I opened them, the tent was gone. I lay on uncovered desert sand. The nomad women were nowhere in sight and the fireball had returned, vanquishing the starry night. I wore a skirt, nomadic patterns in the best colors with four rows of silver piping along the bottom. I ran my hand along the trim as I lifted the rows of fabric up to my chest. I peered down, no underwear.

NYC: EL SOMBRERO

The subway trains were running slow, as they had been as of late.

'...memories I have. Coming back to LES reminds me every time. Like when I was still in college and in the summer I'd go back home to my family's place in Ohio. I had a friend. We were always getting into some kind of trouble.'

Chris, a nothing-exciting-looking kind of American, paused to smile. 'It was the middle of one hot summer and I was missing NYC, so he said, "let's drive up there." And we did. We got into this crappy blue car he had and drove here. I'd given up my NYC apartment over the summer. I brought my address book along, and we were gonna call some of my friends who I thought might still be in town, see if we could crash with them for a night or two.'

Navid sat listening as the train moved south. He had begged the guy handing out the bracelets to let him go to New York. New York City, a Tehrani graphic designer's dream city.

Engrossed in his own story, Chris continued. 'I remember distinctly it was on this trip that he told me his last name spelled "IS A RAT" backwards. We laughed and laughed about it. The name suited him. I was infatuated; he called me his partner in crime. After driving all night, we rolled into NYC about five-thirty in the morning. There was nowhere to go, so we were kind of just driving slowly around the East Village looking for a parking spot, but they were all taken. Daylight had just broken, the car was stopped at an intersection, and I look over and see some people coming out of this mysterious red door of some run-down graffiti-covered building. Looked like they'd been partying. There was this guy who closed the door from the inside. I said to IS-A-RAT, "party's still on." We parked the car and banged on the door. It was *Save the Robots*. At first the bouncer, if that's what you'd call him, wouldn't let us in. See, the problem was: one, it was too late to let new customers in, and two, IS-A-RAT had recently broken his foot jumping off a building. He was in a cast and using crutches, the bouncer said it was illegal to let him go down the stairs to get into the place—not that the place was legal to begin with. We flattered him, bribed him, I don't remember what else we did to him to get in, but we got in. IS-A-RAT hopping down those stairs—I can still remember it.'

Navid was finding it hard to breathe in the small seat between his Host and a hefty woman with braided extensions holding a too-large-to-be-on-a-lap child.

'Anyway, we partied down there with some nocturnals for a few hours. When we went back out to the car, we found the rear window was broken. I'd left my overnight bag in the back seat, and someone must have thought it was valuable. Alphabet City—you know, Avenues A, B, C, D—they were still roughish back then...petty crooks, drugs, your basic scuzziness abounded in the general area.' Chris laughed.

Hoping the American was finally done, Navid said, 'We don't have clubs or rock concerts.'

'You mean no good bands come to Tehran?' Chris asked.

'I mean, we don't have anything. The police won't allow it. There are times when aspiring musicians will try to give a concert. But it is always at someone's house. Every time I tried to go to one it ended badly. The place would be raided. There would be threats that someone was going to be taken away, although no one ever was. Still, the party was over.'

They got off the empty F train at 2nd Ave and walked up the first set of stairs. Gradually ascending from the 'pits of hell,' as Chris called it. Sounds in the station reverberated off the subway tiles and surged up toward the ceiling like a cyclone, building up more power with each turn. They came to the exit and were spat out single file through the revolving turnstile. Up another set of stairs and, finally, light.

Walking east on Houston Street, Chris turned to Navid. 'LES—that stands for Lower East Side, you know.'

'I guess it describes our location,' Navid said semi-sarcastically as he took in the scene. A two-way street with taxis speeding by in both directions. Storefronts with foodstuffs and bars along the sidewalk.

'Katz's Deli coming up on your right.' Chris suddenly realized he sounded like a tour guide. 'Have you seen *When Harry Met Sally*?'

'I don't remember, maybe.' He just watched whatever was available, and it rarely made much of an impression.

'I never liked the place.'

The red and green neon of the sign hit Navid's face as they passed.

'Supposed to be the most famous deli in NYC. The times I went, it was always shitty service. You'd beg them for your sandwich at the pick-up counter and they finally make it for you—corned beef or pastrami, of course—then they throw the plate at you like they did you a big favor. What's worse is, after you finish, they tell you the sandwich is like fifteen bucks and the kosher pickle is five.'

Navid said nothing. They turned the corner and headed down Ludlow. He didn't hear any music, but a garbage truck was revving up way down the street.

'It's kind of like the place we're going now. The Hat's been here forever. Then again, it isn't doing as well as it used to. All the trendies would rather be a few blocks down eating minuscule vegetarian portions at Moby's place than chowing down sizzling fajitas, am I right?...I'm right.'

The stink of rancid lettuce and other refuse lingered. 'New York is always full of garbage. Where does it all go?' Chris pondered.

Navid nodded while he took in the block from the middle of the street. Regardless of the smell, he liked the vibe. Even at eleven in the morning with hardly anyone around, it felt alive.

At the corner of Stanton and Ludlow, Chris pointed out a string of windows. The glass continued around the corner storefront. A door opened onto Stanton directly below the 'L' and 'S' of the black El Sombrero sign, which looked like it hadn't been repainted since the eighties.

Red tablecloths, hiding the mismatched furniture, sat begging for customers. Sombreros were strategically placed to make the place more festive. A gambling machine by the door played its electronic tune as they walked in.

The Spanish waitress's feathered bangs blew out of place as she emerged from the kitchen. Chris walked toward a table by the windows and took a seat. Navid sat down with his anorak on.

She brought over a set of silverware wrapped in paper napkins and a couple of worn menus, then disappeared.

'How often do you come here?' Navid asked.

'Don't get down here as much as I'd like now that I'm up in Harlem. How's about a margarita? I know it's a bit early, but hell, let's go for it. We're celebrating that you made it here, right?' Chris said.

'Yes, it's hard to believe I'm really here. I've never had a margarita.'

'Never? The Hat has great margaritas, the best in NYC, possibly the best in the world. First margarita and drinking it at The Hat...you lucked out, my friend!'

The waitress dropped a bowl of greasy salsa and chips on the table.

'Is the margarita machine working?' Chris asked.

'Pretty sure.'

'Can we have a pitcher?'

She nodded and lazily moved to the bar.

'You know that drinking alcohol is forbidden in Iran, right?' Navid asked.

'So you don't drink? Hey, don't you want to take your coat off?'

Navid shook his head. 'Just because it's illegal doesn't mean that people don't. It's just hard to get a hold of and very expensive. I usually drink "Doggy Booze".'

'Sounds horrible.'

'It's the locally made alcohol. What do you call it...a...a moonshine. Sixty percent proof or more depending on how they make it, and it is never consistent. People die each year drinking bad batches. But sometimes I can get a hold of foreign whiskey or beer.'

The bulky stainless steel machine—a big box sitting on the bar's counter—was vibrating and making slurping noises as it concocted the margaritas.

'I'm a beer guy myself, but a margarita once in a while isn't a bad thing. So you can get arrested if you get caught drinking there?' Chris asked.

'Sure, but most of the drinking is done in private, so it isn't risky. Finding and buying is what is dangerous.'

The pitcher arrived with two big glasses. The waitress poured the first round. 'What will you have?'

Chris opened the tattered menu for a look. 'The best thing here is Sombrero Fajitas.'

'I can try that,' Navid said.

'It's a big meal, but we're celebrating, am I right? Right.'

She glanced down at them. 'So two Sombrero Fajitas?'

'Yes, thanks.' Chris turned to his guest. 'You eat meat, right?'

Navid laughed. 'For Persians there is no problem there. We eat a lot of it. Lamb and chicken—and we have some good recipes too. I remember when I was a boy...one year my family was on an excursion for the *Sizdah Bedar*, Nature's Day. We were camping in the desert way outside the city, and it was very hot. My mother and her sister plucked a chicken while my father dug a hole in the sand. He told us kids to watch, that magic would happen. He plopped the chicken in the hole and covered it back up with sand. I wondered if we were ever going to eat...I was so hungry. He told us to go play for a while. When we returned an hour later, my father called us over and dug the hole open. Like magic the bird was cooked—nearly scorched just from the heat in the ground. It was the best chicken I'd ever tasted. And there are also lambs' eyes. My mother never made me eat them.'

'Eyeballs, hmm.... I'm glad we're having Mexican today.' Chris raised his glass. 'Cheers.'

Feeling somewhat weary, Navid took hold of his glass. 'Cheers.'

After a couple of sips, Navid's head iced over. He dug into his pocket and pulled out his Homas. He took one out and offered the pack to Chris, who looked at him in alarm.

'You don't like to smoke?'

'You can't smoke in here. Back when Giuliani was Mayor, he got this bill passed that totally limits the places people can smoke in public. You can barely smoke on the sidewalk these days.'

'I didn't know.' Navid scrunched the cigarette back into the pack.

'Come to think of it, NYC is pretty smokeless right now in general.'

Navid's expression remained blank.

'It's pretty sad.' Chris said.

'Not so bad compared to Tehran. We live the best we can under the current administration,' Navid said, staring out of the window.

'I don't know, maybe everyone's at work. These days you have to work like twelve hours a day just to make enough to live here. And for what, so you can go out to the movies occasionally, see some arts and culture? By the time you finish working you just want to go to sleep 'cuz you're exhausted and know you have to get up and do it again the next day. What's that Nine Inch Nails song…? *Everyday is Exactly the Same.* You know the one, right?'

'No, but I understand what you are saying. It's the same in Iran. During the Revolution, every day was exactly the same, cluster bomb after cluster bomb. The only thing that was different was where they dropped.'

'It's not like it used to be. Used to live just a couple blocks east,' Chris said, pointing to his right. 'Great apartment, but I eventually had to move out. My boyfriend was on the lease and he…um, well…'

Navid eyes scanned the empty room, his face taking on a troubled expression. 'Well, at least you could live together. I have friends who have been jailed, even though they are always released eventually. But Iran is very open to men holding hands or putting their arms around each other in public. Everyone plays it off that they are "just friends".'

'That's scary stuff. I'd be afraid for my life over there.'

Navid nodded.

Smoke was coming through the kitchen window, the smell making its way toward them. Chris took a look over. 'It's almost ready. Take your napkin and put it over your mouth and nose to avoid the fumes when it comes. If you don't you'll choke.'

Navid sipped his margarita, already feeling the effects of the alcohol, and wondering whether he had said too much.

Lines of smoke traveled up toward the ceiling and spread out, forming a smog that hung over the sombreros as the waitress whisked the fajitas to the table. Intrigued by a place and a food that required this kind of action, Navid got his napkin in place. He resisted the urge to cough.

Once the sizzling died down Chris started to pile the steaming mixture of meat, grilled peppers and onions onto a tortilla, dabbing some sour cream and a touch of guacamole on top of the heap. Navid's eyes followed as he rolled the tortilla into a tube and stuffed it in, continuing as he chewed. 'Do they make you pray like five times a day?'

Navid laughed. 'No one goes to Mosque anymore. I've never been. You think we spend all day praying, right? Maybe it happens in some very religious families or out in the villages, but most of us don't, even if we still say we are Muslim. The fundamentalists don't want anyone outside the country to know this.'

'So the people aren't religious?'

'It's not that they don't have faith. They just don't need to go to a physical place to have faith.'

To Navid's relief, they settled on quiet as they ate, each engrossed in his own memories, but the silence was shortlived.

'Well, it doesn't get any better than this. What do you think? Not much gets going around here this early, but I've still tried to show you NYC as best I can. Best margarita and fajitas in the city, hands down. Right?'

'Right.'

Chris called over to the waitress at the bar, 'Can we get two margaritas to go?'

She hurried to the table. 'We don't do that anymore, haven't done for.... The city stopped us.'

'Listen, my friend is here from Iran. Can you believe it?'

She acknowledged Navid. 'I used to come here all the time.'

'Sorry, we just don't,' she said quietly as she eyed Chris, then picked up as many dishes as she could carry off.

A few minutes later the check arrived, accompanied by two brown paper bags with straws poking out of the tops.

'Hey, thanks.' Chris tried not to let his excitement show too much.

Looking at Navid, the waitress said, 'Have a nice time in New York,' then took off.

Chris picked up the check. 'I'm getting this one.'

'That's very kind, but I would like to pay,' Navid said, pulling out some bills.

'Can I see them?' Chris took the bills and flipped through. 'How much is each of these worth?'

'Last I checked the dollar and toman were about equal. So this 1,000 is about a dollar. But the exchange rate keeps getting worse.'

'How about that. Hey, do you think I could have one just for fun?'

'Yes, and I'll leave one for the waitress too.'

Chris turned the bill over in his hands. 'She'll think she's rich when she sees a note with that many zeros on it!'

As they walked out onto the sidewalk, Chris pulled the brown paper bag off his margarita and found it had been hidden in an 'I ♥ NY' coffee cup. He hadn't seen one of those for a long time. 'Gotta love it,' he said, holding up the cup to reveal the logo with the red heart and the oddity of a straw sticking out the top of the plastic coffee cover.

Navid removed the bag from his drink, crinkled it up and stuffed it into his pocket.

'Only in New York can you sip a frozen margarita out of a coffee cup at noon in the middle of March. I love it.'

Chris seemed satisfied. 'Did I not say I'd show you New York? Right?'

'Right, Chris.' Navid sipped from the straw. *What do they put in these drinks?*

'Let's walk west on Stanton. We might catch a gallery just opening up...Fruit and Flower Deli, Luxe, Smith-Stewart, you know, maybe go to Miguel Abreu on Orchard if you haven't X'd out of here by then.'

The neighborhood was just getting going. A bike messenger rode past them. A malnourished girl in a miniskirt with black and white striped tights bent over to clean up after her mangy dog while it pulled at the end of the leash. She lifted her head as they passed but didn't smile.

Walking along the north side of Stanton toward Allen, it became apparent that something was happening on the other side of the street. A parked taxicab blocked their view, but as they moved closer they could see men kneeling on the sidewalk facing east. Lined up in rows filling the entire sidewalk, their shoes had been discarded in the street. They prayed shoeless, some men wearing socks, some barefoot. Chanting buzzed through the air. Chris hadn't noticed anything like this in the neighborhood before, but his fellow New Yorkers showed no signs of acknowledgement. Those passing closest to the action nonchalantly stepped around the men and their shoes and continued on, not even glancing over.

Navid stopped momentarily to take in the whole scene. He sipped the last of his margarita while he watched. Suddenly he felt very cold.

HEART POUNDING, WITH the absolute urgency that usually occurs only in dreams, Estella raced for the train, making it inside just as the doors of the Acela Express sealed shut. The express was already moving as she maneuvered herself into her temporary workstation, filled with an acute foreboding. *If I don't make it in time....if I don't solve the box....*

She brought out the hard drive, but its perfectly smooth, almost abstract surface was difficult to grip, and it slipped from her hand and beneath the tabletop like a bar of wet soap. Shifting herself awkwardly down in her seat, onto the floor, and under the table to retrieve it, she was reminded of what they called her in the lab. 'Hazardina' was a bit harsh—her clumsiness was never really a hazard, except for one time, and even then it had only set the data collection back by a few months....

The dark space beneath the table seemed to expand as she sunk into it, engulfing her like a child playing in a homemade fort. She grabbed for the box. A series of faintly luminescent numbers scrolled past on the front panel, in constant motion. As her fingertips played across the top of the black casing she felt repeating geometric patterns, jeweled insets that gave slightly and, with every touch, made the surface configuration shift.

The numbers and letters changed faster, accompanied by a strange sequence of almost ultrasonic tones. It was almost as if she could *hear* the problem. A shift in *Sequence 3*. Composition, line, structure, time. Even though she could barely articulate to herself what she was trying to achieve, the entire fabric of the box now seemed to be coming loose, as if a knot had been undone somewhere.

The cover lifted off. *What's inside?* Just four letters, glowing with a strange fluorescence.

X Y Z T

Suddenly Estella felt the ground break away and fall, taking her remaining sense of reality with it and creating a vacuum that sucked in nothing but dread. Instead of moving forward, the train was plummeting vertically. Crawling back out onto the seat, through the window she gazed out in confusion at an array of intersecting translucent planes receding into the distance, and refracted through them, miles below, a patchwork landscape rising up to meet her. As if she was looking through frozen sheets of lake ice, the vision wavered and buckled as the train plummeted toward the parched ground.

Open up the box. Suddenly, without knowing why, she felt an awful, vertiginous sense of responsibility at what she had unleashed.

Gazing down at her hands, she saw blood. Estella shut her eyes and readied herself for impact.

ESFAHAN: NOTES TO SELF

walk out onto street after meal—shahrzad no chez panisse but had its own local flavor—bitter cold, like it was going to snow—not dark but street lamps on and over-lit—very jagged sidewalks connected stores selling clothing and other wares—Mrs. Aghasi said we needed to take bus to museum—so embarrassing, west coast to the core! neck got so numb at bus stop wearing small scarf bracelet guy gave me—their scarves longer and heavier, covering heads and shoulders—wished i brought my winter scarf

bus fairly modern, but nasty exhaust fumes + loud—size of an AC Transit, two entrances/exits—men enter thru front door near driver, other entrance in the middle for women—men sit at the front and women further back—before getting on in the middle, we let women exit—a few in full veils, others jackets and scarves—slow process—women's section packed, men's empty—no seats left for us so we stood—Mrs. Aghasi said not far—too warm—Rosa Parks syndrome, but with gender not race—looking at empty seats at the front just feet ahead and not being able to sit down—Asked Mrs. Aghasi + daughter how they felt about this—has been this way for a long time, didn't think about it—would they prefer to have non segregated buses—said they didn't care

what about veils?—didn't like them but had been doing it for so long—Mrs. Aghasi remembers not having to wear veil, long time ago now—daughter has worn one in public her entire life—if they had a choice, would they stop wearing veil?—answer: yes—do all women feel the same?—some would choose to continue

Natural History Museum—courtyard with fake concrete

dinosaurs—remembered time family went camping, stopped at roadside attraction, I climbed on plastic dinosaur's tail—after Mrs. Aghasi paid, passed another guard—didn't look up—like we weren't there at all

Room 1—wide range of taxidermied animals—various stages of decomposition—as if they'd been there since the 60s and never dusted off—corral in the center filled with rocks, bits of brown shrubbery to make it look like a habitat, various stuffed animals, all just as worn-out looking—began to regret asking to visit museum—boredom turned to disgusted fascination, on closer inspection b/w spotted calf had extra head—one of its four fake eyes missing too, so two-headed calf with three eyes—every single one of the creatures was a mutant

sinister-looking brown cow with two mouths, doubly wicked set of rotting teeth—doubly dead—calico goat propped up on a rod to display his six legs—saddest smile eternally sewn on his face—like puppy dog in the pound begging you to take him home

outer walls w/cages low to ground, built into walls—through grating visitors can view groups of animals—boars, weasels, ferrets??—hard to tell—have to kneel down at each cage + peer into darkness—dead animals are so happy

Room 2 botanical room painted palest lilac—exact color of Grandma's bedroom when she had her house—Nearly two stories high—domes covered in relief patterns built into plaster walls—edges of domes painted metallic silver—fine lined geometric patterns cut into walls highlighted w/chocolate brown—(consider these shades when repainting apartment)—room had end-of-day golden glow, sun filter through windows, bright yellow scalloped curtains highlighting curious speci-mens—stems of various plants or flowers pressed into cheap diploma-sized picture frames—glass crushed specimens against construction paper backgrounds in yellow / robin-egg blue / black—like pressed flowers in a book found years later, turned into grotesque brown shriveled-up version—frames all over walls, others in locked glass cases as if valuable—watercolor drawings too, outlandish drawings of plant cells—RHIZOME OF FILICINAE in English then Farsi text at bottom

whimsical mushrooms, other fake plants growing alongside them—FUNERE, SPHAGNUM, BRYACEAE (look up at Berkeley)—all very creepy—Little fungi worlds forever pre-served—Mycophagists would have loved it

Room 3 size of a big closet—on the walls atypical elevated plas-ter surface maps—seemed even older than other items in the museum—all locations marked in Farsi or Arabic—useless to me

Room 4—grandest room—golden mean of the others, inner sanctum—home to prize specimens—prismatic reflections from stained glass windows—mutant specimens all in jars

Baby with twin placenta frozen in clear box of formaldehyde—Siamese twins joined facing each other floating in space—outer part of display case taped together w/clear packing tape—jars of snakes, scorpions, mutant babies—vessels of ??? stuff, one looked like penises—hard to tell—color mostly flesh-peach, all cylindrical in shape—couple of inches thick, 4–5 inches long—jar had a red cover

framed images of various oddities—as if when couldn't have real thing in museum, next best thing is image of some oddity added to collection—(remember newsprint article of head-conjoined twins)

reproduction of an old b/w photograph of chinese man standing with full-length coat on, pulling up shirt—pants dropped to ground to expose giant scrotum, sagging like bulging water-balloon below his middle, hung all the way down to his shins

daughter saw me looking, asked if I knew about sultan who lived in Esfahan during seventeenth century—told me story in low voice so that mother didn't hear

Shah Sultan Hosein ruled Esfahan during late C17 to early C18—Esfahan at the time was in one of its most glorious stages—over centuries it had risen + fallen as a city of power many times—before Hosein's rule it was up, now it is down

sultan was given nickname Yakhshidir because whenever anyone asked him about matters of state he would reply 'very well!'—more interested in harem + pleasure gardens—had large number of wives, 400 or so, had sex with at least 4 per day—at the time it was thought that, to keep sex drive up, could eat other men's balls—so sultan had entourage out on patrol for men who looked like they might have large testicles—when they spotted a likely candidate, was thrown into jail + inspected—if he had the goods, would cut off his balls + make them into special soup for sultan

sultan went on ruling, eating soup, fucking women until empire invaded by Ghilzai Afghans—leader Mahmud had mercy on him, didn't kill him—instead banished him to small village outside Esfahan—when sultan Hosein heard his fate, begged successor to allow him to take wives, because could not live without his women—successor allowed sultan to take 100 with him—soon Mahmud died, succeeded by another man—when successor heard that the Ottoman governor of Baghdad was sending an army to reinstate Hosein as rightful Shah of Persia, had Hosein's head cut off + sent it to Ottomans

'in the middle east we are more interested in balls than kings'

is it still common for men to have more than one wife?—no, now very uncommon, considered in bad taste—not even sure if still allowed

have to stop writing now—messy thoughts here—full of lapses—add more

remember pink coral clusters in lilac room—remember the scorpion-man

Ck

ARKHAM: A RAT IN THE RAFTERS

Shervin couldn't seem to stop rubbing his eyes. Something dark emerged from the door next to him into the hall. He looked up and focused on the long chestnut strands, matted, nearly dreaded, haphazard bunches of thin braids tied with army green fabric scraps. *Girls' hair*, he thought just as she turned around. *Punk girl.*

'Whatcha doin'?' said a narrow, twitchy face.

'Not sure. I'm a bit confused.'

'You look kind of sickly. Wanna sit down in my room?'

'That would help.'

The skinny girl curled a hand around the door, pulling it open wide enough for Shervin to fit through. She invited him to take a seat on one of the two single beds, and he sat down on the one closest to the door.

She walked over to the kitchenette, opened the mini-fridge on the floor and grabbed a Fuji.

'Any better?' She handed him the water, her small eyes glancing over his face in rapid movements.

'I think so.' Shervin looked her up and down as she stood over him.

She opened her eyes wider. 'I think you'll be fine.' Even with the dark kohl, he thought, the heavily-lined eyes, almost full circles, seemed a little small for her already petite face, an elongated oval with slim, downturned nose and small mouth...there was an abnormality about her features, something that didn't quite add up. But cute enough, with the messy hair, tight-fitting black top and army pants. A rock-and-roll or retro-rave girl, he thought, or some kind of music fan, anyway.

She asked if he was hungry, and before he could answer she was over at the refrigerator pulling out packets. 'Do you like

Totino's pizza rolls? My favorite. At least the pepperoni ones.'

'Doritos?'

'No, Totinos!'

'I don't know what they are. Don't think we have them.'

Shervin watched her tiny hands tear at the big bag, retrieving the heavy chunks and dumping them onto a paper plate. Just as briskly she pulled open the microwave, shut them in, and jabbed at a button to start it up, chattering all the while. 'I know they have lots of trans fat, even more since they phased out the real cheese, but I can't help myself.'

'No real cheese?' Shervin said.

She spun around. 'I'm Megan.' The microwave hummed behind her.

'You know you shouldn't stand in front of a microwave while it's going.'

'Why not?' she asked, wide-eyed again.

'It can give you radiation or cause malformation.'

'You don't say?'

'Well, my mother had a friend who used to work in a microwave factory in Germany, and there were stories. Plus she said they used to make the ducts inside the machines out of cardboard to save money.'

Megan bent down and rummaged through the refrigerator, retrieving a peculiarly shaped chunk of cheddar. When the microwave dinged she popped up again, grabbed the pizza rolls and divided them up onto two plates, then cut the cheese chunk in half and dropped a piece on each plate. She passed one to Shervin and sat back down beside him as he eyed its contents uncertainly.

'Thanks.'

'Sure,' she said, wasting no time in nibbling the four corners off a pizza roll with her unnervingly sharp teeth.

He tried to figure out how he was going to eat the cheese without a spoon. 'Megan, where are we?'

She giggled convulsively. 'Don't be silly.'

'No, I'm serious. I don't know where I am.'

'Maybe you have amnesia.'

'No, I can remember things, I just don't know where I am right now.'

She set the plate down on her lap and studied him closely. 'Well, sometimes we let the older memories go, and only remember the things we can cope with. That's what it's like with amnesia patients.'

'No really, it's not amnesia, it's something else. I'll try to...'

'We're in the Miskatonic dorms,' Megan said, cheese crumbs scattering as she spoke.

'I suppose you're going to tell me you're a psychology student focusing on amnesia.'

'Very funny. No, I'm studying linguistics. I speak many languages.'

'That's commendable. How about Farsi?'

'*Baleh albateh*,' she said.

'What town are we in?'

'In Arkham, silly.' She nudged his shoulder with her own and again emitted the odd, high-pitched giggle.

'Arkham, Massachusetts,' Shervin murmured, and fell silent as he ate a couple of pizza rolls. 'I only know the town from an old horror story. Do you like horror stories?'

'Nah. That stuff is for boys.'

Shervin didn't know how to respond. 'You know, translations of good American ones are hard to find in my country. I finally found a few reprinted in *Danesh va Khial*.'

Megan watched as he finished his snack, her head angled to one side. 'I don't have any classes today. I'm not really engaged until late April.'

'That sounds like an easy schedule.'

'Nah, I have courses. I mean nothing exciting is happening until then.'

'You can always study. That's how I have fun. Sometimes.'

Her face lit up. 'I can show you a place if you like.'

'What is it?'

Megan dropped her empty plate onto the bed and got up. She moved to the closet and pulled out a Gore-Tex jacket, and a pastel-striped knit cap which she pulled over her head.

'Scurry up.'

They walked through the Miskatonic campus to find her Taurus on West Street. As they rode away, Shervin examined the university sign, the kind of stuffy school crest that indicates a prestigious institution. Megan went out of her way to drive over the Miskatonic River, stopping the car on the bridge for him to get out and see the view. From the railing he could make out, amidst the murky currents, the island, and knew that it couldn't be far off now. The gambrel roof could supposedly be seen from the bridge or from the island itself, but he could not discern which of the distant houses it might be.

He was not sure how long he had been standing there, peering through the fog, watching the strange shapes of unknown creatures moving through the gloomy waters. He started when he heard Megan's shrill, piping voice calling him back to the car.

Following alongside the train tracks on Water Street, they came to a quiet stop-signed intersection. Her mouth twitched as if with suppressed hilarity. 'If we turn left here we'll be headed to Innsmouth, and we don't want to go there.' She swung a right, and from the passenger seat Shervin was able to get a different view of the island as they passed over a second bridge back towards town.

Main and Church Streets housed quaint shops, eateries and bars in small, connected storefronts; a few people were out on the street. *The legend of the haunted city of Arkham.* It felt pretty tame to him. Just like any college town, almost welcoming if it hadn't been for the sickly pink and green overcast sky.

Characterful houses, aged yet well maintained, lined the lanes along which Megan inched slowly—very slowly, compared to drivers in Tehran. As he took in the neighborhood, a queer feeling came over him. While it certainly seemed like a 'normal' Western town, even a pleasant one, from what he had read, this New England haunt had a weird and eldritch past. Not just because of the story—there was something else. He strained to remember.

She pulled the car to the side of the road.

'P2.'

'P2?' He glanced over her way as she turned off the motor.

'Corner of Parsonage and Pickman.'

There, from the car window, Shervin saw it. The house exuded prestige, with its traditional design: two tall stories with windows symmetrically placed, just the way it was done in old Colonial construction. The roof wasn't exactly as he had pictured it, though. No windows on the steeper part of the gambrel roof, which instead was covered in moss-slate shingles. It did have a sharp pitch, making the house appear easily three stories high, including the space in the roof. The garret.

They got out of the car. Megan clicked the remote.

He stood on the grass, the troubling edifice towering intimidatingly above him.

'Is it the Witch-House?'

'That it is.' She looked up toward the roof and then over at him.

Shervin's body became numb. 'It's still here after all this time.'

'Well, not exactly. Back in 1931, after the owner, a man by the name of Dombrowski, fled the house, it was condemned as uninhabitable by the building inspectors. A little while later the house was leveled, much to the neighbors' delight. Nothing was built on the land for years.'

'How did this get here, then?' he asked, squinting to see if he could make out any movement in the windows.

'In the eighties, when there was a shortage of available land in Arkham, developers started to get interested. But by that time the Arkham Historical Society had gotten strict about local heritage. The preservation police decided the only way the land could be used was if they rebuilt it to the exact specifications of old Keziah Mason's seventeenth-century house. Not really a problem, because the layout of the house was highly desirable and the right family, one that didn't bow to superstition, could get a very large home in central Arkham for a reasonable price. So, the house was rebuilt.'

'Gads, it looks just like the original. It even looks ancient.'

'Wanna go in?'

'Really? How?'

Megan walked up the slate path and climbed the front steps, Shervin following behind, his stomach knotted while she worked the lock. He chose not to ask why she had a key.

Inside, Megan pressed the code into the security system and pulled him through the door. Well-greased, it slammed shut with little effort on her part. In the entranceway, under a large entry mirror, there stood a console table displaying a miniature ship made of wood and painted in reds and blues that coordinated with the long Persian rug that covered the waxed and buffed wide-plank floors. Where the rug ended, an oak staircase began which ran straight up to the second floor.

Another carpet covered the stairs. The center hall opened onto a formal living room also decorated in nautical style. An oil painting of a shipwreck in a large frame hung above the brick fireplace, and canvas sofas and chairs filled the room, with maritime-themed needlepoint pillows thrown here and there. Everything seemed quaint, orderly, and very quiet.

'No one's home?' Shervin asked.

Megan grabbed the banister. 'Nah.' She scrambled up the stairs.

He paused at the bottom and watched her reach the second story then disappear from sight. The house seemed harmless enough; after all, it was just a replica. *No harm in taking a look at the construction*, he thought. For the more time passed, the more Shervin remembered of the story, and the more he felt himself drawn upward toward the attic room.

He scaled the stairway to the next level.

From the faint scuffling noises behind the door, he surmised that Megan had gone into the bathroom off the second floor hallway. He peeked into the bedrooms one by one, finding each to be decorated with wooden furnishings and warm rugs. The master bedroom had a colorful quilt on the bed. Near the fireplace sat a wooden rocking chair; next to it a small table held a couple of mystery novels.

The toilet flushed and Megan came out. Their gazes converged on the smaller, less ornate stairs that ran up to the next level. 'Wanna check it out?' she asked with a peculiar look on her face. Her hands were clasped together in front of her stomach; she pulled both palms up so that her knuckles cracked as she waited for a response.

'Oh yes.' Shervin eagerly walked over to the narrow set of steps and started up, Megan following behind.

The next level was smaller and darker. The hallway had two

doors, one opening east and one west. Other than these, there was nothing of interest except for the rope hanging from the ceiling. 'For the stairs up to the loft space,' Megan explained as she dashed into the west room.

In the irregularly angled room stood a single bed, some simple furniture, and an old desktop computer on the narrow table in the corner. He couldn't remember if the character in the story stayed in the west or east side of the garret, haunted by the witch and her repugnant familiar.

'Check out the other room.' Her eyes became even wider than before, and he figured she had answered his question for him.

The door of the east room, unlike that of the west, was closed. Megan opened it slowly and they walked in. A mirror image of the west room, all of the furniture in the same position. She walked over to the bed as if she owned the place, jumped up, leaned back on the patchwork pillow shams and pulled her feet—still in combat boots—up onto the covers.

Shervin stood in the middle of the room and tried to get his bearings. 'Mind if we check the measurements?' He pulled from his jacket pocket a minuscule notebook with a matching pen, and a small red measuring tape.

'Be my guest, Shervie.'

Turning the tape in his hand, he moved slowly around the room, looking at the corners and the ceiling. 'This wall is north, right?'

'Yes, that's the one. Uh, why do you carry a measuring tape around with you?'

'Just in case I need it to measure.'

'Okay...' Her nose twitched skeptically.

'Iranians always prefer to carry a measuring tape over a gun.'

He was, after all, a civil engineer, even though his main interest was mathematics. He was not familiar with gambrel roof construction, as it was not popular in the Middle East. But he could now see the construction was pretty straightforward when looking toward the room's outer wall to the east. The line of the roof angled in as it rose up toward the ceiling, at what looked like the same angle he had observed on the steep part of the roof on the front of the house. But what he couldn't figure out was why the ceiling in the room slanted down, when it could have been constructed straight across.

'I thought there was some kind of boarded-up window on the north side,' he said.

'There was, and is, since this house is the same. But you can't see it in here because of the north roof. There's a space between the external roof and the interior wall, like a triangle,' she said.

'How do you know all this?'

'I've spent a lot of time here,' she answered.

Shervin grabbed the chair at the side of the room and climbed up to get closer to the low ceiling. He extended the measuring tape to the corner of the highest part of the ceiling and took a measurement to the center of the room. He turned the other way and measured the slope from the center of the ceiling above his chair to the edge where the ceiling met the north wall. Writing both figures down in his notebook, next he attempted to measure the north wall from the point where the ceiling ended to where the wall angled down to the floor. 'Doesn't add up,' he murmured. Again he recorded the figure in his book.

'Are you sure that centimeter tape is good enough?' Meghan teased.

Flustered, Shervin responded, 'Sure enough, it's the best you can get,' adding: 'Maybe you Americans should change to the metric system rather than worrying about changing your presidents so often.'

Unphased by his comment, Megan seemed content to hang

out on the bed watching Shervin measure. He measured the floor at the widest point from the south wall to the north wall. He measured around furniture from the east wall to the door wall, each time carefully adding the numbers to his book. He measured everything he could think to measure.

Shervin then joined her on the bed and started to calculate the numbers in his notebook. He drew acute and obtuse angles and various other diagrams to help him figure. He carefully reviewed the measurements of the ceiling-slope-to-north-wall calculation, shaking his head, baffled enough that he got back up on the chair to double-check his measurements. When he added the new figures, they did not match his first calculations. He wrote it off as inaccurate measuring on his part, measured again, then sat down only to find that the new tally matched neither the first nor the second.

'What are you trying to do?' Megan exaggerated a yawn.

He fiddled with the bracelet on his wrist. 'I'm just looking at the angles for...'

'For what?'

'Wasn't there talk of a fourth dimension and other indefinite unknown realms either inside or outside of the space-time continuum? The way you get there is by way of the lines, special angles that perhaps lead to other planes.' He gazed at her nervously, still fingering the bracelet.

'It's what Keziah is known to have done in this very room.' She suppressed a toothy grin.

'Right.'

'Cultivating the skill of passing through different dimensions in order to reach unfathomed places,' she said, as if to prompt him.

'Exactly. What I'm trying to confirm is whether this garret, with its irregular folds, allows passage to different places either within this world or outside of it. I also want to know if this type of passage can be replicated in any room—anywhere—if the conditions are right. I mean the mathematical conditions.'

'Are you good at math, Shervie?'

'Good enough, I guess. Math is certainly my main interest.' He grabbed his notebook, wielding it as a mullah wields his Quran.

Megan sat up. 'I think it can be both. Some places are conducive to this kind of travel. I have an artist friend who found that her place was based around the number 13. The measurements were all 13. 13 × 13 bedrooms, the living room 13 × 26, and everything else in increments of 13. Her place was particularly receptive not only because of the measurements, but because the house was also on an intersection of ley lines.' She paused. 'Either a space is already set up for it, or one can master the art of passing through dimensions and draw their own lines anywhere. Keziah could do this. With a little help from her friend, of course.' Again she flashed him the goofy grin.

Shervin was finding it increasingly difficult to assess how serious she was about all of this, and felt confused himself. 'That's very...um...is the 13 house here in Arkham?'

'Nah, Westchester.'

'I still can't make sense of the calculations. Is there any way we can go up to the loft?'

'And have a look around?' Megan leapt to her feet, grabbed the chair and carried it to the hall. She sprang up onto the seat with both feet in a motion so rapid it seemed humanly impossible. A pull on the rope brought down an expandable ladder that had been folded up in the ceiling.

Shervin climbed the wobbly steps up to the garret room above. A single bulb lit the windowless space. The walls were made of wood, with oaken beams running up towards the peak of the house. Shervin thought the floor was slanting down toward the north, which made sense; but the longer he stood in the dark, cramped, musty space, the less sure he became. He began to feel disoriented and faint. Unable to concentrate, his ears popped, and his eyes teared up. When he looked for Megan, who had scurried up the ladder behind him, he could barely make out her silhouette in the corner near the south end of the house, curled up in the corner, the dim light throwing hideously suggestive shadows across her face.

With effort, he began measure the angles. Even though the pitch was not sharp enough to make him fall, he struggled with his footing on the uneven floor, and felt as if he was fighting off some kind of motion sickness. In the end, he could do no more. 'I'm finished,' he said as he started to make his way down the ladder to the level below.

After catching his breath, he tried to make sense of the measurements he had taken. Sat on the chair in the hallway, he was so engrossed in his own thoughts that he didn't notice Megan had scrambled down too and was seated on the floor, her back resting against the west room wall.

Suddenly, Shervin's mind became unclouded, and he began to feel sick. *XYZ for Euclidean coordinates and T for Time*—but how could he travel to a place that didn't even exist? *Slipped outside our sphere to points unguessed and unimaginable.* And then a more troubling thought entered his mind: How was he going to get back when his three-hour tour was up? Would he simply be transported back to Tehran? Or would the XYZT bring him back to some abnormal projection of his city? Some other city altogether?

Shervin reviewed his calculations in light of what he had discovered. If...if only he could make sense of the angles, surely they would provide the answers....

Walter Gilman 3/22/08

I awake from the ongoing nightmare. The continual, ceaseless fusion upon fusion of dream and reality. Ever more distinct on each occasion. I think it will stop, stop at some point, but it never does, the dreams become worse, more maddening. It is this, for the present. What comes next?

For decades Keziah and the old house, distinct dreams—distinct reality. Now some added horror: to dream self as story. The objects— organic and inorganic—nothing but phantasms of the mind, night-gaunts. They are nothing. Or are they? The mind does not play games. Or does it? Plot doesn't matter. It doesn't matter whether the setting is the Orient or the Americas. Does it?

Sound of the story. Wrong, the lack of sound in the story The Abyss, a howling terror of cosmic pulsing. Screams infinite and never-ending. Howls, howl and puncture the ears with debinal.

And then the faithful Brown Jenkin, these nights disguised. She told Shervin enough for me to know. I am in the timeless place, youth intact, as nothing but a potential element of nightmares. My heart ungnawed, existing on another plane (another dimension). See all. I say, Shervin, Sir, it is the surfaces, not only the measurements. Surfaces, young man! Surfaces that fold into yet more folds. Did you hear me? F-O-L-D-S!

TABRIZ: BEDTIME STORY

Wintertide in Tabriz. Hold fast, hold tight.

After dinner Mr. Golshiri asked the Jameson boys, 'Do you like to hear stories?'

The American boys nodded sheepishly, while Mr. Golshiri's own children, who were about the same age, said in unison, 'Oh please, Father, tell us a story!'

'Let us retire by the *bukhari*.' The Host guided the party towards the red and black patterned rug. They took their places on rug pillow-cushions, which were all of the same color and spread out on the floor around the heater. 'We have a long history of telling bedtime stories in our family.' He turned to his wife. 'Farzaneh, bring the candies!'

'Father, can you tell us the story of *The Three Brothers*?'

Mr. Golshiri, a nerdy-looking man with a thick moustache, receding hairline and round wire bifocals, whose mannerisms and overall appearance gave the impression of some socialist intellectual in the old USSR—a throwback to his time in the Tudeh Party before the Revolution—put his hands on his hips, causing his stomach to bulge. '*The Three Brothers*, ah yes. My grandfather first told me the story right here in this room many years ago.'

Mrs. Golshiri brought over steaming chai in Persian tea glasses encased in ornate silver filigree holders with baby-size arched handles. On a separate copper tray, she presented the children with long sticks covered with crystallized sugar, which had a faintly yellow hue—the color plastic turns over time. The Golshiri children stirred their chai with the wooden candy. The Jameson boys licked theirs while staring dubiously into their teacups.

Mrs. Golshiri took her place on the pillow next to her husband, wrapping her shawl around her shoulders. It was clear she was content with how the evening had unfolded.

Mr. Jameson cupped his tea with both hands, trying to get some heat in his palms. He could barely feel the warmth of the furnace drifting his way.

Slowly Mr. Golshiri took to the middle of the room, sitting in the center of the rug so that he could be seen and heard by all. Unhurriedly, he began to tell the story, the story of *The Three Brothers*.

'A long time ago there were three brothers whose father had died. The father had been in debt and so the brothers had to organize the selling of his home and other valuables to pay off his debts. The father had a cow that the brothers thought might be worth some money. So the oldest brother set off for the village to see the vizier, who was the town's minister, appointed by an evil king. This man was known to have bought cows and other livestock from individuals in need. He liked to profit at the expense of other men and therefore was known to be very greedy.

'The brother traveled along with the cow and made his way to the vizier's grand home. He was greeted by the vizier, who told him that he had a few things he had to attend to before he could buy the family cow. He said the brother was welcome to wait in the courtyard where he could eat as much fruit from the trees as he'd like and he could play games with the king's daughters until he was finished with his business.

'The oldest brother left his cow and walked into the courtyard. He ate some tasty fruit and then came across the king's daughters, who were known to be wicked girls. They were gambling and offered him the opportunity to play. With nothing better to do, he agreed and gambled with the girls.

'The girls were far more skilled than the brother and soon won.

Because he had no money to pay the girls, his punishment was death. First they slashed his body with horrendous gashes and then they cut his head off. They placed the eldest brother's head, still dripping with blood, on a long stick, hoisted it up in the back of the courtyard, then continued to play their games.

'The next day, the elder brother had not yet returned and the other brothers became worried. The second oldest brother decided he should go to the village and inquire as to what had become of his brother and their cow.

'Once in town, he was directed to the vizier's home. The vizier greeted him kindly and told him that he was very busy and that he needed to finish his official business before he could discuss his brother and the cow. The vizier directed him to the courtyard where he was also offered the opportunity to eat fruits and play with the king's daughters.

'He too lost to the daughters, as he was not a skilled gambler. His forfeit was the same as his brother's. The daughters eagerly cut off his head and attached it to another pole and placed it in the courtyard next to his brother's.

'A few days passed and the second oldest brother did not return home with news of his brother or of his father's cow. So the youngest, whose name was Kaveh and who was an apprentice of the town's blacksmith, set off to the town to see what had happened. He too was directed to the vizier's home as the townsfolk had seen both men go there.

'When the youngest brother called on the vizier, he was welcomed by the man himself in much the same way his brothers had been greeted. The youngest brother was known to be both curious and smart, and when he entered the courtyard, he decided to take a look around before he ate any fruit or gambled. He went around to the back of the patio and discovered the heads of his two brothers dangling high up in the air.

Their blood had dripped down the poles and dried on the patio tiles, so he knew they had been dead for a while.

'Naturally, the youngest brother was very upset by this terrible sight. He agreed to play with the kings's daughters, as he himself was a fine gambler. He thought he could find out from them what had happened. The girls offered no explanation, and they played a fine strategy in gambling, however the youngest brother was very smart and beat them all. They were forced to pay him his winnings.

'As the brother was still alive, the vizier was obliged to meet with him. The vizier told him that his brother had indeed brought him a cow and that he would pay for it; but he would have to borrow the money from the king.

'The vizier then directed the youngest brother into a private courtyard where he was asked to wait. While he waited alone, an old woman emerged from behind the trees in the courtyard. She told the brother to follow her if he wanted to save his life. The youngest brother did not want to die, so he followed the old woman into her home at the back of the courtyard.

'She said there was no doubt the vizier was planning to kill him; he had a secret room on the premises which had a deep well, and the well had a torture machine built within it which crushed men's bones and turned their bodies to mincemeat.

'The youngest brother quickly thought up a plan. He asked the old woman to go to a store in town and get him some women's clothing and make-up with the money he had won from the king's daughters.

'The old woman did as she was asked and returned with the items.

'Kaveh, who was still very juvenile and had a face that was not yet masculine, changed into the dress. He applied make-up to his face, adding lip color with his fingers and eyeliner to his stunning eyes with a bone-tipped applicator. He transformed into a beautiful young woman.

'The old woman told the youngest son that the vizier would be at a party in the afternoon, so he should go and be presented as her daughter who had come from another village to help her as she had been sick and was weak. He agreed, and so the old woman presented him as her daughter at the party. The vizier, who was known as a ladies' man, was very intrigued by the old woman's daughter whom he thought very handsome. He asked the old woman to bring her daughter to his quarters so that he could be alone with her. The woman refused. He begged her to allow him time with her beautiful daughter. The woman would not allow any such thing. Finally, the vizier said that he would marry the girl if she would bring her to him in the evening.

'The woman agreed after the vizier promised to get the mirror and prepare the henna for the marriage the next day.

'Kaveh, still disguised, entered the vizier's private quarters as promised. The vizier wanted to be alone with her and to have his way with her. But she resisted and said that it was only right for him to show his new bride the rooms of his home. He reluctantly agreed and gave her a tour of the vast home which included fancy salons, a room filled with shining jewels, a room consisting entirely of silver, and a kitchen staffed and stocked with the finest quality and freshest foods imported from all over the world. However, he did not show her the well room. She was persistent and kept inquiring about the one closed door in the house that he had not opened and which she suspected to be the well room. He said there was nothing special in the room. But she persevered, and he was finally convinced to open the door.

'When they entered the room, she asked him what a well was doing inside his house, and he told her it was where he put all the bad men of the town, that he had made a machine inside the well to hurt his victims, and that when they got to the bottom the unfortunate individuals would be stretched by the contraption—stretched to such an extent that all the bones in their bodies would be crushed and they would become mush.

'The girl appeared fascinated by the well and told the vizier that she couldn't quite understand how it worked. She asked the vizier if she could get into the well to see what it felt like just before the crushing occurred. The vizier, who was totally taken with the young girl by now, wanted nothing to happen to her fragile body. Therefore, he suggested that she remain outside the well, and that he would get in and show her how it worked. He told her that when he said "Ouch," she should let him back up. The girl agreed and the vizier got into the well. She began to turn the lever and he started his descent. The girl continued to turn the lever, plunging the vizier deeper and deeper into the well. He didn't even have time to say "Ouch." With every meter his cries became softer and softer until only a faint sound of whimpering was audible.

'Satisfied by what he had done, the youngest son removed his costume and proceeded to take as many items as he could from the house as payment for his father's cow and redress for his brothers' untimely deaths.

'After ten days the youngest son heard that the vizier was alive and getting better. Since he was recovering the king announced that he would hold a party in the town in the vizier's honor. So he ordered the cooks in his kitchen to make a large quantity of halim for the party.

'The youngest son thought this was unjust, so while the king's guards were away, he entered the king's palace, where he knew they were keeping the vizier. He found the vizier alone sipping chai in the kitchen and inhaling the delightful aroma of halim, which was cooking in huge pots for the party.

'First the youngest son threatened the vizier by telling him he was going to cut his head off his body and attach it to a pole and place it in the courtyard. The vizier shuddered and stepped back toward a large copper pot on the fire, as he knew what the culprit was capable of. Then, instead of going for the vizier's head, the youngest son caught him off guard and pushed him into the bubbling halim, where he let off a squeal not unlike the noise a live lobster makes when it is introduced to boiling water. He watched as the vizier's body disappeared into the depths of the cauldron.

'A very short time later, the youngest son, wearing his leather blacksmith apron, appeared among the group of townspeople searching for the culprit. He did this to throw off any suspicion that he was the one responsible for vizier's untimely demise.

'When the cooks returned to the kitchen to attend to the massive pot of halim, they began to stir the pot, which now had one extra ingredient. When their spoons scraped near the bottom, they found something was preventing them from stirring. Ever so slowly, bubbles formed at the center of the pot and, finger by finger, a hand emerged from the gunky substance. Soon a foot ascended from the depths of the halim to float on top. The cooks pulled and tugged and eventually got a hold of the thing in the pot. When they succeeded in bringing it to the surface, they were horrified to find it was the vizier, who still had a look of shock on his face, mouth open wide and eyes beaming at them as wide as big ripe dates.'

At this point Mr. Golshiri smiled. He looked very proud of the story.

'What happened to the youngest son?' a Jameson boy asked.

'He became the most famous blacksmith among the ordinary people all over the country.'

Mr. Golshiri stood up and walked toward the corner of

the room where books were stacked on the floor. He carefully picked one up. On the cover there was a golden vexilloid embossed on a square with solid red borders surrounding an old painting of a battlefield.

'Here! If you want to know exactly what happened to him, then read this abridged translation. Make sure to read the chapter on the *Seven Labors of Rostam*, you will love it! That's my last copy, bring it back next time we meet.'

LOS ANGELES: LOLITA

Kim: A dealer, a promoter? I've seen him before, I'm sure of it. Working some street job, wearing a sandwich board, some club promotion. No, I didn't see him wearing that in front of the black stage or at a party. Just imagined that. Must be high. No one wears those signs.

How did we end up in this room? Where did Ameneh go? Guess she can take care of herself.

Sean: So far gone, so fuckable, no way to resist that. Pull the curtain to separate off the room, a bit of privacy, not that it matters much up in this crash pad.

Join Kim in the middle of the room. Single bed. Cozy

'Can I get you a drink? Something to eat?'

She doesn't reply but slinks her body like a stretching invertebrate, worming around the unmade bed. So obviously wants it. Her shoes are off. May as well dig up some worms.

Kim: Open my eyes and he's on me. His body floats over me. Raven hair falls well below his shoulders, tickling me. Open my eyes again. He moves his face close and I smell alcohol on his breath. He kisses me hard.

Philippe: Look at this little *jendeh*. 'How old are you?' No reply, instead she giggles. Maybe fifteen. They marry them young over there, right? Giggles turn into swelling mirth, too loud to be coming from that small body. Maybe she's older. How can I tell? Who gives a fuck? Strawberry gloss engorges the red of her already full lips, which open to allow the flood of laughter to pass. The laugh is disconcerting, but even in her sexy get-up, more Rue Saint-Denis than Sunset Boulevard, she's still adorable. Innocent.

'Do you have any opium to smoke?' she asks.

Not so innocent, then. 'No, can't get that very easily around here, baby.' She could find some heroin, maybe. 'How about a cocktail?' I say. Major compromise. She's already Xing and who knows what other weird shit she's on.

'I don't drink,' she says.

I pull out a pack of Marlboro Blend No. 27s. She takes out a little Homa. I light us up.

Ameneh: His accent is so Frenchy. I always wanted to go to school in Paris.

'Why are you in America, Philippe?' I ask as he puffs on his cigarette, running the fingers of his other hand up and down my arm, giving me the shivers. We sit on the black leather sofa in this place above the nightclub. I can feel the music coming from below and want to get up and dance. We're in Los Angeles, after all.

'I'm an exchange student. Been here a few months now.'

'Do you like it?'

'It's all right. *Comme ci, comme ça.* You understand?'

'Yes.'

'And you? Your friend said you just got here, no?'

'I came to Kim's parents' house. They are my Hosts, and they let Kim take me out. I was Xing, I'm only supposed to be here a couple of hours, I should have been gone by now. Not sure why I'm still here.' I don't think he thinks I am making sense, speaking good English, but I am.

'Well here you are, *ma chérie.* So you're really from Tehran?' He takes another puff, and enunciates: '*Reading Lolita in Tehran.*'

'Everyone's read it,' I say.

He nods.

I get up and start to twirl around. 'I love to dance!' I scream over the music. I wish there were these kinds of clubs in Iran. Home parties aren't the same.

He says, 'This MGMT mix is wild.'

'Come on Philippe, let's dance. Come on!'

He lifts his small designer-clad frame off the sofa and joins me, whisking me around, both of us laughing. He grabs my arms and swings me in circles for the entire song. Air fills my mouth.

The room is spinning. He guides me back to the sofa where I hit the cushion, feeling dizzy.

Kim: Gamma ray burst wakes me up. Top is off, bra still on, Sean's clothes are off, his T-shirt and pants on the floor. He comes at me at an angle, like a ramp veering upward, the slant turning me on. I'm in no condition to suck, even though it's right between my lips. Get the impression he fucks around a lot. I think he keeps questionable company and probably fucks around with said questionable company. How do I know this?

'There are condoms in the bottom drawer of the armoire,' he says, pointing. He must have read my mind. Or did I say what I thought out loud? I get off the bed and walk then fall to the floor, try to hide the fall by mimicking seductive cat-like crawling as I move along. Pull the drawer open and take out a condom from a blue box at the top of the pile.

Get up and nearly tip over on the way back to the bed. It's kind of sleazy to have a bed in the center of a room, but he's on it. MGMT booming up from below...*this is our decision to live fast and die young, we've got the vision now let's have some fun...* Make it to the bed and hand him the condom. Rest while he struggles to get the latex all the way to the base. It doesn't seem to be fitting. The man next to the armoire, the condom man, tells me that there are Trojans in the drawer too, in a purple box.

'I can get you a Trojan, if that would help.' I look back over and the condom man is gone. Can X make you hallucinate?

Sean drags off my underwear and shoves my bra up over my tits. I lay back, head drooping over the edge of the bed, open and feel him push inside me. He continues to fuck while I watch the room upside-down and pitching gently. Upside-down black entertainment center, an old TV, an out-of-date boombox. The base of a black floor lamp, its cord coiled around in a messy pile, unplugged... Snake charmer. Blood rush to the head.

Philippe: Such a flirt. So full of energy. As we talk I play with her dangly gold earring. Every time she gives me the look to stop, I stop. A minute later I move it again, just enough so that the gold balls at the bottom jingle and the flat petals catch the light.

We hear activity in the room next door. Her friend is screaming off and on.

The noise continues. We decide to go check out what the hell she and Sean are doing, although I am pretty certain he's screwing her.

We enter the room just as Sean is getting off the girl. She's motionless on the bed. Both of us move closer to them. I can see Sean. Damn, his body's sexy as hell. Her eyes are closed.

Ameneh: We walk through the curtain into the room where Kim is with that guy. They're on the bed in the center of the room. I get on there with him. He makes room for me. Kim is next to him, sleeping. Smells of sex.

He starts to kiss me. Philippe moves over to the chair in the corner to watch.

His matted hair rubs against my skin, leaving its oil on me. He takes my face in both of his hands and looks me in the eyes.

'How old are you, baby?'

Kisses me again while he pulls my over-the-shoulder top toward my waist, stretching it out, exposing the fuchsia push-up bra I got in Tehran last year. I remember when I bought it, the boy who sold it to me winked at me like it was a good choice. Pulls off my *tanakeh*.

Philippe is watching us. I look over at him and smile. Kinky.

Philippe: He's going to screw her too, *merde*. Remix of an old song. *Sex I'm a....*

WHEN ESTELLA AWOKE, confused and exhausted from her dream, the hard drive sat on her dresser taunting her, as if aware that she had tossed and turned all night without knowing why. Bleary-eyed, she munched on a stale muffin washed down with soymilk, forcing herself to eat even though she wasn't hungry. *The black box is calling.*

It was time to plug into the thing. She rummaged through a drawer full of cords until she came to a connector that fit snugly in the socket, and attached the other end to her laptop.

A blue screen of death would have been predictably annoying, but instead, when the drive finally span up, it plunged the entire screen into unillumined blackness. The light on the drive glowed, but nothing happened. Ready for the challenge of hacking her way in, she pulled her wavy strawberry-blonde hair back, not bothering to get up to find something to tie it with. This would take skills, and skills she had.

Minutes turned to hours as she laboriously recovered all of the files from the hidden partition she had located. A feast for the eyes: documents, images, archived emails. She couldn't open them fast enough.... One folder full of incomprehensible circuit plans. *Specs for what...? GPUs? Okay, processing power. Then flash memory, GPS locator, standard microelectronic components, but what's the controller for...?* Another containing JPEGs of city locations, aerial view plans, and text files with long lists of surnames, both American and Middle Eastern looking. *Why would they need all of this?* Then cut and pasted bank transfers detailing payments made throughout the first part of last year, and archives of what seemed to be long email exchanges in the same Arabic script.

Sure enough, many of the documents featured Kade's name. But Estella still couldn't make this unlikely pair add up: preppy Kade and his imaginary billions, his 'cribs' and 'rides', always working on *something big*, and the gentle Amir, apparently so disinterested, so committed to his work above all else, keen to make his way in the US and help out his parents back in Iran? Amir, who had now 'gone away' as he warned her he might—with Kade?

Estella continued to scan the drive item by item. Amir had definitely been working overtime. The technical documents referred to hardware she had never even heard of, and the code used a bewildering array of libraries and APIs he had evidently hacked together himself. 'Tests', 'deployment location', 'device activation'. *What the hell has Amir gotten himself involved in?* Horrified, she reluctantly googled bits of information that she had found. Strings of words, names, component IDs, anything that would give her more to go on.

An hour later her phone vibrated and a fluorescent green Android robot came on screen locking the phone. A geek for hi-tech, she had the latest phone which, as a student, she couldn't really afford. *Must be updating.* She connected the charger and forgot about it, engrossed in the plot unfolding before her. The more files she opened, the less she was able to hold back the sinking feeling, the dread at her worst suspicions, and then her shame at the excuses she was already inventing to rule out her own involvement: *not friends, just acquaintances, fellow students...I wouldn't exactly say I knew him....* If she destroyed the box now, would that just look more suspicious? Increasingly outlandish scenarios played out in her head. *It's not paranoia if they're really out to get you*, she joked feebly as she peeked through the window blinds. Sure enough, a sleek black car. So what. A car.

The phone buzzed again, went dark, and restarted itself.

DENVER: CENTRAL LIBRARY

Even though Purim is in the air and she has a guest in town, Eva has something she needs to look up, so they head to the fifth floor of the Central Library, the postmodern architectural mish-mash Michael Graves created as something of an ode to information and knowledge. Eva suggests to Mahasti that she might like to wait for her in the periodicals section, and drops her off at the first group of chairs she sees. Newspapers spread out before her, Mahasti starts leafing through the issue on top, in fact people-watching more than reading—the library is a happening place: young people carrying books, women with baby carriers, couples walking along hand in hand. She pulls out a petroleum-smelling lip balm, applies it, then discreetly makes a kiss-smack into the air. Glancing down at the page, she spots a photo of Ahmadinejad.

Further Pressure on Tehran over Nuclear Plans: The Iranian government once again finds its nuclear power program frustrated as the UN Security Council adopts resolution 1803, extending travel restrictions and asset freezes and instituting a travel ban on additional Iranian entities. The resolution also forbids Iran from buying a range of nuclear and missile-related technologies, and calls for countries to inspect suspect cargoes to and from Iran more closely. The international community was warned to exercise vigilance over public financial support for business with Iran and transactions involving Iranian banks.

The resolution names Bank Saderat and Bank Melli specifically. Discarding the article, she turns her full attention to the passers-by.

THE DISTRICT: NINE WEST

She couldn't help it, every time she had the boots on and walked outside, she would sing: *These boots are made for walking, and that's just what they'll do. One of these days these boots are gonna walk all over you!...* It was always under her breath and she followed the refrain by saying *Strut it girl. Strut it.* Then she'd move along, shifting her shoulders forward and back as she walked, feeling so Latina. The guys on the streets of New York City liked watching her strut in the boots too. A guy on Park yelled 'Strut it, bird!' one time. She didn't know why he called her a bird though. They did look like Nancy Sinatra's patents, only her Nine West version was regular leather, not shiny and plastic looking. She wouldn't be caught dead in those kinds of boots. On sale, she had got a great price on hers with her employee discount.

It was Saturday, and Xiomara had her favorite boots on because she was going out for drinks after work with a friend from Daffy's. And whenever she wore her boots out, she felt lucky—she could always take home any guy she wanted at the end of the night. But her daily routine had taken an unexpected twist. No longer in Midtown, now she found herself strutting along with her Hosts, and even though she was taking in all of the scenes—bizarre as they were—she could still hear *These boots are made for walking...* repeating in her head. It was actually a fine road for strutting. She managed to tune the song out by talking to her Hosts as they walked. They had commented on her nice boots, these women who were taking her to the exceptional shrine.

Just as Xiomara had lost the urge to sing, another tune presented itself. She realized a moment later that it was not in her head but coming from a nearby street. The sound of a cheap electronic melody like that of a musical greeting card only much louder, with the same tune on repeat: *Da-da-daaa-daaa da da. Da-da-daaa-daaa da da*...coming nearer.

'What's that song?' she asked her Host, Zammy.

'Just the garbage truck song.' Zammy patted her guest on the shoulder as they continued to walk.

This didn't make sense. '*Que lo que*, why is the garbage truck playing a song?' she asked.

'To let everyone know it's coming.'

'Gotcha,' Xiomara replied dubiously—*Like, why would you want to know?* But as it played over and over, she still couldn't name that tune.

As the garbage truck made its entrance, street cleaners jumped off the back and placed empty garbage bags at the gates of each house on the block.

'What are they doing?'

'Dropping off the recycling bags.'

'Is being green really big here?'

'What do you mean?'

'Like, do you do a lot of recycling and nature shit in Iran?'

Zammy stood motionless, then announced, '*Sizdah Bedar*! *Sizdah Bedar*. I forgot it's on Tuesday! It's a national holiday. Everyone goes to places of nature away from their homes and enjoys the day.'

Vashti, her second escort, elaborated, 'In ancient times it was to get rid of the Demon of Drought, and since it is on the thirteenth day of *Farvardin*, it is to get rid of the unlucky number thirteen.'

'There's a holiday for that? No one gets time off for Earth Day in my city.'

'Only one bad thing, you can't leave your house unattended because it's a big day for burglars. Since they know everyone is gone, they sneak from house to house looking for gold and jewels.'

As the truck whizzed off, she finally recognized the melody. 'The garbage truck plays *Happy Birthday*?' she exclaimed. 'Weird.'

'Is that the song? What's wrong with a truck playing that song?'

'What, that's not weird like?' Xiomara insisted.

Her Hosts offered no response.

They made their way into a grand public courtyard where the women handed her a *chador* they had pulled from a plastic bag. 'You have to wear this inside the shrine.'

Xiomara unbunched the wrinkled ball and put it on, as did Zammy and Vashti, who had only been wearing scarves and long-sleeved smocks. A man holding big bunches of fresh green herbs wrapped in newspaper asked if they wanted to buy any. The women shook their heads, and he was gone.

They approached the women's entrance to the shrine and went through the security check. Inside, a few women were working behind a counter. Vashti told her she needed to take off her boots. Xiomara slowly unzipped them and placed them up on the counter along with their sandals. An employee shoved them in a cubbyhole on the wall, just like at a bowling alley. Barefoot, the women were ready to enter.

Inside, some women were seated on the carpeted floor in various places, while others waited in line to be near it. The shrine, a tomb of Imam number something or other—Xiomara had forgotten as soon as she was told—was surrounded by gold bars, so you couldn't really touch the tomb. It didn't stop the visitors from stretching out their hands toward it, trying to reach it; some were even kissing the bars. Close to the Imam, many of the women were using their voice to create a repetitive *kal-kal-kal* sound in unison. On the other side of the tomb was the men's part, from which Xiomara could hear what sounded to her like deep murmurs of despair—or, on second thoughts, drawn-out groans of delight.

Taking their place on the carpeting in front of the gold, they sat quietly. Xiomara thought about how this set-up was the distant relative of a Santería shrine. Primary red, royal blue, bright green and gold, and the decorations—it all seemed like another version of altars she'd grown up with in Bayamón. She was Catholic now—no weird shit, thank God—but she remembered well enough.

The women exited through a door that took them back to the shoe locker, where the attendant gave Xiomara back her boots. Zammy passed her a tip. As soon as they stepped out into the courtyard, the women took off their *chadors* and stuffed them back into the plastic bag. They moved through a long stuccoed corridor full of arches. Motorcycles lined the walkway, but the women passed easily through.

As they emerged onto another street, suddenly everything went blue. The cement walkway was painted a clinical blue, as were the walls of the buildings and the street poles. The sky, whited-out by the sun, was the only thing besides the pedestrians that was not some tincture of blue. Xiomara noticed a woman walk by with a fresh bandage over her nose. Another passed with the same bandage. Everyone who passed in the other direction—men and women alike—was wearing a nose bandage.

'Why they all bandaged up?' Xiomara asked.

'Nose jobs. Iranians get nose jobs.'

'What...Why?'

'Because most Iranians have very big noses.'

'I'm sure that's not right.'

Vashti replied, 'Oh, but it is. It's nothing to be sorry about, just a fact.'

'My nose is *way* too big,' Xiomara said.

'Why don't you take care of it?'

'I never thought of a nose job.'

'You can do it while you are here. You have two hours left. This is the rhinoplasty district. I'm sure they'll be happy to fit you in since you are so pretty.'

Xiomara thought about it. Maybe that's what she needed, maybe the guys might.... 'Even if I wanted one, I can't buy that,' she replied.

'Nose jobs are affordable for everyone.'

'Like how much?

'You just pay what you want.' Zammy and Vashti smiled as they weaved through the oncoming traffic.

'I pay what I want?' It sounded better than a going out-of-business sale. 'I only have dollars though.'

'You can use that. There is a place for every price range, and dollars are always good for bargaining.'

More and more patients filled the streets around them. They were coming out of the storefronts and immediately closing the doors. The windows were darkened so Xiomara couldn't see inside.

'Why don't we see if they can take you?'

This can't be true, she thought as she felt her nose and nodded hesitantly.

The women stopped in front of the nearest door, which happened to be opening. A woman wearing red lipstick and a bandage exited, beaming as she walked by.

In the small waiting room, Vashti lifted a trapdoor built in the floor. 'Good luck!' she said, and motioned for her guest to go into the floor.

'What should I do? I can go there?' she asked, peering down into the hole skeptically.

'Just go down the chute, we'll wait up here for you.'

The chute was made of stainless steel and angled down like a slide.

'Down there, really?'

'Go on, we did it. There is nothing to be afraid of.'

She sat down on the floor and stuffed her booted feet into the chute, then reluctantly pushed off from the edges of the trap. Before she knew it she was speeding down like a luger in the Olympics.

While she was recovering, I tried the American patient's boots on behind the curtain. Giti Pashaei! Glorious Giti, our beloved chanteuse. I started to sing the song 'Gol e Maryam', a long-lost tune from my brain's storeroom.

MOUNT ST. HELENS:
LEIURUS-GIGANTOPITHECUS

Free Associations. The slope of the terrain was quite steep and the snow heavy, but Sahara was sheltered in a covered niche. Walls of densely packed snow protected her small urochrome-tinted armor from the frigid wind; normally robust and durable, here she was weak and struggling. But هيس would look after her. The fire that هيس had built just outside the cubbyhole provided her with enough warmth, but for how long, she wondered? The burnt-orange and propane-blue flames were steadily melting the snow around her so that slush dripped onto her semi-translucent abdomen, getting caught in the grooves between segments of the chitinous exoskeleton and drizzling off in fine streams. She gazed fixedly into the fire built on the slanted hill and tried to guess how long it would be before it went out. The wet wooden stems هيس had used kicked up extra smoke, which weaved through the tall redwoods up into the white sky. She wondered how old the trees were.

Hopefully هيس would return soon. She felt terribly out of place, suddenly transplanted into this alien landscape. To date, her life had been limited to the desert, and then the cramped flat in Tehran with هيس. She knew she wasn't supposed to ever get scared—that was how she was, and surely one reason هيس liked her and had chosen her as his companion. But she couldn't lie to herself: she was more terrified now than she had ever been.

The fire produced more smoke as the flames dwindled.

She heard rustling and movement but couldn't see down the hill from her mini-igloo. She was relieved; the cold was causing her legs to freeze. Was هيس coming back?

The noise continued for minutes, building to a low, dull thudding that seemed to be moving nearer, yet nothing materialized from the white-out. Should she go out and have a look?

'هيس, is that you?'

The ground below her shook, the rumbling sending vibrations through her minuscule body. Through the tendrils of smoke she saw brown—a set of enormous furred feet, which would have looked like fur boots were it not for the twelve bulbous toes protruding from them. It was an animal, and a big one at that. Sahara shivered and retreated further back into the niche.

The melted snow splashed under the huge feet as the thing shifted position. And then suddenly it was right there, a gigantic face, intelligent like هيس's, but dark, shaggy, animal-looking. The thing was kneeling down and peering into her niche. With nowhere to hide, she crunched up in the corner as far away from the opening as possible.

'What are you doing?' said the beast, its voice deep but surprisingly gentle.

She cleared her throat to speak loud enough so that it could hear her. 'I'm waiting for my companion هيس.'

'Why do you have a fire going?'

'To stay warm. I'm very prone to the cold.'

'Regardless, you can't have a fire here. They'll see it. We have to put it out.'

'But then how will I stay warm until هيس gets back?' Her initial terror easing a little, she surveyed the beast's broad face. When he turned to the side, she saw that his head curved sharply at the back. A heavy brow line over his eyes, he was somewhat like هيس, but not exactly. This creature had hair all over his face, and stood at least two feet taller than هيس. They were not the same kind of thing, she decided. She would have to be on guard, ready to sting if necessary.

'Where did he go, this هيس of yours?' said the beast.

'To Seattle, to locate an indoor place for me. I'll die out here.'

'Seattle!' the beast exclaimed incredulously, 'That's far from here. He'll never make it.'

'He's human, he can travel fast. But it would be too cold for me, even if I rode on him.'

'Well, we're near Mount St. Helens here. It's pretty far from Seattle, I know that much.'

'We were supposed to arrive in Seattle though. Someone was meant to be here to meet هيس. I just came along for the ride.'

'As you can see, you have not arrived. Seattle is a big city, this is the mountains.' The beast looked around, muttering to himself as if mentally weighing up some decision.

'I'm not sure what to do. I'm terribly cold.'

'We could take you to our complex. It's not far from here. You can warm up.'

'That's very kind. Would هيس be able to come along too? We could wait for him a bit longer.'

'He's a human though? No, I'm afraid not. We don't interact with humans. We've evaded them this long and we plan to continue doing just that.' His eyes followed her as she crawled away from the corner.

Sahara hesitated. If she left, هيس might never find her again. A clump of snow fell onto her tail, another onto her face. 'Could you make an exception for هيس? He's a really nice guy.'

The beast's face hardened. 'He's a human. Sorry, no exceptions.'

'How far is your place?'

'Very close.'

'Maybe we could go there just long enough for me to warm up, and then I can come back and wait for هيس.'

'If that's what you want to do.'

'I think so, otherwise I will die. A deathstalker is a survivor.'

'I can understand that.'

Impure Mixtures. The beast's brown furry foot kicked slush over the remnants of the fire to douse it, careful not to push any into the hole. With the embers gone, Sahara could focus her eyes properly on the creature. His fur was matted, and he was rougher and larger than she had initially thought.

Sahara slowly emerged from the hole, stretching her feet. She maneuvered around the fire mess and looked downhill. There were more than one of him. All of them the same, tall and woolly all over, and talking amongst themselves as they approached. But she wasn't afraid of them—she was a deathstalker. How long would it take هیس to get back?

The first beast looked down at her, nearly frozen and slowly turning from yellow to albino in the open terrain. 'You don't look too good. We'd better get you inside. My relations are fine with you coming to our dwelling. How should we should carry you?'

There was no time to feel self-conscious, although she was embarrassed at her vulnerability and dependency. 'On your shoulder, if your place isn't too far. That's how I ride on هیس.'

Wasting no time, the beast kneeled down and brought his shoulder close to her. She moved swiftly, clambering up the curve of his back to grip his burnt-cinnamon-scented fur.

Without saying a word, the beast started down the hill. Too weak to ask his name, Sahara just hung on for her life. Wind stung her face and blew snow in her eyes as he trudged endlessly downhill. To try and keep her mind off her frosted shell, she imagined what the beasts' homes were like. Maybe they were cabins and had wood-burning fireplaces, maybe they were *ashayery chadors* with kerosene heaters. So long as it was warm. She sank into abstracted dreams of white sun-scorched deserts.

She was momentarily shaken awake when her carrier made a misstep in the snow. The drifts here were higher, and the beasts had to work hard to get through. A few of them carried carved diamond-willow walking sticks that they jabbed into the white crust to keep their balance. The pines were shorter in this section of land, and the ground was littered with countless fallen logs around which the creatures had to navigate.

Transversal Contagions. When she awoke the next time, she found herself on an undersized bed on the floor of a cramped cave. The earthen walls glowed fluorescent orange from glass ball lamps lit at various heights throughout, each containing a bright gooey substance that churned hypnotically inside the sphere. She had never seen anything quite so intense. هيس's time as a chef had enriched her color sense and vocabulary, and she imagined how he might have described it. Carrot purée with mango-pomegranate-blood orange, lit up like a flambé.... As peculiar as the substance was, though, the orbs within which it circulated were even weirder—thirty centimeters in diameter and perfectly round, as if they had been hand-blown by a glassmaker, yet she could see no break in the glass where the substance could have been added. Even odder was the fact that they seemed to hover in the air of their own accord.

No one was around and, already feeling better, she shifted her body over to the closest ball. The orange was giving off heat as well as light, and it felt as if she was basking in a neon sunset.

Hearing vague echoes outside the room, she peered curiously around the doorway. A narrow, rounded tunnel ran as far as she could see in both directions, with doorways carved out of the rock intermittently along her side of the tunnel.

The echoes became louder and traces of light flickered across the concave walls. A few beasts appeared where the walkway curved out of sight, each carrying a wooden stick at the end of which hovered a glow-ball similar to the ones in her room, about two and a half meters in the air above them, almost touching the ceiling as they walked.

They made their way over to her. Among the group she recognized 'her' beast. 'Have you rested enough?' he asked her.

'I feel better. How long was I out for?'

'A few hours your time.'

'Really?'

'Really. We'd like to take you to Hex-25. We can talk there if you like.' He sank down to his knees and without further questions she clambered onto his shoulder again.

Out of the harsh external environment the beast seemed far more reserved. It looked as if he had groomed himself, possibly taken a bath. She saw his profile, his cheeks quite rounded, the brow jutting out prominently. 'Where is Hex-25?'

'We've got to cut through some tunnel lines, that's all.' Sahara hung on to the beast, his orb beaming warmth down on her as she rode.

They motored along the tunnel. She had been in a near-fatal state a few hours before. Now she no longer felt the dull ache of the cold on her exoskeleton, and her color had started to come back.

'You blacked out, but we got you here,' the beast said.

'Where are we?'

'We're in the Lava Tubes right now.'

'What is lava exactly?'

'It's a bit hard to explain, but it's the substance that a volcano makes.'

'Oh yes, that's what it is.'

'The Lava Tubes are created by the lava running through and then cooling down, making this kind of space.' He stopped walking and placed his glowing stick in front of them. 'That's lava in there, too.' He pointed to the glass ball.

'Cool!'

'No, it's hot.'

How did you get it in there?'

'It's hard to explain. But it's our own invention. This is how we heat and light our complex, and we use it for other power too. They're called Lava Lamps.'

'Good name.'

'We think so.' He started to walk again.

The beast pointed out lava pillars in one tall tunnel; he said that they were the only pillars in the tube system. Another tunnel had shark's-teeth stalactites hanging from the ceiling. Most of the tunnels had dwelling rooms attached, where he said they slept.

Passing through a room glowing iridescent blue, Sahara inquired why it had this peculiar color.

'The blue helps our biological clocks.'

'Certainly makes me feel calmer.' She glanced towards the beast's face. 'How big is the tube complex?' she asked.

'It's huge. They know about Ape Cave to the south, but there are thousands of lava tubes over here. They just don't know how to get to them.'

'They?'

'The humans. They start their expeditions, and then stop every time there's the slightest hint of danger. Understandably, no one wants another 1980. We lost tens of thousands, and they lost many too. Even this January, they called off an exploration because of a little steam coming out of the lava dome.'

'But you don't want them to find you.'

'True. We hope they don't dig deeper.'

Epiphytic Transplantations. They rounded the corner and arrived at a set of uneven stairs chipped out of cooled lava. The others, who had mostly remained silent, turned to her beast. He nodded, and they proceeded upward. The stairs wove around large rock formations and brought them to a landing where the ceiling was covered with hundreds of short, spiked lavacicles. To the left, an iron railing was built along a partially open wall. As the beast moved towards the railing, Sahara could see the landing overlooked a gigantic open space.

'So what do you think?' the beast asked.

She looked out over Hex-25. The outer walls were hardened lava, and she could see cuts of jagged stone in places all the way up. Mostly though, the walls of the loosely hexagonal room were covered in vegetation—plants of all kinds, growing in black containers that protruded from the rock walls, and apparently organized by species. Long pathways made of wrought iron clung to the walls at various heights, with stairs connecting all levels. Boxes filled with gravel and plants occupied almost the whole floor of the room which, from Sahara's vantage point, looked to be about half the size of Azadi Square. A few beasts watered plants with hoses on the main floor, while the foliage up on the walls was misted with an automatic irrigation system. Sahara could make out vines laden with eggplant, tomato, giant zucchini, and other unidentifiable produce.

While the lush, fertile vegetation was awe-inspiring, it was nothing compared to the enormous glass ball hovering in the highest part of the room. Similar to the lava lamps, it was of far more intimidating dimensions—at least fifteen meters in circumference. While made of the same clear glass and perfectly round like the smaller models, this version fed into tubes that ran down one side of Hex-25, where they connected to metal machinery on the main floor. The orange lava shifted non-stop inside the glass, lighting the giant space.

Sahara's attention was drawn to a curious contraption under the ball, made up of panes rotating around and around, each a flat, circular disk of a different color, together making up an entire spectrum. The light from the lava hit the panes as they spun, sending prismatic projections across every surface, from the walls to the plants on the main floor. The beasts themselves were hit with the full spectrum every minute.

'I'm not sure what to think. It's very beautiful. What is it all for?'

'The Hexes are where we grow our food. There are a number of them down here.'

'How does it work?'

'The basic idea is that, using the lava, we generate a full spectrum with the revolving prism. You see? It's more complex than that really, it's something we invented. But you see, the spectral rotation provides a kind of artificial sun so that plants can grow down here without natural light. The hydroponics on the floor use this kind of light to grow as well, and it's also good for our health and mood.' With his finger, the beast made a circle in the air then added dots for eyes, a nose, and finished his air drawing with a curved smile.

Sahara attempted to return the smile. 'What about those colored tubes?'

'Various uses. The black ones are raw energy that will be converted into power and distributed throughout the complex. The red tubes filter the sulfur dioxide out and send it to our winery.'

'Cool.'

'It has taken years, but we're finally self-sustaining down here. No need to go up onto the surface any more.'

Teratological Combinatorial Processes. One of the beasts pulled a plaid wool blanket from his bag and spread it out under the lavacicles at the center of the landing. He detached his lava lamp from its stick and let it hover in the air while he neatly folded up the wood.

'Let's have a seat.' He let Sahara off his shoulder onto the soft blanket. Another beast pulled out an assortment of plastic containers holding raw cut vegetables and a dip, and poured root beer into small glasses the size of Dixie cups.

'I'm not going to beat around the bush here. We may be self-sustaining, but we're still at risk. Our kind needs to get stronger if we want to survive,' he said.

'It's sometimes harsh here,' the beast who was pouring root beer said. They all nodded.

'Can you learn to be better fighters?' Sahara thought it an appropriate question.

'No, we know how to fight. We mean another advantage.'

'Like what?'

'We aren't sure—that's why we want to ask you. We don't get many visitors around here, and we could use your expertise. We're thinking about doing something for our kind similar to what we're doing with produce modification and enhancement.'

'You mean with your...race?' She wasn't sure what to call them.

'Exactly.'

'What are you guys called, specifically?' Sahara felt embarrassed asking the question.

'They call us Bigfoot, but that's pretty derogatory, don't you think?'

'Yes.' She couldn't help but stare at their feet.

'Then there's Sasquatch, which basically means wild man. That's no better. We are Gigantopithecus.'

'That sounds fancy.'

'Indisputably. We are a unique species and need an exceptional name.'

Sahara looked around. It was dark in the space, nice and damp but not too chilly. Truth be told, she could be comfortable in this place. She liked the beasts' utilitarian approach to living and their curious inventions. She momentarily remembered هيس, and wondered whether he had come back for her, whether she was still his, whether this was a betrayal, an infidelity.... But Sahara wasn't one to linger over decisions. Deathstalkers don't waste time. Without too much contemplation she said, 'My expertise. Well, I'm quite prolific.'

'Your point being?'

'I mean I am a prolific breeder. I can breed and breed many. That's what a deathstalker scorpion does. I have the fairest traits of all arthropods throughout the world, some of the finest poison. My only weak attribute, as you may have guessed, is that I get into difficulty in bitter cold.'

'True,' they agreed.

'But it's not enough to make me a bad seed. What I'm asking is, what would be the outcome of a combination of, say, *you* and *me*?' She pointed her front claw at each of them in the room.

'Bigfoot and scorpion?'

'You seem surprised.'

'Oh no, it's just that none of us have ever conceived of such a combination. It may be a stupendous proposal, just a deviant and unlikely one.'

'Imagine your fur, my sting. Nothing could stop us.' Sahara said in a serious tone.

'Well, this might prove quite the thing, if I do say so myself. A teratological experiment, you might say.... When you mentioned bad seed, it reminded me: have you ever read *Des monstres et des prodiges*?'

'I don't read French.' She threw up her claws.

'*Monsters and Prodigies*, Ambroise Paré's book on teratology and cryptozoology. He was a human, a sixteenth-century French surgeon. Paré believed that his teratological treatise should be incorporated with his works on surgery and practical medicine. He thought the problem of taxonomy was more twisted and deformed than monsters and deformities themselves.'

'So how is it relevant to us?' Sahara scanned the other beasts, who were listening intently as they chewed on their carrot and celery sticks.

'For Paré, what was truly monstrous was taxonomy itself. What he asked was this: How is it possible to build a monstrous order or taxonomy to bring all fiends, rogue beings, demonic deformities and divine marvels into the fold?'

'Interesting,' she said, still not entirely sure of the pertinence of these musings to the beasts' practical problems.

'I only mention Paré because the idea started with him. He created a paraphysical model in which singularity, planes and forces were the main components from which the taxonomic system was concocted. Basically, forces were derived from different fields or spheres and varied from occult-paranormal all the way to mechanical-physical forces. In Paré's system, most of the taxonomies evolved out of interactions between the elements. I could tell you the specifics, but there is something more.' The beast abruptly broke off and shot a meaningful glance at his relations.

'The specifics aren't that important. What's the big picture?' Sahara said.

Her beast hesitated. 'Well, the specifics are important...'

'How so, Beast?'

'AD. The *Arbor Deformia*,' her beast said shakily.

The others became rather nervous and agitated, but tried to

hide it by sitting as still as possible and gazing fixedly ahead, refusing to meet her gaze.

'I'm listening,' she said. Her deathstalker impatience was starting to show. 'I suggest you get to it and tell me so we can formulate our plan.' Surprising herself with how aggressive she sounded, she wrote it off as the result of having to speak up over the noises coming from Hex-25 below.

'All right, then. *Arbor Deformia* is a schematic designed after the Paréan system of teratological taxonomy. Taking up this idea of a monstrous taxonomy that must include all monsters and all deformities, AD is an arborescent model in the tradition of the early trees of knowledge, elements, demons and celestial bodies. The *Arbor Deformia* follows the tradition of arborescent distributions, where the idea of the tree is the ratio of two operations, contraction and expansion, which are represented by two folds, roots and branches,' the beast explained.

'How did you come by this *Arbor Deformia*?'

'We don't know the exact origin of the book. Further research might prove helpful,' said the root beer beast, and made a circle in the air and added a smiling face inside, only this time he fashioned an air wink. 'But the published schematic including notes is in our library all the same. Marked "Restricted".'

'Have any of you read it?'

'Oh yes, and it's quite popular with the teenagers,' a beast said.

Her beast added: 'AD includes mention of other forces and planes that account for those causes of deformities that are absent in Paré's taxonomy. And there is speculation as to what those forces may be capable of.'

Some of the beasts seemed to tremble as they contemplated the implications of this last suggestion.

As if reciting from memory, hers continued: 'AD describes

five forces and two planes. There are occult forces, geopathic forces, mechanical forces, hereditary and biological forces and inter-specific biological forces. The plane of the differential and the plane of geo-mechanics are the receptive planes for forces. The plane of geo-mechanics is not directly involved in producing deformities and monsters, but it connects two different forces, which can cause abnormalities.'

'How does this any of this relate to our proposed project?'

'Be patient. Listen. The last two forces, the hereditary and inter-specific biological forces, make the organic fold of the tree over which non-organic forces grow and blossom. Unnatural conceptions between pigs and men or ants and lions are classified as inter-specific biological deformities, while deformation by a corrupt seed belongs to the hereditary forces or forces associated with the lineage. AD shows the proportion of its branches to its roots, of the inorganic arms to the organic appendages. Monsters, frauds, marvels and mutilations are the fruits of this proportional relation.'

At last she saw what he was getting at. 'Now we're talking. You can call it an unnatural conception if you like, deformity or mutation—it doesn't matter. The liquid sky is needed to push the water to the bottom of the mountain. You understand?' Sahara asked.

They beasts looked at each other, puzzled. 'Not really.'

'I can breed a legion with little effort. It might seem slow at first, but watch it multiply. So what do you think?'

'It sounds like the kind of thing we were looking for,' her beast said.

She asked, 'When do we begin?'

'Soon?' He eyed the scorpion apprehensively.

'How about right now?'

Communicant Vessels of the Highest Connectivity. 2018: Leiurus-Gigantopithecus, count: 122,079.

WHEN MORNING CAME, the fear that had expanded in the dark leaked into the outside world and hung like a smog Estella was powerless to disperse. Upon waking she had cursed herself and immediately deleted all local traces of her searches for XYZT, the hardware IDs, the investors mentioned in the emails. *How could I have been so stupid?* Like it or not, she was now implicated too, along with Amir and Kade. But in what?

The students she passed on her way to Stata seemed to regard her strangely as she walked around campus going through the motions, her inner dialogue chattering and screaming for attention. SUVs with tinted windows, the kind of vehicle in which a senator would be chauffeured, cruised the roads around campus without any apparent destination. Massachusetts plates with glowing red letters and numbers. 328, 2EK, 735…. She found herself wondering whether they would know that she was memorizing the plates, realized that was insane, then berated herself for even entertaining the thought of 'them'. *Enough already. More sleep needed.*

When she came out of the library in the afternoon there were no more SUVs, but in their place had come a second phase of lurkers: wrecks, junkers that no one would want to own—running loud, dents, license plates thrown on the front dash. The curious thing was that they shared something in common with this morning's models. She began to notice that all of their headlights were on, and then, more precisely, that only the left light was working. She wondered how many other irregularities and inconspicuous details she was missing, and began to look out for patterns.

Estella is...acting totally rational, honestly. Someone had told her that you don't exist if you're not on Facebook. She had an account, but never posted. But all of a sudden she was way popular. Requests around the clock, potential friends from every corner of the world. Friending none of them, she had only profile pics to go on, and they were just more paranoia fuel. First it was the hip-hop drug lords clad in gold chains from Africa. 'Do you have something for us?' Then the potential traffickers in Southeast Asia: 'We pay top dollar, you know what we want,' followed by the arms dealers in the Middle East. And someone from North Korea. Their walls were filled with content, but it all looked fake, manufactured. *What the hell do they want from me?*

Facebook wasn't even like she remembered it. The dashboard looked different, was it a new version? There were glitches as she scrolled. The icons on the left pulsed, switching faster than she could blink. Friends' physical locations came on screen blinking in red over their names. Her friend Christine was currently at a grocery store near campus. She didn't remember this as a feature. *Have I been hacked?* She closed out, but tiny 'F' icons flashed insistently in the taskbar.

A hundred times she started to write an email to Amir, to confirm that all of this was nonsense, that he had just taken an impromptu vacation—and stopped halfway through, realizing that they would be in her emails too. Any communication would only complicate the situation further. Face it, Amir doesn't do vacations, if anything he would treat himself to a week of Xbox and Cheetos.

She deleted the drafts and dived deeper into the black box instead. *I'm missing something.* The same objectless sense of urgency as in her dream. Hours passed. The phone vibrated off and on. She had no food left in the studio. Still she continued.

On its opening page, one corporate-style presentation document featured a circuit diagram of components embedded in a flexible bracelet. The accompanying notes, composed in Kade's signature bullshit style, made Estella's runaway thoughts suddenly switch tracks—from terrorism to venture capital. *A world-changer. Bigger than the airplane, bigger than the internet.* Amir's tracked changes added a note of sappy utopianism: *connecting us, united cultures, removing barriers, positive cultural exchange...help broker a cease in hostilities at this difficult time...power of democracy.* She read on with increasing incredulity. *Jeez, guys are such megalomaniacs. These two are as bad as each other.* On the point of exhaustion, as she wearily scanned the final paragraph, obviously intended as a big reveal to potential backers, everything imploded, the impact of what she read flinging her straight back into dream mode. *Bracelet form factor proven to enable full body dislocation capabilities...platform to be trialed in New York and Tehran... Tests will be transported instantaneously, remaining with Hosts for a period of three hours...proof of concept...a chance to invest in the future...A future that will be shaped by the technology we call XYZT.*

ST. LOUIS: CHINESE TAKEAWAY

'Take some more of the General Tso's Chicken, would you? Let's finish it off,' Andrea said to her guest.

'I'm really full.' Maryam stared at the pile of white cartons with wire handles.

'It's good, right? You have Chinese back home?'

Maryam licked her lips. 'We have one Chinese restaurant. It's on the food floor at the mall. I ate there once. This tastes better.'

Andrea scooped the rest of the chicken onto her Styrofoam plate. 'It's so popular here. We have it at least once a week since we work so much. It's a healthier alternative to Burger King if you order some dishes with vegetables. Did you know America invented Chinese takeout? I mean this kind of takeout.'

Maryam was surprised. 'Really?'

'It's different than the stuff they make in China. I have a friend who went to China on business, and he said their food tasted totally different. He couldn't eat it.'

'Have you been there?'

'Oh no. I've traveled a lot here, though. Been to nearly every state except Texas, Alaska and Hawaii. They're next on my list. The US is such a big country. Unlimited vacation possibilities!'

'What about Europe?'

'We have Las Vegas.' Andrea leaned toward her guest. 'They have the Eiffel Tower, Egyptian pyramids, and a Sphinx. You can ride a gondola down the Venice canals. You don't even have to leave the country to see the sights. Why would you bother going halfway around the world, with the airline tickets and all the other expenses? Las Vegas always has deals.'

Maryam frowned. 'It's not really the same.'

'It's even better, trust me. Oh, and if we want to go somewhere exotic and warm, we can go to Puerto Rico. Did you know that's technically the US?'

'No, I didn't.'

'Take a fortune.'

Maryam stared blankly at her Host.

Andrea mixed up the four cookies on the table. 'Go on, you pick first.'

Maryam picked up a fortune cookie and tried to read its plastic wrapper while Andrea contemplated which of the remaining three she was going to pick, then grabbed the closest cookie, ripped open the wrapper and broke it in half.

'Well, what does yours say?' said Andrea between crunches of her cookie.

'*Don't let the past and useless detail choke your existence.*'

'That's a good one. Mine's silly: *If you and your countrymen do not look beyond green pastures, you will find yourself surrounded by dirt in the New Year.* I guess I'll have to wait until next January for this one.'

'Our new year just passed two days ago.'

'I'll use your New Year's then.'

'Wouldn't that mean you're already standing in dirt?' Maryam suppressed a smile.

'That's silly. It's just one of those throwaway fortunes that doesn't make sense. Oh, guess who invented fortune cookies...?'

KERMAN: SOMETHING IN THE WATER

The worst can't happen because the worst does not bother itself with humans.
Anything else that happens is just trivial.

I find myself on a narrow street, cars parked tightly on one side, doors to different buildings on the other. As I walk to the nearest doorway, an entrance to a multi-level apartment building, a couple cross my path. They both give me really scathing looks and start hissing confidentially to each other once they have cleared me. I see that she is wearing a scarf. I need to get the scarf on. I put it on as I stand in the doorway. The buzzer system has ten buttons; I press them all and wait. No one answers.

I walk to the other side of the street and lean up against a parked car to get a better view, hoping the person who is supposed to meet me will come out. Fifteen minutes pass. The thick layer of dust on the car makes smudges on the back of my skirt.

Another man walks by. He looks flabbergasted when he sees my skirt. Okay, so it's short, but I got plenty shorter. Not a mini by any standards. And I just got it dirty.

Another thirty minutes standing in the middle of the street. One pedestrian and one car pass during this time, and neither stops to help. I am quite sure the driver was snickering at me as he drove away.

I'll have to walk to a busier road. I look around at the small shops crammed between more apartment buildings. People are carrying out plastic bags of food from the store to my left, but it doesn't look like a regular deli. The store to my right has a couple of sinks sitting out on the sidewalk.

People walk past me in both directions, all of them gawking

as they pass, most looking down at my lower half. *Yup, I'm not from here, okay?* When they're about to look me in the eye, I look instead at the drain between the sidewalk and the parked car in front of me. The trench is wide and deep. Some kind of red stuff floats along on the surface of the water like oil on top of a puddle. Almost stagnant, but slowly shifting. Watching the red helps distract my attention away from the stares.

An older man stops. He asks, 'How are you?'

'Okay. I could use some help.'

'No matter, what do you need? Where are you from?'

'Queens,' I say, but before I can tell him any more, he shakes his head like he doesn't know where Queens is and starts talking about the US and the president and politics, stuff I don't wanna hear about. I finally succeed in telling him that I am lost and that I can't find the family I was supposed to meet. He says that maybe I should wait at my hotel and they will find me later. Thanking him for his suggestion, which is of no help, I go back to looking at the drain so he won't talk any more politics.

I start to think that a hotel might not be such a bad idea, that I can get a room and just wait until I'm outta here. I see a taxi inching its way up the street. I walk over to the driver's side, he rolls the window down and I tell him I want to go to a hotel. He understands hotel, but when he asks me which hotel. I say, 'NICE HOTEL.'

He says loudly, 'GOOD HOTEL.'

'Yes!'

He waves me into the back of the cab. We get off the slow street and turn onto a road filled with more traffic, which leads to a roundabout with a fountain in the center, maybe Iran's grand piazza. Cosmetics stores line the streets in all directions. I should have written down the street name but it's already too late.

Every road we drive on is filled with activity. A man buying a newspaper at a small stand, folding it and putting it under his arm. Women covered in black fabric standing in line outside a bright orange bread store, out front a metal table where customers fold the bread and put it in plastic bags. A store selling canvas tents, some in stripes and some in solid colors, a woman wearing a black tent at a sewing machine in the front window.

We seem to be driving further and further from the center of the city. Everything is spreading out. One street is lined with car part shops, some with cars parked in front and men working on the vehicles right on the road. Further down, a number of used vacuum cleaner shops line both sides of the street. Outside a washing machine repair shop, a man is dragging an old avocado-colored model toward the doorway. Stores selling huge pots and pans in silver and copper, followed by metal shops where welders work on the sidewalk sending out blinding molten orange sparks.

The driver slows and points to a hotel. It looks grand from what I can see, so I tell him yes. He pulls up as close as possible. But I had completely forgotten about paying, and I can't remember how much money I have; when I look inside my purse for my wallet I find twenty-two dollar bills and some change. Figure I'll use my credit card for the room. We were driving for a long time, so I hand him the twenty and tell him I only have dollars. He nods and shifts through a thick pile of bills pulled from under the plastic cover he uses to shield the dashboard from the sun. He gives me back five 1,000 bills—'Tomans,' he tells me.

A doorman opens the door and I walk into an impressive lobby, two stories high, grand, with gold everywhere. Kind of like the Palace Room at Villa Russo.

I walk toward the front desk, up to the single attendant on duty. 'I need a room,' I say.

The attendant starts to speak in Iranian and motions with his hand for me to stay put. He must be going to get someone who knows English. To my left on the counter are hundreds of tiny national flags, each propped up on its own little table stand. Must be every country in the world, I'm guessing. I look for the US flag, but haven't located it by the time the attendant returns with an older gentleman.

'Yes, Missus?' the gentleman says to me.

'I'd like a room, please.'

'Oh Missus, where is your husband?'

'I don't have a husband.'

'Missus, you are traveling alone?'

'Yes, I'm alone.'

'So you don't have anyone else with you, Missus? What about your father?'

'My father? What does he have to do with it? I just want a room.'

'I see.' He looks disappointed. 'Missus, you know it is customary for a woman to travel with a tour guardian if he is from another country.'

'What the...' I manage to stop myself in time. 'What is a tour guardian?'

Taken aback by my response, the man pauses and pulls at his earlobe, in obvious discomfort. 'Missus, please wait.' He exits through the same door, leaving me with the attendant, who begins to sort through small cards, trying to look busy. I glance back at the flags and continue my search. Italy, Spain, France....

Some guests in the lobby have been peering at me. When the man returns, I am anxious to get the room.

'Missus, I checked with the hotel manager, Mr. ASJDJHJF, and he tells me that we will do you a favor and allow you a room with no guardian.'

I want to tell them what I think of that, but I am too tired to argue.

'But Missus must cover himself properly in the hotel.' As he says this, he lays a black piece of felt fabric on the counter and pushes it over my way.

'What am I gonna do with this?' I ask.

'Cover your legs.'

I take the unsewn fabric and unroll it, looking at its dimensions to figure out how I should cover myself, and finally deciding to wrap it around myself once and tie it at my waist like a swimsuit cover.

The men watch attentively as I put it on and they seem satisfied, the older gentleman now willing to proceed. 'Passport please, Missus,' he says in a reserved voice.

'I'm sorry, I don't have my passport with me. I have my driver's license though. Will that work?'

'No passport? How then did you come to Iran?'

'I didn't bring it.' I say, avoiding the question.

'Missus, what country are you from?'

'America,' I say.

Their eyes widen. The attendant starts flipping through the cards faster. 'You know Missus, we are to call the police if we find anyone traveling without a passport.'

'No. Please don't do that. I'm only here for a short time, and I only need a room for a few hours then I'm gone.'

'A few hours. A few hours only?'

'Yes.'

'Wait here.' Straight away he leaves the front desk. Each minute he is gone is excruciating for both me and the attendant. There are no new arrivals, no guests asking for help, no phone calls. Just the shuffling of those damn paper cards. The longer the man is gone, the more worried I become that he is calling the police. I don't know anything about the police in Iran, but I don't wanna know any more.

I walk over to the flag display. One, to continue my search, and two, to test the sari, which is now my new skirt, to make sure it doesn't fall down when I walk. And three, to step away from the attendant.

Ten long minutes pass, and still the manager has not returned. I convince myself that he must have called the police and that I'd best get the hell out of there.

'I've changed my mind. I'm leaving.' I walk rapidly toward the exit and see that the attendant has made a dash for the door to alert the other man that I am on my way out. The doorman tries to communicate with me, but I don't understand. I open the door myself.

I motion for the first taxi in the line, and the driver wastes no time in picking me up.

I get into the cab and tell him 'Hotel.'

He looks at me puzzled. We go back and forth for a few seconds and then he says, 'Hotel.'

We pull away, and I find that we are speeding back toward town. The back of the cab smells of raw tire and burnt peanuts. I notice the fabric around my legs and realize that in the commotion I did not return it to the hotel or pay for it.

While we are driving the taxi driver says, 'Hotel in Kerman.'

'Kerman,' I say, and the conversation ends there.

The ride is about the same length as last time, and when he drops me at another hotel he holds up five fingers.

At first I think he means a five star hotel, but when he shakes his head, I pull out a 1,000 toman bill.

The décor in the new hotel looks like some old Comfort Inn I wouldn't want to stay in, but whatever. 'English,' I say to the attendant at the desk, a woman wearing a blue headscarf that matches her uniform.

'Yes.'

'I want a room.'

'For you only?'

'Yes, I'm traveling alone in Kerman for one day. I'm going to meet my family tomorrow.'

'A single room is 340,000 rials. You are foreign, so you pay 549,000 rials.'

'That's fine.' With no real idea how much that is, but relieved nonetheless, I take out my credit card.

'We don't accept credit cards from outside Iran. Cash only.'

'Oh, well, I suppose I could go to a cash machine.'

'There is a cash machine outside Bank Melli down the street.'

'Where do I go?' I look toward the door.

'Out there and *gauche*,' she says, directing me with her hands.

It's getting dark, and more people are coming out. I seem to blend in better now that my legs are covered, and only get the occasional glance. Everyone is rushing, but I'm not sure where they're going. Coming home from work? I inhale the exhaust from the cars, the smells coming from the takeout restaurants, and another repulsive smoky smell that seems to fill this whole city.

I see the bank coming up on my left, with a bizarre little awning hanging just over the ATM machine. The customers' heads almost touch the underside of it while they stand waiting. When it is my turn, the machine takes my card and I wait for the screen to come up. Green fluorescent letters, like an old computer, displaying a message I don't understand. Then the message disappears. I press some more buttons but nothing happens.

The man next in line steps forward and looks at the screen. He asks me if it is an international card or Iranian and, when I tell him, shakes his head and says that they don't work in Iran.

I decide I should go inside and try to find out what happened to my card, but when I get to the bank's entrance, a metal gate is positioned in front of the doors with a big chain and padlock.

I walk back to the hotel. 'I wasn't able to get any money from the cash machine. Can I have the room and I will pay when my family arrives?' I say, hoping the woman will oblige.

'No, you must pay first.'

I tell the woman I'll come back, and then walk out, this time in the other direction.

A couple of blocks in and the streets get darker. There are still people out, but now I see only their shadows, the women in full black fabric turning into negative ghosts that only become visible as we meet head on. The side of the street I am walking on has a cover over the sidewalk, similar to one of those blue temporary construction walkways in New York City, but here it looks permanent, attached to a long, boarded-up building. There are men lined up in front of it at various intervals: some are selling things like cheap tools, plastic toys and other useless items, all set out on the ground. I see one woman sitting on the sidewalk with an ornate skirt of blue and black sequined fabric spread out around her, in front of her a pile of brown grain. She takes a small silver cup, fills it with the grain, then pours it back into the pile, over and over again. She has a deep red mark on her hand near the thumb, a cross but with two circles at the base. She looks up at me helplessly as I pass.

Next, a group of men holding wads of money in their hands. Some have makeshift tables displaying pigment-stippled currency of different sizes. As I pass they say 'Tomans! Tomans!' It's very dark in this stretch, but I can still see their faces. I realize that they are money converters, so I decide I should change my remaining dollars into Iranian money. I stop at the most respectable-looking display.

'I'd like to change some dollars into Iranian money.'

'Dollars?'

'Yes, dollars.' I pull out my money, knowing I'm not going to get much in return.

The man snatches it and motions for me to pour the change out onto his table.

He counts the money three times, then he pulls out two 1,000 toman bills. I take the money and thank him. As I walk on, the men who have seen me exchanging money become aggressive, trying to get me to change some with them as well. 'Lady, Lady. You change money?'

I walk by rapidly, making a sharp right at the end of the block. The sidewalk is a mess of patchwork concrete. I can feel the unevenness under my feet, the same as it is all over town. My foot catches on the corner, twists and drops into the deep gutter, and I fall into a channel the same size as the drain I saw when I first arrived. My entire lower half disappears below ground, my skirt is wet up to the knees. With difficulty I lift myself out, cursing my own dumbness because I knew these gutters were all over the place around here.

I see a couple of the moneymen coming toward me, shouting at me. I start walking as fast as I can. My ankle is in pain, but I am able to get far enough away that the moneychangers give up and turn back. I look at my hand—pebble indents and small clumps of abraded skin.

The next street is busier. I walk along for a couple of blocks, passing meat store after meat store. My leg and ankle are really hurting, so I pause in front of a butcher shop window to rest. Severed lamb's heads are presented on metal trays, lined up in rows. Red tongues piled high on another tray. A bowl of eyeballs staring crazily up at me. Ground hamburger placed next to slimy, purple-brown sacks, livers perhaps? The butcher, with bushy moustache and hairy arms, comes out wearing his bloodied apron and carrying a cleaver with fresh blood on it. Daniel Day-Lewis in *Gangs of New York*, only hairier and scarier, he approaches and looks at me questioningly. I shake my head and move on as fast as I can.

The street becomes narrower and metal racks for hanging carcasses fill most of the walkway. The animals' bodies are lean, I think they are mainly lambs, although I am not sure. I have to turn my shoulders to the side to pass. The rotting-flesh stench has been getting worse as I proceed down the block. A plastic bin sits next to the drainage ditch near an empty carcass rack with watered-down blood in it; I look into the gutter and see a burgundy mess floating on the surface.

It says *Pizza* on a sign outside a restaurant, and I realize that I should eat. Inside the cramped place there are a couple of small tables with chairs at the front, a counter towards the back. I look at the menu—photos not only of pizza but also of fried chicken, hamburgers and sandwiches. I step up to the counter. The clerk is wearing a paper hat and plastic gloves. 'Gimme a slice.'

The clerk calls to the back of the shop and someone starts to prepare the pizza. He pulls out a tray, gets a small Pepsi from the refrigerator and places it on a tray. Then he gets two packets of ketchup and one of mayonnaise.

He rings up the bill on the register. I take out my two 1,000 bills and hand them to him.

He shakes his head and makes a gesture with his hand that might mean *more*.

I say, 'I don't have any more.'

He talks to me in his language, and we can't get anywhere. He finally points towards the right, suggesting I go to another store. Maybe the pizza is cheaper next door.

The restaurant next door is smaller and has no tables or chairs. The combination of orange tiles and bright fluorescent lights hanging from the ceiling nearly blinds me. I walk to the display case. Fried triangles.

'What are these?' I ask the questionable man behind the counter, who keeps looking over at the small TV set propped up in the corner.

'Sambouseh,' he says. 'Very good.'

'Okay. I'll have a Sambouseh.' Before he does anything, I show him my two bills. He gets a bag and fills it with two of the fried triangles and grabs a 7-UP from the portable cooler on the floor.

I hand him the last of my money, hoping he will give me some back, but he doesn't. I thank him and pull some tissues from the box sitting on the counter.

On the street, I bite into one of the triangles. Crunchy, definitely fried. Inside, a mixture of diced vegetables, maybe meat. It's very tasty, reminds me of an eggroll but with a more Indian taste.

After walking less than two blocks, I have devoured the Sambousehs and 7-UP. I don't know what else to do, so I just keep walking. It has become dark, each unidentified noise scarier than the last. I find myself in a neighborhood with a park hidden behind a fence across the way. Couples are sitting on the benches, and there is a woman with two children playing on the ground in front of her. Looks safe enough. I sit down on a bench toward the back of the park so I won't be bothered, and massage my swollen ankle. How long have I been here? Exhausted. Maybe I'll lie out on the bench and take a short rest.

My eyes half open. Not fully awake. The lights in the park are off. Groups of people are standing around, young men talking loudly and smoking. That smoky Kerman smell. Too sleepy to get up, will rest just a moment longer.

People are hovering over me; the men are taking off their jackets and piling them up over my legs. I lay on the ground looking up. I can't move.

The park is even darker. They are shouting in Iranian. My head hurts. A woman props me up with something soft.

دکتر خبر کنید، این خانم صدمه دیده.

One of them runs off. I wonder how long I have left. *They said three hours only.*

تا الان داشته دور خودش چرخ میزده و جیغ میکشیده،
« Butcher, stay away! Butcher don't get me! I'm a New Yorker! »

بابا این آمریکایی ها خیلی پارانوئیدن.

حتماً به خاطر اینه که یک چیزی تو آبشون هست.

'Have I been hurt?' I mumble weakly from down below. 'Has someone hurt me?'

The woman holding my hand says, 'No dear, we Iranians love the American people.'

CERRILLOS: PEACOCK ANGEL

'Did you enjoy seeing the ghost town, Ashkan?' Karen asked, setting a piece of chocolate mousse cake in front of me on the wooden table tagged *Smith & Hawken*.

'Yes.' It was a half-truth. I stared at the mountain range in the distance, trying to focus my eyes as she poured coffee into my oversized terracotta cup from a stainless steel carafe, then into the other two cups on the table. Her feet made no noise on the flagstone as she headed back toward the patio doors leading to the kitchen. I was alone again.

It wasn't that I hadn't enjoyed seeing a real American ghost town. It's just that I was so tired. And anyway Cerrillos seemed fake, like the sets you see in spaghetti westerns. In fact the movie sets seem more authentic, but I guess that's what set designers aspire to. Peter said that Santa Fe and Albuquerque have tried to turn their ghost towns into profitable tourist attractions, heavily promoting the Turquoise Trail, Route 66 road trips and Gold Rush themed bed and breakfasts. It must be working, because Cerrillos was packed, with tourists snapping photos outside the post office and buying souvenirs in the Casa Grande Trading Post.

Karen and Peter Johnson have been kind enough; they showed me what hosts show guests around here. They gave me a tour of their ranch, a one-hour 'hike' over some of the seventy-five 'acres'—about thirty hectares—of their property. All of this has left me tired, especially since I didn't take my afternoon rest as I do back home.

Supposedly, in the 1880s Cerrillos Hills was full of mining activity. Karen and Peter's land has many remnants from that time—ruined stone structures, the remains of dwellings, dirt roads with abandoned wooden wagons in various states of decay.

They say they are authentic, that these relics were here when they bought the property a few years ago after selling their house in Napa Valley, but I'm not convinced. It's not like with old Persian artifacts; these are uniquely American, and I don't have the expertise nor the interest to assess them. We walked for quite a while to get to an important landmark: a wagon wheel, laid out on the ground next to a three-sided wooden box and some scrap metal. The place reminded me of the mountains in Iran, although this terrain is slightly different, more desert-like. We saw the stables and the horses, and they opened a pen so that I could stand inside with the peacocks. I felt at home with *Malik Tavoos*. And the goats—Peter wants to try making goat cheese, possibly start selling it.

According to Karen, theirs is a traditional Santa Fe house, a sprawling, single-story building. She pointed out the adobe detailing as we walked the rooms. Peter's brother Adam owns stuDO, a big architecture and design firm in the Northeast, and apparently he had done most of the design for the house. The open living room had refurbished oak timbers from the nineteenth century, and the vigas and beams on the ceiling were from the Jicarilla Reservation. The walls and ceilings were made of hand-troweled plaster. Rounded adobe-type fireplaces in every room and an outdoor fire pit. But somehow, like the ghost town, the house felt staged. The 'southwestern' tiles on the walls and countertop in the kitchen, the western knick-knacks throughout, the adobe woven rugs—it all felt fake.

I looked down at the fork. She did not leave a spoon.

*

My mind has turned to the Peacock Angel, as it always does when jump-started by a reminder and during a leap year. Head turned to the right, white beak curved down, looking smug. One black eye surrounded by bare white skin, crown on the head waving. His neck and front body vibrate a metallic indigo blue, glimmering. Indian, oh Indian Peafowl! Tavoos. Things change. Spinning clockwise and his head is gone. A swirl of white lines spiraling out, black crosshatching into darkness, elongated feathers spanning out. Eyespots, at first a hundred, then a thousand. A thousand nestled, iridescent, green-burnt sienna-turquoise blotches eyelining a thousand centers—the kidney-shaped black pearl eyespots. Oh thousand-eyed cosmic wisdom! Oh change! Fan of motion. Layering. Aid to camouflage, aid to see. Spinning clockwise. Use the wire-threads to weave into one eye and out of another, symmetry then asymmetry. Wire-threading a line through the layers, wire-threading multiple layers, stitching, shading through black. Axis of evil, axes of evil. Malevolent fowl. Coherency and incoherency, generation of planes: kelly green, ultra blue, flywing, black pearl, one after another.

THE SUN WAS already shining in Boston when Estella awoke and immediately felt the knot in the pit of her stomach. It didn't help that her brain was physically pounding, her head aching as if she had had a full night of drinking. She dragged herself up. With nothing in the kitchenette, she was forced to go out for some tea, which would surely make everything clearer. *I'm still missing something.*

Too weak to focus on the people around her and their activities, all she could do was to make her way mechanically. As she waited for her server to pour the chamomile she was reminded of the last time she had stood in the line, and clutched her bag more tightly. She took the drink and grabbed the only open stool at the bar, too frail to take it back home. Pulling off the cover, she took a sip as the warmth of the steam hit her face. Halfway through the cup, she knew where she was going next.

It was no luxury condo; many MIT students stayed here because of its proximity to campus and the cheap rents. Estella slowly climbed the stairs and found 3B. She knocked. Nothing. To her surprise, when she turned the handle it jiggled loosely and the door opened.

Jeez, this is one room I never wanted to see the inside of, she thought as she scanned the place with distaste, her nose screwed up. The smell of dirty clothes wafted up as she walked over the piles. *The guy really is a jock.* The total disarray of the room belied Kade's constant talk of his meetings and deals.

Her eyes shifted to the rickety desk in front of the room's only window. Its empty surface was covered only in scratches and peeling paint. She ran her hand over the table, catching dust at the outer edges. *This is not right.* Below the table a mess of unattached cords trailed from the surge protectors.

Kade's bookshelf was filled with course books, manuals, and biographies of self-made millionaires, but alongside them she spotted a bunch of his notepads. Easily missable, but not to her. Many times she had seen him doodling in the books instead of paying attention during class. She pulled out the purple book from the shelf, the most recent one—she remembered because she had thought it strange that such a masculine guy would pick an Easter-egg-colored book.

As she flipped through the notepad, she noted once again references to 'Tests' and 'Hosts', dates and locations, interspersed with childish doodles. The last entry, adorned by a control tower being struck by lightning, was just a date and two locations: *March 22, 10am, MSG NYC. Grand Bazaar Tehran. It's happening today. Right now.*

A sheaf of loose papers fell from the back pages of the notebook. Legal documents. Non-disclosure agreements, retainers, draft agreements for sale...all very formal and officially stamped by notaries. Each one signed by a different entity, and all countersigned by Kade himself. No mention of Amir.

Concerned we weren't ready but Kade has pushed things forward. Her mind turned back to Amir's cryptic message, and for the first time she felt a pang of fear for him. On many of the pages of Kade's notebook every reference to Amir had been crossed out. It was as if he had been systematically deleted. *Somewhere along the line things went very bad between Kade and Amir. But did Amir know this?*

She steadied herself. *Cease and desist. Just quit meddling and destroy the evidence.* But then she thought of Amir again, trying not to notice the pull of tenderness toward him that had begun to form in her. She took out her phone, cursing its sluggish response. Amir's number didn't connect. *He must be in Tehran. He needs my help.* But to get to Amir, she would have to go through Kade.

Estella eyed the diagram of the two locations, then snapped the notebook shut and dropped it into the bag alongside Amir's hard drive. *10am, Madison Square Garden.*

THE BOARLETTE OF YASOOJ

'This whole discussion reminds me of a story I once heard about a Boarlette who lived in Yasooj:

'A married couple living in the village of Yasooj in Kohgi-luyeh and Boyer-Ahmad Province had been trying for many years to have a baby. They had sex daily for two years, and yet the wife never became pregnant. Desperate, one night the wife decided to pray to God so that she and her husband could have a baby. "Hello God, it's me, Nazgol from Yasooj. Can you get me pregnant? I don't care if the baby looks like a boar, just let me give birth to a child of my own."

'Nine months and nine days passed, and the woman gave birth to a baby girl. But the baby was not a regular infant: it was a baby whose outer skin was that of a boar. Nevertheless, the couple gladly accepted the baby because it was theirs. Later, when the woman and man took their baby out and about in the village, everyone laughed and called her Boar-Baby. But the couple didn't mind, because they loved their child very much.

'Years went by, and the Boarlette started to grow up. Since no one in the village wanted to be her friend or teach her anything, she had to watch and learn from others at a distance. When she was old enough, she set out to the mountain ranges near Yasooj to look around. There she roamed through the oak for-ests, all the while seeing the Dena Summit high above her. One day while she was out on one of these adventures, she observed village girls collecting wood for their families' cooking fires, so she collected some wood and brought it home. Her mother and father were very pleased, and so it became Boarlette's job to find the firewood.

'On one of Boarlette's trips into the forest, she spotted a spring flowing with water. She was in need of a bath since her human skin often became hot and sweaty under her boar suit, which was full of folds. Since no one was around, she shed her skin to take a bath. Boarlette was apprehensive of removing her boar skin—she did it only when absolutely necessary. She very much enjoyed taking a bath in the spring, and so it became a regular routine for Boarlette to bathe on her firewood trips.

'One afternoon, as Boarlette was bathing, the village's young prince rode by on his horse. As the sun hit the water on Boarlette's glowing skin it sparkled, and the sparkle reflected on the tip of the prince's silver sword, so that he stopped to see what it was. It might be an animal he could slay and bring back to the castle for cooking, or a thief hiding in the forest, he thought to himself. He got off his horse and sneaked up behind the trees until he had a view of the spring.

'His eyes widened as he saw a beautiful young girl with long flowing dark hair. She had the most delicate body of soft white flesh, firm but voluminous young breasts, long slender legs, and what he imagined were the tiniest of feet splashing around in the brook. This Persian maiden was a sight to behold. The prince hid behind the tree, watching her scoop up water that then ran down her body in the most appealing way. When the maiden was finished, she walked over to the side of the spring, got into a boar skin suit, and trotted off like a boar!

'The prince was shocked by what he had seen. He returned home still thinking about the beautiful girl who became a boarlette. He couldn't control himself—he needed to know more about this mysterious girl in the forest. He went riding each day around the same time and hid in the trees, hoping that the girl would return to the same spot.

'Sure enough, nine days later she returned. First the boar turned left, then right, but she did not see anyone around, for the prince had found a fine hiding place. Then she shed her boar skin and emerged as the fair maiden. She frolicked and played in the water, sometimes using her finely formed fingers to massage her milky skin or to run through her long, curled tresses. Eventually the girl emerged from the water and returned to her boar skin suit. As she was putting it on, the prince came out of hiding and called to the maiden. "Hail, fair maiden. I am the prince. I know that you are not a boar, for I have seen you in the brook. Will you speak with me?" Boarlette recognized the prince and was embarrassed that he had seen her not only naked, but also getting into her boar suit. She disappeared through the thick trees so fast that the prince couldn't catch her.

'"Oh where, oh where did my Lily-Head go?" the prince kept repeating, for he had fallen in love with Boarlette. After days of sulking, the prince decided he needed the help of the king and queen. He told them his story and begged his parents to help him find the boarlette in Yasooj village so that he could convince her to come out of her boar skin. It was his heart's desire to marry this beautiful Lily-Head. The king and queen thought their son was crazy, but he threatened to kill himself if they did not help.

'The next day the king sent armed men and a representative from his court to the village of Yasooj to find the family who had a boarlette. It didn't take long for the other villagers to point out the couple's home. The representative knocked on the door and announced that the king wished to purchase their boarlette for a large sum of money. The couple looked at each other and at Boarlette and told him that their boar was not for sale. She was all they had, they loved her dearly, and no amount of money would change their mind. The representative nevertheless decided he had the authority to take the child without their consent, but he left some money as a goodwill gesture. The couple was devastated. The only thing that made them feel better was the thought that the king's court would tire of playing with Boar-lette and she would eventually be sent home.

'Boarlette arrived at the king's castle, where the prince stood at the gate waiting eagerly to see her again. He told her that he knew she was a beautiful maiden inside her boar suit and that she should come out and talk with him. When Boarlette did not speak, the prince got down on one knee and proposed marriage to her right then and there.

'Still Boarlette said nothing. But soon enough the wedding preparations began. A non-stop party preceded the wedding day, lasting for eight days and eight nights. Guests talked of one thing and one thing only throughout all of the festivities: the wedding night, when the prince would have to go to bed with his wife Boarlette for the first time. All sorts of terrible jokes and gossip spread throughout Kohgiluyeh and Boyer-Ah-mad Province. She was still known as Baby-Boar in Yasooj, but other names were circulating: the Boar-Bride, Boar-to-Be and BaBaBoardumb. The prince didn't care, because he knew the truth about his Lily-Head.

'They were married in front of thousands. That night, the prince entered Boarlette's boudoir and begged her to come out of her boar skin. But Boarlette just teetered back and forth on her hooves, looking up dumbly at the prince. The prince finally decided that he should treat an animal like an animal. He got a stick and spanked the rump of Boarlette, not too hard and not too soft. Boarlette started to talk with her human voice from within her boar suit. The prince told her how much he loved her. Eventually she emerged from her boar skin and let it drop to the ground, leaving her standing naked in front of the prince. In no time their marriage was consummated. After a few days of nonstop lovemaking, the newlyweds emerged. The entire vil-lage, including the king and queen, was shocked to find that the prince had been right all along. Boarlette was the most beautiful Persian maiden they had ever seen. Now she was to be known only as Princess Boarlette.

'The prince's cousin was so amazed at what he saw that he decided he too would get a boar and change her into a beautiful girl as the prince had done. The king and queen tried to convince him that Boarlette was a special animal, and that this wouldn't work on normal boars, but the cousin did not listen. He went out and found a boar in the forest and brought it back to the castle. He married the boar, and on the wedding night he entered its chambers. He began to talk to the boar as the prince said he had done, and when the boar did not "come out," he hit it with a stick. This enraged the boar so much that it pulled free of its chains and leapt at the cousin, biting him with its sharp boar's teeth, ripping the cousin's face into shreds, followed by his penis. But the boar didn't stop there; it began to eat away at the cousin's chest until it had opened a passageway straight to his heart. The boar then took out the heart and chewed it up like a tasty snack.'

'It's not a good story.'

'Why not?'

'First off, it portrays boars in a negative manner.'

'It is an old Persian fairy tale, one of our best.'

'Well, it shouldn't be told anymore then.'

'Can't it stand as it is? Those were different times.'

'I don't know. It also reflects poorly on women. Beating her with a stick, whether a woman or a boar, is just wrong.'

'Okay, I suppose. It's politically incorrect. You can't have that in the story.'

'The story of the pretty girl marrying a prince, she's attractive only after taking off her boar skin, giving into society's idea of beauty...who's to say she makes a prettier girl? Maybe she's a lovelier boar. It's just another way to promote those patriarchal messages we have been trying so hard to get rid of since I don't know when.'

'If we can't tell this story, then what story can we tell? What would your ending be?'

'Well, maybe we boars could revolt and take over. Maybe Boarlette could put her skin back on when no one's looking and go into the forest and round up some other boars. She could convince them to devour all of the humans and take over the castle.'

'But that would be politically incorrect as well! All stories are politically incorrect to someone somewhere.'

'I suppose.'

VIRGINIA: HAM

Mr. and Mrs. Peterson excused themselves to go check on the meal. Zahra smelled a sweet aroma coming from the kitchen. Her thoughts about the experiment and how she was feeling were sidetracked when a dog came running into the room and jumped up on the sofa next to her. Initially surprised and frightened by the animal, after inspecting it Zahra realized it was cleanly groomed, and not at all vicious.

Mrs. Peterson popped her head back into the living room. 'That's Pippi. She's an English springer spaniel. Don't worry, she won't bite. After the kids left, she's like our baby. She's utterly spoiled. We love having her around.'

'Cute.'

'She's named after Pippi Longstocking, because she's orange and her ears look like pigtails, see? I'll be right back.'

Zahra knew that Americans loved their pets. Pet ownership in Iran was not as common as what she had seen in the Hollywood movies she watched on satellite. She remembered hearing about what Americans had done for homeless animals after the Katrina disaster, so she could understand about the dog being spoiled. Zahra stroked Pippi's smooth coat, partly to hold the animal down so that it wouldn't jump up and lick her face.

Mrs. Peterson returned to the room with an album filled with photos of her grown children. She went through it with her guest page by page.

Then Zahra was led into the formal dining room. Mrs. Peterson had lit two tapers, which stood monumentally on both sides of the flower centerpiece, an arrangement of white daisies with lilac-tipped edges in a wicker basket that was a bit too small for a table seating eight. Mrs. Peterson noticed Zahra looking at the flowers.

'They're a gift my daughter sent for Easter. She's stuck up in New York.'

'They are pretty.'

'Of course they are. It's an FTD.'

As the three sat down at the table, Pippi took her place under it. Zahra inquired about the menu.

'We always have the same thing for Easter,' Mrs. Peterson said with pride. 'Frank, will you get the ham?'

Mr. Peterson pulled his armed chair back from the head of the table and headed to the kitchen.

'We have a Southern Glazed Ham. It's a specialty here in Virginia.'

Zahra didn't want to have to tell her Hosts that she didn't eat pork.

'And here's the sweet potato casserole.' Mrs. Peterson pointed at a dish that was topped with a thick crust of toasted marshmallows.

'We have green beans with the Campbell's cream of mushroom soup sauce and onion sprinkles. It's my favorite. Top it off with some cranberry sauce like we have at Thanksgiving, deviled eggs and these soft bun rolls. I have pineapple icebox cake for dessert. I'm sure you'll like it.'

'Does ham taste like boar?' Zahra remembered how her brothers used to hunt the creatures in the forests along the edge of the mountains on the outskirts of her town.

'Well, I don't rightly know. Is a boar pork?' Mrs. Peterson asked as Mr. Peterson walked in with the steaming platter and placed it on the table, a large hunk of baked ham scored with perfect diamond patterns, studded with cloves and dripping with thick brown sauce. The plate was garnished with canned pineapple rings and maraschino cherries.

Not that she was feeling comfortable to begin with, now

Zahra's thoughts shifted from present company to wondering whether she had already eaten pork.

He took the electric carving knife and plugged it into the nearest outlet. The tool vibrated and Zahra jumped in her seat. Pippi positioned herself on the floor next to Mr. Peterson in case any scraps fell from the table. Slowly, with surgical precision, Mr. Peterson sawed back and forth, cutting the succulent flesh into quarter-inch slices until there was nothing left to carve.

SISTAN-BALUCHESTAN:
BUGSAM DASIES

As I backed my head carefully out of the tree, weighty oblong fruits trailed over me, releasing a comforting scent of lemon custard and Orangina. The tree was one of many symmetrically placed around a long narrow pool with sandstone sides. The inside of the pool was studded with turquoise shards that pulsed, seemingly folding over and into one another as if they were moving. A sculptural trompe-l'œil perhaps, as the water itself was still and the light did not shift.

The journey and the speed of arrival had induced a panic attack, and I was having trouble breathing. Looking around me, the courtyard seemed more like a fortress—the place looked as if it had been built to stave off an invasion. Four bulky retaining walls enclosed the space, built so high that no one could see in or out. If you were to stack four men on each other's shoulders, the one on top still wouldn't be able to see over. Towers rose up from each corner.

A buzzer sounded, reverberating around the courtyard. I heard activity in the largest building, a fair distance to my right, and saw the doors of the wall towers open. Men appeared, one from each tower, wearing light robes and cloth head coverings. Their figures melded with the sky, only the silhouettes of their machine guns standing out as they paced the tops of the wide exterior walls.

I moved back to the tree I had been hugging for cover. Hadn't I gone looking for adventure, volunteering to be a Test? But now, nervous and scared, I was trying to hide. I'm the kind of guy who always keeps out of trouble. Frankly, guns scare me. Machine guns terrify me. One of the two guards I could see was speaking into a handheld radio. I wasn't certain whether they had seen me, but they weren't firing, at least....

The buzzer sounded again, and the guards returned to their posts. I breathed a sigh of relief, which was followed by a jump of the heart and a pang up the spine when a door in the building behind me opened. This time there was no question of hiding. The man who entered the courtyard headed straight in my direction, shuffling briskly across the dusty slabs, looking directly at me as he walked. He was undersized, not even five feet tall, yet his demeanor struck fear into me. His stride picked up as he closed in on me. His plastic-sandaled feet stopped abruptly. He was close enough that I could smell him. It wasn't body odor, more a pungent whiff of some food you'd rather not ingest. Russet eyes close together on his face, skin tone dark. He beckoned me with his right hand, then started towards the source of the muffled noises I'd heard earlier. Usually I would have questioned where we might be going, but in this instance I remained silent, nothing leaked from my mouth. I wasn't sure he spoke English, anyway.

The structure we were walking toward was the largest building on the courtyard, and ran the length of one entire wall. The facade's construction was simple, but there was nothing modest about it. Fifty wood-framed windows, each a grid of dark panes, reflected us back in multiples like smoked glass mirrors. Along the far side ran a long set of doors, reminding me of those at the entrance to a theater. Made of metal, they were painted the shade and shine of a bright red Mercedes convertible.

My escort pounded on one of the doors and it was opened by a security guard wearing the same outfit as those I had seen patrolling from the towers. His machine gun shifted over his shoulder as he talked animatedly with my escort. I kept my eyes closely on the weapon.

I could hear people talking and moving around inside. I had just started to think about formulating in advance some plausible explanation for how I had come to be there, when someone else appeared in the doorway.

'You are the Test?' The few words had a calming effect on me. He was also wearing white, but his robe was made of finer linen, as was the puffy turban on his head. Though he was clean-shaven, his ebony hair flowed out from under his head covering, and twisted down his shoulders in healthy curls. Was he wearing black eyeliner? He reminded me of what a wealthy prince would look like, and so, since I had no way of knowing his name, I immediately began to call him 'Prince' in my head.

'Yes,' I managed to say. I could feel cool air carving its way through the swelter to my face and hands as I stood just outside the door.

'You will be my guest of honor. This is where I entertain. We have a party.' His eyes penetrated mine.

'I...' He stopped me by putting a finger to his lips.

Stepping into the building onto a square landing, I noted the security guards stationed to the right and moved slowly and carefully around them. Inside there was indeed a party: laughter, music, the clanking of plates, all of which had been completely inaudible from the courtyard.

Everything lay below, down a flight of steps from the entry landing, so that, before we walked down, I had a bird's-eye view of the massive complex he said was his entertaining space. The ceiling of the single-story structure was high, as the place was partially below ground. Light filtered in from the windows along the outside, reinforced by a kaleidoscopic stained-glass drop ceiling that provided artificial illumination from above. Semi-open rooms were built haphazardly all over the vast space. There was no repetition, no miter-box order to the rooms, probably no ninety-degree angles in the whole place. I saw stone and glass, carved rock, and even fabric. But because the outer walls were built out of raw concrete, the Prince's space had an earthy, cave-like feel. The largest open area was near the back wall. A long piece of white fabric was rolled out on the floor, running parallel to the wall—it reminded me of something a bride would walk down at an outside wedding. The stained glass, various floor surfaces and rug coverings, the pathways curving around, fountains and foliage in odd places—it all reminded me of looking down on the Candy Land board game from above as a child. I wanted to play.

Once we were down on the main floor, I found it yet more curious. The first rooms we walked by were filled with chaise lounges, frilly patterns, potted ferns, and resting women who watched us sleepily as we passed.

'How is the US these days?' the Prince asked as we walked.

'Not too bad.'

'Are you sure?'

I didn't know what he meant. 'Pretty sure. I'm doing fine.'

We glanced into a room whose walls were carved out of shiny Mount-Rushmore rock, with numerous flat-screen TVs embedded into the bulbous stone, all showing different programming. A few men sat on mattresses holding a dozen remote controls.

The prince turned to me proudly. 'We have over six hundred satellite channels available. Would you like to watch anything?'

'No, I...'

'Not your thing,' he nodded approvingly. 'What about films? We have those too.'

I politely shook my head.

We passed a moss-covered fountain with a squat palm growing from it. Further on, another room was a sea of deep red. 'Is that coral?' I asked.

'From the Persian Gulf.'

My initial thought was that insanely large chunks of

fire-engine-red coral must have been glued together to create the impression, but on closer inspection it seemed to be one seamless reef. Inside, a few children amused themselves with PlayStations, the screens built into the coral just as the TVs had been.

The brick path forked and we took the left way. As my Host casually strolled along, he fell silent. I stayed quiet too, even though I had a million questions.

The area we approached next seemed the loudest in the entire place. The walls were golden, possibly of real gold. All of the activity revolved around one of the tables. I couldn't see because my view was blocked—alarmingly—by a herd of animals. Creatures with short, light silver fur, standing upright around the table! These fantastic beings held themselves like men, but they were considerably larger. Boisterous, overpowering and masculine, they had the physical fullness of bodybuilders. Horns protruded from their heads, and each wore only a cloth draped across its groin.

Three beautiful women with long, flowing hair, dressed in translucent mesh skirts made of enough layers to conceal their legs, stood near a golden counter. Halter-tops scantily covered their full breasts, and gold coins dangled from the tops, adding yet more sparkle to the ostentatious setting. Towering glass jugs whose forms emulated the women's hourglass figures sat on the bar. The waists of the green-tinted bottles were wrapped with twine, they were filled with a dark red liquid, and alongside them stood an array of golden goblets.

Still, I couldn't take my eyes off the beasts at the table for long.

'Lynoil,' the Prince called loudly toward the table. The one that seemed to be in charge didn't hear the prince. He said to me, 'These guys are the deavs. They get a little out of control.

But I invite them often. Always good to have some deavs in your corner, particularly in my line of business, know what I mean?'

'Of course,' I nodded, having no idea what he meant.

The Prince moved closer to the deavs. 'Friends. There is someone I'd like you to meet.'

The deavs turned towards me. Their gaze was difficult to hold for too long. They had no pupils; their eyeballs were a glossy black. Some held fistfuls of money, others goblets of the red liquid. 'Who's this you've got here?' one of them asked contemptuously.

'Our honored guest. He's from America.'

The deavs snorted and crossed their arms over their chests as if they were hugging themselves. A gesture for 'nice to meet you' in Deav, perhaps. I didn't know whether I should make the same gesture back. I decided not to, and just blurted a feeble 'Hello.'

'Hey, do you want to get in on the action?' the deav closest to me asked.

'Action?'

'We're playing for high stakes. But don't tell anyone.' The deav winked. 'It's illegal in this country.'

I glanced down at the table and saw a game with dice, something like backgammon. 'What are you playing?'

'*Takhte Nard*. Do you have any currency on you? Care to give it a try?' The eyes of the assembled deavs grew wider, some shooting out fiery sparks.

'I don't know how to play.' The black eyes were chilling, and once again I had to look away.

'We can teach you.' He called to one of the women behind the bar. 'Get him some drink.'

The Prince stood quietly beside me, looking on.

'No, I think I'll take a pass on...*Nard*.'

'That's no fun. Where's your sense of adventure?' the deav

asked as he moved next to us, towering above. 'How about one little wager, just for fun?'

I'd never been a gambler. The only gambling I had done had been slot machines in Atlantic City, and I really wasn't interested any doing any more. Adventure, though—now that touched a sore spot. 'Okay, what do you propose?'

All at once the atmosphere lightened. The women brought me an oversized goblet filled to the brim. One of the beasts raised his glass high. 'To the American, and to the steep trip ahead.' They raised their glasses. The deav next to me clanked his goblet against mine so hard it spilled. He laughed. I tasted the drink—musky, earthy wine, with a hint of spice.

The deavs became even more rambunctious, high-fiving each other and joking around. 'Normally we wouldn't wager with a human unless the stakes were higher, but since you are the honored guest, how about this: Since you're not from around here, we won't play *Nard*. You see the dice over there? You name the number you will roll, and you can have all of the money and gold we are betting here today. But if you do not roll the number you name, you give us all of the money and gold you have on your person.'

I was too freaked out that I was talking to these animals to think clearly about the odds. But I didn't like gold, so I had none of it *on my person*, only cash.

'But you don't know how much money and gold I have with me.'

'That's why it's called gambling!' They jostled one other, chortling vigorously. One deav punched another.

'Okay, I'll be adventurous.'

'Now we're talking, human.'

The women refilled the goblets. The beautiful server in the green skirt came between myself and the deavs as she filled mine.

As she poured she whispered, 'Do not pick number nine,' and swiftly stole away.

The prince said confidentially into my ear, 'The deavs like this kind of game because it's all chance. No thinking involved.'

The head deav handed me the dice. 'What's your number?'

'Twelve?'

'Are you sure you don't want to pick nine?' It looked like the deavs were holding their breath as they waited for my answer.

'Nope, twelve is the number.' I rattled the dice in my hands.

'Lynoil, you heard him. Listen, his number is twelve,' the Prince said as he scanned the deavs' faces.

'Sure, sure, it's twelve,' Lynoil replied, looking down at the gold wristwatch on his arm.

The party was getting ear-deafeningly rowdy. Some of the deavs had their arms around one another; there was lots of camaraderie going on. I set my drink down and cupped my hands to give the dice a good shake.

To be honest, I was hoping I would lose. The thought of having to take their money and gold was too much.

I threw the dice.

The noise, the movements of the intimidating creatures, the ministrations of the serving girls, all suddenly seemed inaudible as everything paused for an instant, frozen in time. Except for the dice...the pair rolled down the table twisting and turning, highlighting momentarily combination after combination of dots. With every tumble I tightened my fists harder. *Please not twelve. Oh God, not nine.* All eyes in the house focused intensely on the table. The dice neared the far end of the table, abruptly coming to rest just short of the cushioned edge.

The deavs moved in faster than foxes after a chicken, inspecting the numbers closely, their heads blocking my view. 'It's ten,' one of them shouted.

'Ten,' they all repeated.

'Sorry to say, you lose, American.' Lynoil said. 'Come on, show us what you have.' They moved closer.

I took out my wallet, with a roundabout figure in my mind of what it contained, and counted the notes. One hundred, three twenties, a five and six ones. 'One hundred and seventy-one dollars.' I placed the pile on the table with the hundred on top.

'That can't be,' one of the deavs said.

'Can't be. What about your gold?' They eyed one another skeptically.

'I don't carry gold,' I said.

'Don't carry gold?'

'You should always carry a bit of gold bullion in case of emergency. Never know when you might need it.'

'You're right,' I agreed, even though the thought of carrying around bars of gold seemed preposterous to me.

'You think your American dollars will get you out of any bind, right?'

I didn't respond.

'You know, American, you'd better reevaluate the whole situation. While you didn't win our money or gold today, know this: gold is the only currency that works anywhere.'

Some of the deavs were muttering under their breath; I heard one say the US dollar was going to have a fate worse than the Iranian rial. Another repeated 'mark my words' over and over. Dollars are necessary, but they aren't quite as important to me as all that, so I just brushed off their admonishments.

But the deavs weren't going to be so easily placated.

'That's really all he carries? I don't believe it. He might be trying to pull the wool over our eyes. What about your pockets?'

I pulled a set of keys and a cell phone out of my pants pockets, and turned out the fabric. I glanced at my phone as I set it down—no service. I fished through all of the pockets in my jacket, producing some Kleenex, a film ticket stub, a quarter, a dime, and two pennies—my change from buying coffee that morning.

'Sorry, I forgot about the coins.' I placed them on the table. The deavs were really wearing me out.

They went silent, shaking their heads.

Now the Prince stepped in, with a diplomatic tone. 'All right my friends, he's given you all he has. We're going to eat. Care to join us?'

But the deavs were obviously disappointed. 'We've just started here. Would *you* care for a wager before you go? Of course, you know the kind of stakes we expect if we play against you.' The Prince laughed off the offer, said his goodbyes, and directed me out of the gold room and onto another path.

The route we took was narrow. As we neared one of the rooms that led off the passageway, I noticed heavy smoke coming from inside, hazing up the corridor and filling it with a fruity tobacco aroma. The closer we got, the more the smoke thickened, making it difficult to breathe.

I peered into the smokehouse, my eyes stinging. Walls were lined with makeshift wooden shelves filled with rows of glass waterpipes in different casts: pink, blue, red, many clear with the image of a man crudely painted on the front. Colorful flexicord pipes dangled from the ceiling. A small stove had been built at the back, where a man stood holding a wire coal basket. Slowly, he took a coal from the fire. *Put it in the basket*, I thought to myself. He put it in the basket.

Old men wearing rounded hats lined uncomfortable-looking benches, they were smoking hookahs through flexible cords attached to the glass waterpipes resting on the floor. The cords, trailing from the ceiling and coming up from the floor, began to look scarily snakelike to me. *I'm getting tired*, I told myself.

The coals on top of the waterpipes smoldered and glowed pink with every inhalation. The old men held glasses, tiny clear glasses, their contents as lambent as the glowing coals. The Prince's eyes scanned the occupants of the room indifferently. They waved at us languorously as we left.

We arrived at the area with the white wedding carpet, where a crowd seemed to be waiting for something or someone. The Prince was spotted immediately. Cheerful greetings were called from afar, and those nearby approached to shake his hand and kiss him on both cheeks. I felt awkward as a stranger in such fond and familiar company.

We began to walk the length of the white fabric, which was now covered with monumental bowls of fruits and nuts. Bolster pillows were placed along the table runner and countless people were already sitting on either side, picking at the fruits and sipping tea. Following the sound of heckling and unruly laughter, I spotted the deavs; they sat in a long line on the other side, goblets in hand, talking over one another. One or two acknowledged me testily as I passed by following the Prince. At this point, I found it harder and harder to walk, feeling sleepy.

I was fairly sure we were headed to the center of the cloth, where mattresses were covered with an array of woven rugs and silken fabrics, and two guards sat either side, each cradling a machine gun. I figured this was where the host of the party would sit.

We stopped in the space between the guns. The music ceased, then the Prince called out to his guests in a language I did not recognize, before switching back to English to present me as 'the honored guest'. Most of them politely acknowledged me, but then started to chatter amongst themselves while still eyeing me. The music, a band playing traditional instruments, started up again.

All of the seats in the immediate area were filled. I figured that, in a situation like this, one's placement at the party must be a matter of family connections, social clout, or eminence in business. Since none of the above applied to me, I felt rather unqualified. Yet here I was.

Waiters, at least twenty of them, brought out trays with glasses of a pasty white drink and heaps of mint. The Prince told me it was *doogh*, a drink made of yogurt that is served chilled. It was sour, and didn't quench my thirst—in fact, it made me thirstier.

Next, salt was served in multifaceted metal containers. As it was being distributed, the Prince said to the party, 'Salt is served so we can never be enemies.' I couldn't tell whether this was a joke or not, but everyone nodded. He told his server to take some salt and cucumbers to the rest of the deavs in the golden room.

Elderly women wearing dull, flowery fabric veils brought flat wheels of bread the size of extra-large pizzas. Steaming platters of beef kebabs and tomatoes followed, along with mounds of white rice covered with golden yellow grains. The guests heaped food on their plates, and the buzz of conversation dwindled as everyone ate.

Once everything had been consumed, the guests moved more slowly, resting lazily on the rugs, draped over one other. It was about all I could do as well: feeling heavily disoriented, I leaned back on a silk pillow. The prince was telling a story in what I assumed was Baluchi. He had told me that many of the guests were Baluchi, although some were Sistani, and had given me the short version of how the province became Sistan-Baluchestan. Unable to follow the narrative of his tale, I entertained myself by watching his gestures and asking idle questions in my mind. The longer we sat there, the more I wondered whether he was one of those Middle Eastern oil sheiks. We were outside of

Zahedan in the south of Iran, he had said. I wondered why he hadn't told me his name, or asked mine. But none of the other guests called him by name either—at least I hadn't heard them doing so.

I had almost forgotten about the guards behind me until one of them shifted, which started another line of inquiry. If security was so heavy, as I understood it might be for someone like this, then why would he participate in this 'XYZT' experiment? Why risk having a stranger enter your house, let alone someone picked randomly off the street?

When the music stopped, the Prince must have thought I was bored, and began to talk to me as we watched the musicians pack up. 'Did you know Sistan-Baluchestan has a long history of poets and musicians, the finest in Persia?'

'I did not.'

'We have the myth of Rostam, and the poets.'

'You mean modern poets or old poets?'

'Mainly old. Like Farrukhi Sistani. He was an eleventh-century court poet. My personal favorite.' He raised his eyebrows and recited with great relish: '*Bring forth new stories since the new has a different sweetness.*'

'That's a brilliant one,' I said unable to come up with a better response.

'I like the idea very much. But Iran can never let go of its history, even a little bit, so it has a hard time "bringing forth the new".'

Once the musicians had departed, an aged man took the floor, carrying two musical instruments that resembled wooden flutes. The prince nodded towards the feeble man. 'He is a famous *don-ali ney* player, the only person in all of Iran who can play this elusive instrument. He calls Sistan-Baluchestan his home and enjoys playing for fellow countrymen more than anywhere else.

You know, it's nearly impossible to master the art of playing the *donali*. It's made up of two parts. They are like *neys* but different. One is considered the male *donali*, the other female. They have to be played simultaneously.'

'How does he do it?'

'Not many know. Some believe that, during a performance, he goes into a trance, which allows him to travel inwards, then outward far beyond himself, and then inward again. The process generates new revelations.'

As the man took his seat on the ground, the servers delivered a kind of rectangular portable grill, more fancy than you would use at a tailgating party, made of fine silver with elaborate patterns carved into the sides and onto the handles. Out of the corner of my eye I noticed plainer versions of the same thing being set down the length of the table. The guests became more lively as the servers also distributed waterpipes.

Holding both instruments and alternating between blowing and using his hands on the holes, the *donali* player started to play. It was hard to concentrate on the music as the servers kept bringing over more items for the grill. First they brought coals, which were added on top of already existing ash, and shifted around with fancy silver tongs until they glowed red. Next, the Prince's server brought a tray that held a few pipes and a plate of what looked like unwrapped Tootsie Rolls. The Prince reviewed the selections and took a pipe—a long dark model with a round white porcelain bead at the end and a needle dangling from it— along with the plate of burnished-brown rolls.

'Would you like to smoke?' He scanned my eyes for an answer.

Smoking has always been out of the question because of my asthma. Anyway, it's unhealthy. He could see my hesitation. 'I don't smoke because I have asthma.'

'Have you ever tried opium?' The prince asked.

Opium? 'No.'

'Don't you want to be more adventurous?'

'Did I say that?'

'Smoking a bit of opium won't bother your asthma. It will calm and soothe, I can assure you.'

My asthma hadn't been acting up lately. A few puffs on a pipe wouldn't kill me, would it? He continued to look at me, waiting patiently. The other guests were watching me too. 'I'll give it a try.'

The prince seemed pleased, and started to prepare the pipe. He placed a lump of brown on a hole at the top of the pipe. Next he took a red-hot coal from the grill with the tongs and held it on top of the opium. Eventually he inhaled deeply, drawing the smoke through the pipe. Eyes closed, he exhaled the smoke in my direction.

As it wafted over me I realized what I had smelled on the man in the courtyard earlier. The entire length of the white carpet, groups huddled around opium grills. The room, despite its sprawling size, was becoming hazy.

On my first attempt, I coughed violently. The second time I was able to take in the smoke, and allowed it to take over me. The others had their turn, and eventually I was handed the *vafoor* again. This went on for some time, although I cannot be sure quite how long. When the smoke entered me, my inner senses swirled around outside my body. The room changed along with my senses. I felt as if I could just drift away, float off quietly.

If I had known anything about opium, I had long forgotten it, except for faded mental images of an oriental opium den in a long-forgotten movie. And didn't *Wizard of Oz* have a field of poppies that put Dorothy to sleep? Dorothy, my mother's name. Dorothy, far from home. Slumbery.

The *donali* man rocked from side to side as he played one instrument then switched to the other. Sometimes he blew into both at once, his fingers sliding up and down the wood.

People were still passing the *vafoor*, although more often than not I declined to take my turn. It didn't seem to matter, for proximity to the smoke was all that I needed to be suspended in a state of quiescence.

The Prince lay back, and together we stared over at the musician. The music was separating the room into pockets of space whose divisions and folds I followed until I could no longer focus. I closed my eyes. Each time I opened them, the man was still playing the pipes, but every time the music was different, although the song continued uninterrupted.

'*Donali* is to wake up the herd. It is finally time,' the Prince said.

A group of women draped in yards of flowing chiffon over saris, each in a unique color ensemble, now filed out in front of the player, gold jewelry hanging from their ears and foreheads, sequins on their diaphanous scarves sparkling in the candlelight. Rich trims lined their clothing. Their feet were bare.

The Prince's voice seemed to come from far far away, even though I knew he was right by my side. 'They are *Bugsam Dasies*. Not traditional Persian dancers. This dance is mysterious. Some say it comes from the Hindu tradition, although these snakes come from Pakistan, not India.'

My mouth moved slowly, the words slurring into one another. 'Dancing...with snakes?'

'Dark sorcery. Snake dancers. Not dancing with snakes, but *as* snakes.'

None of them was more than twenty years old, some considerably younger, although they all were around the same height, creating consistent order across the carpet. Their faces were so incredibly tender, fragile, with painted eyes and lips standing out from flawless skin. How could they be dark?

At first the Bugsam Dasies' soft movements were easy on the eye and perfectly complemented the mild, hypnotic, lyrical notes of the *donali*. Their hips pendulated back and forth in rhythmical slow motion. They moved in unison, hands reaching up at the same time, feet shifting together, each move heavily choreographed for visual consumption by the audience, or maybe for melding with the music.

They put their hands on the backs of their heads and twirled, then lifted their appendages as if they were waving snakes. Back and forth they swayed, shifting and twisting through the lingering wisps of opium smoke, their movements telling a story in a language I felt I could almost understand.

The instrument played on without pause, leading them, moving them, shifting them.

And then the Bugsam Dasies turned away and repositioned their heads over their shoulders, looking back seductively at us. Taking their cues from the music, shifting as the sound of the *donali* shifted. Becoming more intense in their gestures. Rotating hips that remained unseen beneath their costumes.

As the dance continued, they moved further apart before my eyes. I could do nothing but watch. Colors flashed. Girls. Out of sync, the movements made little sense. I tried to focus my attention on the nearest Dasies. The blue and green girls. The dance was faster even though the tempo of the music remained constant. Then I saw only one. The most beautiful. Blue. She swirled, for me alone. Body rose and hovered in the air like the music. Costume merged into background then reemerged, metallic sari piping and golden bangles leading the way. Face was no longer anything but a blur of motion.

Over time, the music drove her to expand higher and higher towards the ceiling. A blue bounded sail, cerulean ribbon twisting around a maypole, a roll of fabric extending from floor to ceiling. Spiraling snake.

Gathering my accumulated energy, I was able to widen the

focus of my attention to take in the rest of the room. Then I saw what was happening. I had not been visually seduced by the blue girl. No. I understood what real seduction was when I saw all the snakes extended toward the ceiling, spinning, moving, reaching higher. Columns of color holding up the ceiling, swaying with ever-greater abandon. The tails of the Bugsam Dasies—once their feet—lifted up off the ground and began to move freely in the air.

I closed my eyes and let the music take me. When I was once again able to lift my eyelids, I saw the snakes canvassing the ceiling, moving along it, twisting and turning over one another, intertwining then separating.

Then they were riding the concrete wall down towards us, slithering along every possible surface. And all the time that little man sat blowing out what now seemed to be directions for the slots or positions the snakes should take up. Now in line with the music, now out of line.

One eye was able to open halfway. It was dark, but not too dark for me to see fleeting lines of color roaming along the floor, across the tablecloth, over the sleeping guests. I felt them brush over me.

When I awoke, the Prince was no longer by my side. The musician was gone, the snakes gone. I needed the bathroom, so I got up and stepped over guests. Some were sleeping, others talking in hushed tones. Light-headed and barely functioning, I approached the waiters standing along the wall.

'Where is the bathroom?' I asked. They directed me through the door the food had come from, but didn't move from their position.

Alone I walked along the brick path, which sloped down sharply. The ceiling was a series of curved domes fashioned out of old bricks. For a moment I was in the Oyster Bar at Grand Central Station. Then I was back. The walkway was lit with gas lamps.

I made my way toward an open doorway from which a strong smell of opium emanated. As I looked into the low-ceilinged room a number of pairs of reddened eyes immediately turned to scrutinize me, like beady-eyed animals scouting in the dark. But the room was fluorescent bright. The eyes belonged to young boys, maybe teens, standing zombified around a wooden table strewn with basketball-sized clumps of the same substance we had smoked, but mushier. Some of them were kneading the stuff like bread, others were rolling it into thin tubes. Along the white-tiled walls of the reeking, windowless room, stacks and stacks of clear plastic bags were filled with the brown stuff.

Not a prince. He's a drug dealer.

When I noticed a couple of guns lying on the floor next to one pile, I smiled at the boys and started to back out of the room.

'Hey, where you goin'?' the tallest demanded. He wore a hooded sweatshirt, and was the only one wearing sunglasses to shield his eyes from the light.

'Back to the party.'

'Come here a minute.'

The smell was making me sick. But on the other hand, they had the guns. I moved back into the room a few steps. They continued to work with their hands as they eyed me.

'How do you know Gary?'

'Gary?'

'Gary Ebrahimi. You know him in the United States?'

'I'm not sure what…'

'You're American yay?' The leader stopped kneading and pulled up the sleeves of the hoodie like he was readying himself for a fight.

'Yes. Why?'

'Just curious how you know Gary. If you knew him there.'

Were they talking about my Host? 'You mean the owner of this place?'

'Yay.'

'Why would I have known him in the US?'

'Because he's from there. Yay.'

'Gary is American? I just met him here.'

'Why you invited to the party? Aren't you Agency?'

'It's a long story. I'm taking part in an experiment.' I was hoping they wouldn't ask any more questions.

'The one he funded?' He pulled the Oakleys away from his eyes so he could look me over without the tint. 'They picked you as a Test?' he asked sarcastically.

'I guess so.'

They remained silent.

'I'm going to go back. You guys hang in there.' I gave another feeble smile and started nervously towards the door, testing to see if they would allow me to go.

'*Khodafez*,' they said.

'*Khodafez*,' I repeated.

A CAR WITH one headlight on followed along at a slow crawl as Estella made her way to the station. Then she sensed someone tracking closely behind on foot. *Coincidence. Keep going.*

A block from the station, the woman moved up alongside her. Estella froze.

The woman came closer. She was wearing a scarf wrapped around her head. 'Estella, listen,' she said in a low voice, 'I'm here to help you, you have to listen.'

She called me by name. Estella stopped apprehensively. 'Who are you?'

Her eyes pleaded with Estella, but it seemed as though she didn't know what to say next.

'*Open...open up the box.*'

Unable to process what was happening, Estella broke into a sprint, and the woman did not try to follow.

'They aren't who they say they are,' she called after Estella.

A few feet from the station entrance, a couple barred her way. The woman looked no older than a teenager, petite, maybe five foot one, in funky clothes, a couldn't-hurt-a-mouse type. The man was wearing a drab suit and overcoat combination. The seemingly incompatible pair positioned themselves between Estella and the stairway.

'Estella, where are you going?' the woman said loudly.

'Why?' She shifted to the side, scoping out a way around the couple.

'Take a walk with us around the block.' The man moved closer, towering over her intimidatingly, his arm moving around her shoulder as if to usher her away.

'Do I know you?' she asked, backing off.

'We're from the Federal Bureau of Investigation,' the man said in a low voice, peering down menacingly at Estella.

The FBI doesn't just stop people on the street. Estella pushed down her fear and replied: 'And I'd believe you why?' She glanced at the badges they waved in her face, realizing she had no idea what they should look like. 'What do you want with me?'

'Let's take a walk, we shouldn't stop moving,' the guy said more urgently, lifting his arm as if he was going to grab her and pull her along.

'I'm not going anywhere with you,' she said in a steady voice.

'Do you have the specifications? With you? This is a matter of national security,' the woman hissed urgently.

'I've done nothing wrong. Why are you following me?'

The woman tried to frown sternly at her. 'You are a person of interest to us.'

Holy fuck.

'Estella, you've done nothing wrong, but if you have these documents in your possession, your safety is compromised. You can mitigate the risk by cooperating.'

Mitigate? 'I'm leaving now,' Estella declared, and moved off into the crowd to see what they would do next. The couple stayed where they were, muttering into their sleeves. *They're not going to stop me*, she thought, and headed for the train. *Don't look back to see if they're following, keep going.*

The doors of the Acela Express sealed shut. She was able to find a four-seater with a table that wasn't occupied. It would take precisely three hours and thirty-five minutes to get to Penn Station.

Slowly she raised her head above the seatbacks and peered down the car looking to see whether she had been followed. Clusters of cloud-blue tweed upholstery, broken up by only a few passengers—a couple of Boston women on a weekend shopping spree, maybe going to see a Broadway play, a man in business casual, and a shady guy sporting a Red Sox baseball cap. *Never trust a sports fan.* But who could she trust, anymore?

The train was already en route when a young guy entered the car: no hustler or skank, just a standard issue college student. He stopped at Estella's seat. No surprise, guys were always hitting on her in public places. His eyes lingered on Estella's hair, the tips of each strand sparkling red from the sun strobing through the train window.

'Are you going to work on your laptop?' His dark brown hair, clean-shaven face and beige jacket all reconfirmed the run-of-the-mill impression.

But Estella's paranoia was in full-on activation mode. 'Huh? I don't have a laptop.'

'You're not going to work?' He pointed to the table in front of her. 'Why else would you need a table?'

'All that was available.' Estella acknowledged him as little as she could in the hope that he would move on.

He nodded, while tracing the topography of her space with his eyes. He looked as if he was going to say something but changed his mind, then quickly moved off, balancing his walk against the acceleration of the train as he headed toward the front car.

Overwhelmed, she closed her eyes as *Zombi Anthology* looped back to Sequence 1. The Acela was breezing south through Rhode Island at 150 miles per hour, rocking back and forth, the cabin humming. She fell into a sleep, this time dreamless.

After what could have been a minute or an hour, she awoke with a start.

Open up the box.

Sinking down into her seat below the eyeline of the other passengers, scanning the space to make sure she was out of sight, Estella once more carefully took the hard drive from her bag and began slowly turning it over in her hands, feeling with her fingertips for a seam or a catch in the smooth plastic exterior.

The cover yielded slightly at two points on the underside and she was able to carefully slide off the casing. Inside, taped on top of the black painted aluminum shell of the drive, was a chunky plastic band with a small numerical display in the center. She immediately recognized the design from the circuit diagram she had seen the previous night. Weighing the bracelet in her palm, Estella sensed the heavy mass of the circuitry embedded in the metallic interior of the bracelet: it was a perfect three-dimensional incarnation of the prototype she had seen in the files.

Sliding the casing back onto the black box until it clicked into place, she fastened the device on her wrist and folded her sleeve down to cover it.

Estella dashed off the train, pushing her way past leisure walkers. Roaming Penn Station, she found the best route heading east and moved towards it. People streamed past her, obstacles in the way of her getting to the scene. She kept a lookout for anyone who could be confrontational. The station's shoddy yesteryear modernity, paired with the music streaming through her headphones—Giallo, resonance of Argento, seventies synth, but a recent recording—made her feel as if she had landed at a commuter space station built in 1973. Clunky departure boards with red LED messages pulsing along the bottom, low white ceiling tiles, dirty air-vents...the place smelled as if it was being pumped full of stale air.

After twenty minutes of shuffling around, she had not yet found the escalator to where she believed Kade must be set up, based on the diagram he had made in his notepad. She stood in the center of the underground tunnel looking at all the directions branching off, conscious of the strange weight of the device on her wrist.

NEBRASKA: AKSARBEN 41°15'0"N, 96°0'0"W

Although a little off-balance and unfocused, I was still able to swing around to where the voices seemed to be coming from.

He had the air of a cowboy, with his dirty jeans, worn brown boots and denim jacket, dark messy hair and stubble. Maybe a modern cowboy. But I don't think they have them anymore.

He was saying to a woman, 'I'm going to turn myself in.' Then he repeated the phrase again.

I was just outside the open doorway of a narrow storefront. No door, just a space about four meters wide, open to the elements. I didn't look up to check, but I suspected a security gate must come down at night to secure the premises. It was odd, though, since it was so cold. The interior pulsed with a blue fluorescent glow, a type of light I recognized well from back home.

He was leaning against the laminate countertop so that his body was open to me. He saw me arrive, yet didn't move from his position. Beneath his beet-brown moustache his lips moved as he conversed with the woman behind the counter, his eyes focused on me all the while.

'No, I gotta do it.'

A car engine started behind me. I didn't look back but instead moved inside towards them. Next I said something that surprised me.

'Don't turn yourself in. Don't turn yourself in.'

'And why not?' His elbows rested on the counter.

I had no idea why not, to be honest. Looking closer, I saw that the yellow plastic containers behind them were marked 'Pennzoil'. Forced heat moved sluggishly through the space. *Because. Because I have to think of a reason. My head hurts, thoughts so fuzzy. I don't know exactly how I got here. Too much flowing through my mind.* I didn't know why he would be turning himself in. What had he done? Was he a criminal? His eyes didn't say criminal to me. His low-toned voice gave off a sensitive-guy vibe that ran contrary to his cowboy roughness.

'Because we're supposed to have dinner.'

He laughed.

I realized immediately that what I had said was ill-timed, and for two reasons: Firstly, how could *I* ask him to dinner given the present circumstances? And secondly, it was not time for dinner around here, even though the air felt heavy outside. It was closer to *nahar*. 'Lunch, then.'

His demeanor shifted from amused to pensive and, after a beat, he replied. 'To be clear, you will take me to lunch if I don't turn myself in?'

'Yes.'

'Are you sure you want to have lunch with *me*?'

'Yes.'

He shook his head and smiled. The woman said nothing but shifted uncomfortably in her place as he disappeared into a back room through a small white door with a shiny golden doorknob.

I realized that, since I'd asked him, I ought to pay. I glanced down at the handbag dangling from my forearm: a classic tote, brown with the LV initials. *This is not my bag. And I'm sure it's not a real Louis Vuitton.* I moved to the counter and placed the bag on it. The woman moved closer.

Unzipping the bag, I found stacks of money inside, many bills in rials. *This isn't my money.* I tried to stuff it into the inside pocket so no one could see it, but there was too much. I closed the bag hastily, not sure whether or not the woman had seen the notes.

'Are your toes cold?' she asked knowingly.

I looked down at my feet, I hadn't thought about them since arriving. *Yes, they are. Very cold.*

'Icicle digits,' the woman proclaimed as she sunk behind the counter and popped back up holding a pair of boots. The boots were made of off-white fur—long, dangling real fur—goat hair, I think. They were big and clunky, and radiated warmth. 'Why don't you put these on?' She dropped them heavily onto the countertop.

I took them while I pulled my toes out of my *Zanjan* sandals; my bare soles touching the dirty linoleum sent shots of superfluid helium up my legs. My feet dove into the colossal boots. '*Motshakeram*,' I said gratefully.

'They use those mostly at the ski chalets, you know, for when you aren't skiing. But they've been under here for years.'

'I feel better already,' I said, as my feet continued to sink into the fake fur interior, softer than the goatskin on the outside.

The cowboy returned, closing the door behind him, putting his hands to his mouth, blowing on them and rubbing them together in a peculiar warming ritual. 'Let's go,' he said, and headed outside.

I followed behind, finding it difficult to walk in the gigantic boots. We moved swiftly away from the paved road where the cars were pulling in and out to pump gas, and followed an asphalt path behind the building. The boots had good traction, but my feet were too loose inside for me to have much control over where I stepped. Still, I pushed forward, holding my *manteau* smock tighter against my chest to fend off the wind trying to make its way into my shirt. At home, out of the available options I prefer to wear a *manteau* instead of a full veil *chador*—but here the head to toe coverage would have afforded more protection from the elements.

We walked a series of paths, some narrower than others, that ran along the rear of what I assumed to be industrial buildings. They blocked out the sky in most places, and I saw only the deep moth-grey of the outer cladding. But even hemmed in by buildings on both sides, the wind still tracked us, at times assailing us from front and back.

No one was in sight. He was getting further ahead and didn't look back once to check on me.

We came to a high-walled courtyard, six hundred square meters at a guess, lined by tall buildings up on a higher level. Most likely living complexes, they had fire escapes, and from a few of the windows hung flags or clothes.

The boots sunk into deep drifts with every step as we walked across the courtyard, and with every step it was harder to drag them out again. I was becoming physically exhausted, sweating under my arms. Still, I moved as best I could, clutching the handbag as I walked. *I don't remember why I'm here, but I know that I have only three hours.*

On the other side of the courtyard a series of narrow steps, a staircase without railings, led up to the higher level. He struggled to climb them as nothing had trampled down the white since it had fallen, and he lost his footing, falling onto his side then his back. It didn't deter him. He got up and continued the climb.

As he neared the top, I began my own ascent. One step at a time, I lifted the boots and positioned them with care.

After what seemed an endless struggle, I made it to the top. The cowboy was waiting nearby under the awning of a lit building. I saw him shaking snow from his exposed stomach.

Out of breath, I made it over to him, still carrying the bag full of money.

'Why is it so dark?' I asked.

He looked me up and down. 'Calm before the storm?'

We stood there for a long time.

'You still want to take me to lunch?' he asked, looking down at the bag.

'Yes, I'm hungry.'

THE LULUBI

What's that up ahead? We never see men on this road. He's waving at the truck, what does he want?

Should at least stop and see, no harm in that. Foot on the brake, bring her in. Kill the engine.

We watch him come over to the window and speak to the Lulubi in the truck. 'Can you help me?' he asks, his beady eyes glancing inside the cabin. This tall, solid man with foreign clothing, who is he?

'What are you doing on this road?'

'Not sure. I've just arrived. No idea where I'm supposed to go. I don't think I was supposed to end up on a road in the middle of nowhere.' He looks down at the dirt road.

What should be done? Best stick to the rules. No interaction at all, it's the best way. 'You are not nowhere. You are somewhere. Sorry, can't help you.'

'Just like that? You can't help me? C'mon,' he pleads. 'Where are we?'

'In the Zagros Mountains.'

'The Zagros Mountains! It looks so remote. I really need your help!'

'Wait.' We could leave him as we left the man seen by the river in 6831L.L. He could fend for himself, as that other one did. Likewise the nomad of 4551L.L. Or the intruders of 3085L.L.

'Please.'

'Wait.' On the other body, we could bring this one back to us. The man looks as though he could be helpful with the operations. A half-meter taller than us, and look at those arms. Will we be mad?

He shuffles his feet back and forth, raising a plume of ore-colored powder. The residue clears. 'Better come along with us then.

Shouldn't be out here on your own. These parts aren't very safe, you know.'

After a great deal of praise and thanking, he silver-streaks around the front of the truck. He is agile and as he runs, even for this short distance, his arms pump back and forth, pushing his body forward faster. A moment later, he is sitting in the passenger seat quietly, looking at the instruments on the dashboard.

Start the truck after three attempts with the choke and rev her up. The tires roll over the uneven road as we move into a tighter and less friendly part of the mountain.

When he finally speaks, he says, 'I'm Mike, how about you?'

'Lulubi.'

'That's an original name. Is it Iranian?' he says.

'It's Lulubian.'

He shakes his head. 'Never heard of it.'

'You don't know the Lulubi?'

'Afraid not.'

'Lulubi are very, how do you say, wait…famous.'

'Not ringing a bell, but then again I don't know much about Iran's history.'

'Lulubi go back before Iran, before Persia.'

'That's very old.'

'Very old Lulubi.'

We drive along Fiydajooj, the road Mike had been standing on, until we reach the Khor Vinede fork. Take a right. The trees growing up and out from the mountains mask the view of the sky. Can make many go mad, these mountains.

Keep waiting for him to talk, but he says nothing, his hawk-eyes alternately watching the gears as they shift, and gazing out over the road and the obstacles on it.

Don't trust this man.

We pass Koojavinpep and have just made it to the top of Koojavinpep Mound when he asks a question. 'Where are we going?'

'Wait.' Need to concentrate to navigate around the tight turn coming up, down a narrow pass that leads into the deep valley. He understands once the truck starts shaking along the dangerous path. It is barely a road anymore.

Once in the valley, put the truck in park, but only for a minute. We can't afford to linger for too long. Mike is still waiting for an answer.

'Going to Lulubum, of course.'

'How far is it from here?' he says. Followed immediately by, 'Do they have a phone I can use? My phone gets no service here.'

Lulubi don't ask more than one question at the same time. Ask one, wait for answer, then ask another if necessary. 'No phones get any service this deep.'

'Well, how can I make contact then?'

'Who are you trying to call?'

He pauses and answers, apprehensively, 'I'm not sure.'

'Then you don't need to make a call.'

He is looking pretty miserable, hot and sweaty; the bumps in the road must have worn him out. We are used to this.

'Lulubi,' he says.

'Yes?'

'How far do we have to go?'

'Not too far. We should be there by nightfall.'

The man twists his head over the dashboard and up towards the sky, but we are too low in the valley. The trees and mountains overshadow the road, he won't be able to see more than a stone loaf's worth of sky.

'It's still light out, if that's what you're checking,' we say to him.

Mike nods.

Time to head on. 'The next part of the drive is through the road known as Zig-Zag. But this isn't a normal zigzag road. It bends and twists, at various gradients, at the same time weaving through many unlit caves. Plus, at the highest elevation, there is the Line-Spot.'

Mike takes a deep breath, nods, and we notice him tightly gripping the handle above his window as we set out on Zig-Zag Road.

We make it through the worst of the Z's and draw near to the Line-Spot. 'Maybe you should close your eyes for the part coming up.'

'Why?'

'It makes many sick.'

'I'll manage, Lulubi.'

'Suit yourself.'

We are finally at the highest elevation, and all Lulubi lend their attention to this one in the truck.

'What is that?' Mike says, placing a hand over his gaping mouth.

'The Line-Spot.'

We get out of the truck and walk over to the front of the vehicle. Tires positioned exactly where they should be. Lulubi are experienced at this. Lulubi glance over the edge to remind us what will be involved if we fall. It must be two hundred meters down, but it's hard to tell. Zagros is always shifting. Today two hundred meters, tomorrow two hundred and ten meters, next week one hundred and ninety. The rock rises and falls like a tide.

Back in the cabin, Mike is spooked. 'We can't be going over that, that...that...What is that?'

'Lulubi already said it's the Line-Spot. It connects us to the other side of Zagros.'

'Okay, it's called Line-Spot, but what *is* it? And how are we meant to get on it?'

'You ask many questions at once, Mike. Line-Spot is made of stone from the mountain. Lulubi constructed it many centuries ago. Fine work, we must say, as it still stands today.'

'Yes, but that long slab runs all the way between the two mountains with no support under it. It's at least fifty feet long, and only about six feet wide. This is a big truck. There aren't even any guard rails!'

'Why do you think we drive this old truck when we can buy a new one? Because the tires fit perfectly on Line-Spot.'

'You probably only have a few inches to spare on the outer sides of the tires. Plus the stone is sagging in the middle. It's not a flat surface—it's dipping. How can this truck get across that?'

'Mike, we have been doing this for a long time now, delivering our bread every day. We are excellent drivers. Lulubi have never fallen off Line-Spot. Maybe you should close your eyes as suggested.'

Mike squirms in his seat and eyes the door as if he is going to get out, but he remains in the truck. He closes his eyes and sits perfectly still. His actions say we should proceed.

Rev her up and begin the slow drive over the stone. Angled just right so tires stay on track.

After thirty minutes we are on the other side of Zagros. Park her up to take a short rest.

'You can open your eyes. We made it, you see?'

Mike opens his eyes. He looks down at palms covered with beads of sweat.

'Would you like a drink?'

'Yeah. That was the scariest thing I've ever been through. I don't know what to say.' He takes the bottle of water handed to him, 1969 brand, picked up in town.

'Lulubi do it everyday, so it becomes routine, but we know

what you mean.'

'What did you say about bread delivery?' Mike says.

'We are breadmakers, and every day we drive to the nearest town outside of Zagros and deliver our fine breads in the back of this very truck.'

'I thought I smelled something good. Hey, my dad was a truck driver, I would ride along with him when no one could watch me at home,' Mike says. 'It's a hard life on the road, glad I didn't have to do that.'

'So you know Lulubi?'

'Can't say I do.'

'If you knew the Lulub…' Lulubi pauses. 'You really don't know the Lulubi, Mike?'

He shakes his head, still drinking from the water container.

'If you knew the Lulubi, you'd know that we haven't had the best reputation over the centuries. We are known to be a warlike and sorcerous tribe. Some people have even called us the bogeyman, which is not accurate. In the past, it may have been that the Lulubians were sometimes thieves, sometimes fought unnecessarily, and even used black magic. But it can all be attributed to Zagros, so forget about it. A few centuries ago, Lulubians decided to try to change our reputation for the better, even though we still are at the whim of the Zagros. Nevertheless, we decided to make bread. That's what we do.'

'I see. Why bread, though?' Mike says, beginning to calm down now that Line-Spot is behind him.

'Lulubi like bread. We are fine breadmakers, Mike.'

Nearing Lulubum, we slow the truck down through the last tunnel and proceed between the small cleared fields, the only open space in Lulubum. None of us are there, as it is already getting dark. We will all have gone back to home base for the night. As we ease her into the loading dock behind the main warehouse and let the engine wind down, Mike looks around eagerly.

'Are we here?' he says.

'Lulubum. Mike, the rule is nobody outside the Lulubians is to ever be here, so there is no way of knowing how we are going to react.'

'What do you mean?'

'There may be…some negative feedback.'

'Negative feedback? I'll only be here for a few hours.'

'A few hours? Negative feedback is a nice way to put it. There might be some bad actions. Bad feedback, you see.' We don't want to tell him too much. What would be the point, now that he's already here?

'Because you're helping me?'

'No, because nobody except Lulubians is supposed to be here.'

'I'm sure they'll understand, given the situation,' Mike says. Not sure we agree. Will have to discuss the idea carefully.

'Wait.'

Lulubi appear along the rock where the loading dock is carved out, up near the trees more Lulubi, and more. Without any noise, we surround the truck, aware of the foreigner.

'Get out of the truck, Mike.' We move toward the back of the vehicle, where the road offers more space than the rocky terrain along the edges of the loading dock.

Mike stretches and looks around.

Slowly Lulubi emerge from all over home base. Some say 'Kiúruum' in hushed voices. In a matter of minutes, Lulubi approach the man from all directions, an arm's length away from him. He hovers over them, standing silently, not knowing what to do.

'Wait.'

A discussion breaks out in our native tongue that lasts over five minutes, some of it heated, spoken in raised voices. We agree to keep the man to work at the bakery. We don't trust him though. Skeptical, but figure we will give it a try.

The human looks scared to death.

'Thought you might be a god, but now know you are just a man,' we explain.

'I'm no god, that's for sure.'

'Am Lulubi,' Lulubi says.

'Am Lulubi,' says Lulubi next to Lulubi.

'I am Mike.'

'Lulubi,' the rest say at nearly the same time.

'Why are you all named Lulubi?' Mike scans the crowd.

'In Sumerian language, when a word is repeated twice, it means you are emphasizing its power for a reason. Lu means faceless people: LuLu means millions of us. Do you like bread, Mike?'

'Of course I do.'

'Glad. It's important to like it, when you make it. Since you will help us make bread, it will be easier if you already like it.'

'Well, I'd very much like stay and help make bread, but I'm only going to be here a short while longer.' Mike looks down at something on his wrist.

'Where will you be going? We have brought you here, and you will be staying here. Unless you can find a way out of Zagros on your own.'

'I'll be transporting out very shortly, so that won't be a problem,' Mike says confidently.

The man doesn't understand about Zagros, although we should try to get more information on this transportation he is expecting.

'Then please join us for dinner before you leave.'

'I don't see why not,' Mike says.

We guide him toward the dining room in home base, but as we are walking there is a slight shift. It is funny to see how Mike reacts.

After nearly a minute of dancings and faultings, the man regains his stance and the ability to speak.

'What was that, an earthquake?'

'It was just Zagros shifting mildly.'

'It felt like an earthquake. I mean, I've never felt an earthquake, but it seemed like that's what an earthquake would feel like. You call that *mild*?' he says incredulously.

'The dance comes nearly every day, and many are much stronger.'

'How can you live with that?'

'This is our home. We have been living here for a long time.'

'Don't people get hurt?'

'Of course, and our buildings get damaged regularly, especially the caves. That's why we need your help around here. You seem very well exercised. You look like you would be able to lift twice as much as us,' we tell him as we head towards the dining room.

'Well, I work out regularly and rock climb at Chelsea Piers. I thought you wanted me to make bread though.'

'That too.'

In the dining room we place Mike in a seat at the center front table along with many elder Lulubi. While we wait for the dinner to be prepared in honor of the human, we talk with him.

The Lulubi on kitchen rotation arrive at the table and present Mike with the selections. 'There are five main types of bread produced in Iran. All regulated by the government. We are proud to say we make them all and make them in the most superior way.'

'Looks good. Smells great too,' Mike says.

'We have the classic flat round bread, bread used for eating with kebabs or walnuts; the sandwich bread, a basic bread; the rectangular stone bread which is bread baked over pebbles—that's why it has all those bumps on it; then there is the sawdust bread, covered with real sawdust from our workshop. Lastly, our own invention, the salt bread, which is available only in Lulubum at this time.'

'I'll have some of each, if you don't mind. I'm very hungry.'

'Be our guest, try them all! We approve.'

'This salt bread has a unique taste.' Mike stuffs more into his mouth.

'The salt is mined here in the Zagros from the salt mounds. That's what makes it special.'

We eat our dinner along with Mike. Discussions at the various tables are lively, nearly all revolving around the discovery of the man named Mike and deliberations on work plans, proposed sleeping quarters, and his *Suvolon* pack, arrangements that will need to be made as soon as possible. Lulubum has not known such excitement since 7212L.L.

After dinner, it is determined that the human must be tired. He is complaining of feeling dizzy, his feet are falling asleep, so he agrees to take a short rest before he transports out. He is led to his new cave abode by the Lulubi who found him on Fiyda-jooj road.

'So you will be able to rest here tonight,' we say.

'Thank you. But I'll only rest a short while. My transportation is scheduled in the next few minutes.'

'We are not sure if that is correct anymore. You see, when you cross over Line-Spot to the other side of Zagros, schedules no longer work in the same way.'

'What do you mean, Lulubi?'

'The surface shifts create distortions that can vary widely. The dancing earlier could have thrown us off by a few hours, or a few days, or even months. The more dancings occur, the more time outside of Zagros becomes detached from Lulubum L.L time.'

'How can that be?' Mike says, examining his peculiar wristwatch closely.

'We know this is true because when we deliver the bread to our contacts in the town outside Zagros, they tell us we are never on schedule. We think we are perfectly on time, but they say that we skip days or deliver twice in one day. Or other timefaults occur, like when we went to deliver the bread one day and the town was not there, but it was back again on our next visit.'

'That's hard to follow. I'd need to know more to understand. But this shouldn't affect my travel. My time is actual time, so it's not important where I am exactly,' Mike says in the same confident tone.

'We will leave you to rest. If you are unable to get your transportation, then we will see you tomorrow morning for a tour of our operations. Goodnight to you, Mike.'

'And to you, Lulubi.'

As we walk back through Lulubum we feel another surface shift occur, a weak dance, but a shift nonetheless.

CHICAGO: INSIDER OUTSIDER
(THE BOX OF ROBBERS)

Feeling the pain as his limbs contorted into nearly impossible configurations, Emad managed to shift enough to take a deep breath inside the black space, turning himself on his side and bringing his knees up closer to his torso. He was then able to ease forward his left arm, which had been twisted behind his back. Terrified of the dark, his panic grew with each gasp of stale air he took. His present situation was not quite what the young man in Tehran had promised. A certain McFarland family was expected to be awaiting his arrival. Using the elephant in a dark room method, Emad carefully started to feel his way around to discover the boundaries of the space.

After an awkward series of shifts and tugs, he was able to get his lighter out of his pants pocket and flick it. He was inside a wooden trunk that seemed to be decades old. With his free hand he tried to push the lid open, but there was no give. He gave a spirited kick to the far side of the box, but it did not yield.

The trunk could easily be Persian, used for traveling, or even an adapted icebox, like the kind used years ago to hold blocks of ice during the broiling summers. So maybe he hadn't even made it to the USA. Maybe he'd been knocked out and dumped into a trunk in Tehran. The beginning of a murder mystery. Stuffed alive into a trunk. He knew corpses had been found in such trunks.

Unable to come up with any better plan, Emad proceeded to scream and bang on the lid of the box, but after what seemed like a long time, nothing at all had happened. He remembered the young man had told him he would return after three hours. Could he make it for three hours in here? His body was becoming increasingly sore with every minute that passed.

To conserve both fuel and oxygen, he continued to flick the lighter at what he believed to be twenty-minute intervals. At first he cursed himself for never wearing a watch, but after some contemplation he changed his mind, as counting the minutes would only have made the ordeal worse.

Suddenly, a curious noise from outside alerted him, and he re-lit the flame once more. A faint sound of rustling and a weak vibration of the trunk floor convinced him to overcome his fear and call out.

'Help, is there anyone out there?' he called in Farsi. No answer. The vibrations below became stronger.

'Help!' A second time, in English. 'Help me, I'm in the box.' A tapping on the top of the trunk. 'Yes, yes. I'm in here!'

A sharp kick to the side of the box caused him to drop the lighter.

'What's in there?' said a male, American voice, slightly quavering with either surprise or fear.

Emad's clamor had attracted the attention of a tall, thin man who at that moment just happened to be pacing the boards of the attic peering into boxes, rifling through papers, and inspecting long-forgotten pieces of dusty silverware. The man was apprehensive as to who or what might be inside the traveling trunk studded with brass-headed nails.

'Please, please help me out. Can you get this thing open?'

'Why should I do that?'

'Because I'm going to die in here, that's why. Please, I beg you, open the box.'

Out of curiosity, and against his better judgment, the man decided to help. The trunk had a curious old lock, but the key was nowhere to be found in the attic. He remembered seeing a basket full of keys on the shelf of the linen closet he had just rummaged through on the floor below. Moving swiftly to the lower floor, he retrieved the basket and climbed back up the winding stairs to the attic.

Both men heard a loud click as the lock opened and the trunk's heavy lid popped up, propelling a cloud of dust particles through the beams of sunlight coming from the dormer windows. One peered into the trunk, and the other peered out.

Slowly the insider unpacked himself, wincing at his limbs' revolt against the sudden freedom. He stepped out onto the floor, cracking his neck and knuckles. Looking around, he quickly determined that he was not in Iran. United States! He took off his hat and bowed to the man who had freed him.

'Who are you? How on earth did you get trapped in there?' the outsider said.

'Permit me to introduce myself. I am Emad. I seem to have ended up in the trunk by mistake. Fortunately, you found me before it was too late. And you must be Mr. McFarland.' Emad offered his hand.

'Ah, no. I'm not.' The man looked shiftily around the room, his eyes settling on an oversized camper's duffle bag.

Emad now noticed that his rescuer was wearing gloves and had a gun sticking out of the waistband of his pants. 'Sir, are you burglarizing this home?'

'What if I am? I've saved your life, so you'd better just keep quiet, you hear me?'

'Of course,' Emad said calmly to the burglar. 'I don't even know if this is the house I am supposed to be in. I just ended up in the trunk.'

'Don't play that routine with me. I warn you, I have a gun and I won't hesitate to use it on you if I have to. I've used it before.'

'No need to worry. I am grateful for your efforts in freeing me from the box. Please go about your business. But, may I ask, where am I?'

The burglar started to wonder whether this trunk guy was off in the head. Maybe he hadn't been getting enough air in there. 'You're in Chicago, on Prairie Avenue.'

'So I did make it. Did you happen to see anyone downstairs or see any food prepared?' Having escaped his immediate predicament, Emad was now keenly aware that it was past lunchtime.

'No one's home. That's why I'm here, duh,' the burglar said. 'I did see an Uno's deep-dish pie in the refrigerator. Why do you ask?'

'Well, because I am to have lunch today with the McFarlands. Is this their home?'

'I don't know or care who lives here, but there's some good stuff I've found.' As if glad of the chance to boast of his good fortune, the burglar began to pull items from the bag one by one: an armful of trinkets, a heliotrope evening dress made of velvet, brass candelabra and a mantle clock. Digging deeper, he retrieved a Bible, a box full of silverware, a copper kettle and a fur overcoat. 'I left the pie behind.'

'So you've robbed a lot of houses in Chicago?'

'Well, if you must know, I'm just getting started. I was very well respected in Italy, though.' Realizing he was saying too much, the burglar turned away and started to pack his loot back into the bag.

The doorbell rang down on the main floor. 'Curses. Who's that?' he said, dropping the bag and pulling out his gun.

Emad, who had been standing near a front dormer, glanced out and saw a man in a brown uniform leaving the front of the house. He was walking towards a mud-colored truck marked UPS. Emad had an idea that would put him in the McFarlands' good graces for sure.

'It's the police!'

'How many?' hissed the burglar.

'Looks like a quite few,' reported Emad dramatically.

'Maybe I tripped a silent alarm.'

'Maybe so.'

'If I'm caught they'll deport me for sure.'

'Listen,' Emad said, trying to move the situation in his favor, 'We are both immigrants here. You have saved me, so I will help you.'

'What do you propose?'

'Get into the trunk, so the police will be unable to find you.'

With no time to think, the thief stepped into the chest. As he crouched down he said, 'Don't keep me in here too long.'

'Oh, no. I know how tight it is in there.'

Emad turned the key in the lock. When it was secured, he thought he would go downstairs to find out what an Uno's deep-dish pie was. But first he should clean up the robber's mess and return the items in the bag. He picked up the weighty duffle and headed down. Dropping the bag on the living room rug, he started to take out the items one by one to determine where they belonged.

At that very moment the front door opened and a group of people swarmed the entry hall, all talking at once.

The Hosts had returned. Emad stood up and cleared his throat to get their attention. 'Sir, greetings from my country,' he intoned as he bowed to the group of six, the bag at his feet, candelabra and furs spilling out across the pile carpet.

A young girl with blonde pigtails let out a piercing scream.

'Get back, Martha,' said an older woman, pushing the girl behind her legs defensively.

'What are you doing in our house?' demanded a man who looked to be the head of the family.

It was beginning to dawn on Emad how the scene looked from their perspective. Somewhat crestfallen, he prompted them:

'I am the Test from Iran. We were to have lunch together today.'

'Omigod, Iran? This guy could be dangerous,' the younger woman shrieked, as if Emad weren't there.

'He's robbing us blind. Look what he's stealing!'

'Oh no, sir, you see, there is a burglar in your attic who helped me out of the trunk. But when I got a chance I put *him* inside so he couldn't rob you. Now I am placing the items he was stealing back where they belong.'

'He's mad,' the father muttered. 'Unstable.'

'Middle Eastern,' the woman added.

'I'm perfectly sane,' Emad insisted, but with little hope of turning the situation around.

'My cousin's a police inspector. I'm going to call him right now if you do not leave immediately.' The older woman pulled a phone from her handbag.

'But, I… umm…'

'My mom told you to get out, you, you burglar!' Martha cried, peeping out from behind her mother's legs.

Feeling bad that he had already caused such distress, Emad headed for the door, the throng of appalled family members parting to let him through as though they were afraid he might touch them.

As soon as he stepped outside, Martha slammed the door behind him. He didn't have a proper coat, and his stomach was growling. But at least he wasn't stuck in the trunk.

KADE HAD SUSPECTED that the New Yorkers would be an un-relentingly tough crowd, something they would probably take as a compliment, which it was not. He had already heard more than one say, 'Why would I want to go to Iran?' He had managed to successfully recruit some Tests, but it was tough going.

On seeing Estella approaching, Kade was at first bemused, and then his whole body tightened in panic. He scanned the table in front of him as if it might be possible to conceal the remaining bracelets from her, but she was already right there in front of him.

He greeted her with phony nonchalance. 'Stell, what are you doing in town?'

Approaching carefully, she said, 'I didn't want to bother you, but I got this message from Amir. I realized he might need some help.'

'Message? Why would he contact you?' Suddenly Kade's voice took on an aggressive edge. 'You wouldn't be here if you knew what was good for you.'

Estella's lips pursed. A gust of wind blew over her from behind. 'Why?'

'I don't have time to explain.'

'You don't have time to explain about what you're doing here with Amir, or about how you've sold him out?' She put her hands on her hips and gave him a look that left him in no doubt as to her determination.

Kade deliberately softened his voice. 'Hey, Stell, I don't think you understand. This is something that's going to be important. For people from different cultures to come together. Amir's in Iran. But things aren't working quite smoothly. I've gotten a couple of distress calls from him on the satellite phone.'

'Eliminating borders, great. How's that working out for you? And for your new business partners?'

Kade said nothing.

'What is XYZT, Kade?'

He cleared his throat and looked down at the contents on the table. 'Well, our technology transports people, without the need for state bureaucracy....'

'To Iran?'

'There are...interested parties in the country.'

Estella's eyes scanned the devices laid out on the table.

'So what happened?'

'I'm not sure, we had problems with coordinates. The connection wasn't good. Something about too many people or the police. He did say "police." He's in trouble, Stell.'

'You mean your deal's in trouble?'

'There's nothing you can do here.' Staring down at the ground, Kade followed the fluttering movements of the discarded green and white confetti and garbage left over from St. Patrick's Day that was blowing slowly along the concrete. 'The phone isn't working from my end.'

Estella pulled back her sleeve to reveal the XYZT bracelet on her wrist. 'Then send me.'

Stunned into silence, Kade stared at the bracelet. *They don't call her Hazardina for nothing. She might screw the whole thing up. But everything is hanging on saving these Tests. The only other option is to just walk away.*

She woke him from his thoughts. 'I can go, let me try. It's just an experiment, right?'

As if in a trance, Kade wordlessly pulled out a black headscarf from under the table, punched Amir's GPS location into the touchpad, and coupled it with Estella's bracelet.

The device constricted around her wrist.

Kade pointed to the escalator, and Estella began to walk.

THE YAZIDI MOUNTAINS

Ēzidi, people of the Peacock Angel, greet you.
You must travel some distance.
First, remove anything you are wearing that is blue.
In case you have packed a snack, do not bring lettuce or okra.
If you have either, dig a hole in the ground and bury it before
proceeding.
Make sure not to utter the word 'Satan' on your journey.
Satan, the truest monotheist: when he was asked to kneel before
humans, he refused, for he believed only in the glory of god.
Do not spit on the earth, in water, or into a fire.
Release the animal from its pole and mount.
Mule knows the way.

The open clearing, the negligible winding trail, mountains in the background—I'm definitely alone, except for the mule. Glancing around, I can understand why the special instructions. The mule brays and shuffles his feet while he looks over my way. Don't know how Peter got the insider info but, sure enough, the tip-off was good, and I wanted to be a Test. Only, when the guy put the bracelet on, he also pulled out this scroll of shiny paper that he said was received from the Host.

The mule is outfitted with a soft woolen saddle and a series of gunnysack pouches that bulge out from his body. As I draw near to the animal he emits another braying cry. When it is done, I slowly shift closer. It appears he isn't going to bite or resist me. I open the closest burlap flap, where I find bottles of water, and the other pouches have additional supplies. How long am I going to be riding the animal?

Let's see, I don't have anything blue, didn't wear jeans today. No greens either, so I guess I'll get going. I untie the animal's reins. Haven't been horseback riding for years, but I figure getting on a mule is much the same process—only the fabric saddle is more of a blanket, really—no stirrups. I jump up and over him, which it turns out isn't that hard to do.

Agitated, the mule makes jerking motions, then turns around and starts walking along the thin-grooved path carved into the dirt. I breathe a sigh of relief and figure I've done my part for the time being, I can relax as the mule takes me to my destination.

Hour 0–1: While riding, I think about what has happened and the engineering of the experiment, and try to grasp exactly how I got here. I was hoping to see various types of Iranian architecture, gather ideas for the firm, but all I see is nature. The landscape reminds me of Peter's land in Cerrillos.

Take a drink of water and eat some of the bland food in the pouches. Most of this hour spent travelling up a lightly pitched hill. Resist the urge to say 'Satan' out loud just to see what might happen.

I work on the Brestrial residence plan in my head. I wonder if we can go ten stories below ground without obtaining a NYC permit. I should know the answer, but as I am riding it does not come. Also, I wonder if we can get permission from the church to cut a main door entrance; if not, what are the other options on how to gain access? Bomb shelter layouts could prove helpful, although we would have to do something edgy, in a panic-room-kitsch sort of way, for it to work. Even then it may be passé.

A flying bug comes my way and asks me what's the first image that comes to mind when I think of 'devil worshipers'.

Embarrassingly, the first thing that comes is heavy metal teenagers listening to AC/DC and Mötley Crüe, banging their heads to the sound in an old Cutlass. The bug replies, 'Then you will do fine, for devil worshipers are not we.' After the bug leaves, I realize that I've been talking to a bug.

Hour 1–2: The terrain becomes much coarser. The mule is overheated and huffing. He stops from time to time to rest, but I remain on his back. As we turn a corner, a slew of navy birds nestled in Joshua trees lining the path peer out at me. I've seen these kinds of trees in the Mojave Desert. And then peacocks. As I pass, they whisper, or I believe they whisper, for I can't quite hear them. I think they ask my name, and I tell them. They hiss, or the trees hiss. Their opinion, apparently, is that I am not a descendant of Adam and should not have been given the name. I shrug and tell them it's a popular name. They continue, whispering that, before there was a difference between the sexes, Adam and Eve both had jars that held their unique seeds. When the jars were opened, Adam's held a handsome male child, while the woman's jar was full of insects and poisonous animals. Yazidis descend from Adam alone, while other humans such as myself come from both jars. The mule and I leave the trees behind and continue our journey.

Where is he is taking me? I'm becoming more and more unsettled, but I don't dare get off.

Hour 2-3: The mule and I arrive in a town. At least, the place looks like it was once a town—a few buildings remain, crudely made structures, no useful ideas to take note of for stuDO's new look: abandoned shacks.... All of them are empty, but I get the sense that the place was recently occupied. As if the Ēzidi have just bolted. As we near a post like the one to which he was originally tied, the mule brays again, his whole body vibrating as he makes the sound. I get off and tie him up, and he drinks from the water bin at his feet.

Nearing the third hour mark, just hanging out in this ghost town. Waiting. The mule says nothing. Impatient, I steel myself and yell out into the emptiness: 'Satan!'

MADISON: EASTER SUNDAY

Rouzbeh Rabiee attempted to work out how many hours he had been in the US. He had become increasingly troubled at the strike of each hour. Confused by the Tehran time still showing on his wristwatch, he resorted to counting on his fingers, counting off not ten but twelve hours since he had felt Iran's sun on his face. He was pretty sure it had been twelve hours.

Rouzbeh could tell that the Millers were just as keen for him to leave as he was to get back home. Calls made from the Miller's home in Wisconsin were not going through. No one could make sense of the strange noise at the other end of the line.

Rouzbeh's thoughts brightened for a minute as he sat on the single bed in the extra bedroom. What if the experiment had not worked as it had been described? He was already well over the three hour time frame. From his childhood, he remembered the unauthorized translation of the Narnia books, with its badly photocopied illustrations, and wondered whether, when he finally made it back to Iran, it would be as if no time had passed, and they wouldn't even have realized he had been gone. He nervously ran his hand over the mustard colored bedspread. He was, he thought, quite lucky that the Millers had an extra room for him to stay in overnight, although Rouzbeh wasn't looking forward to being dragged along to 'church' tomorrow. Maybe he wouldn't still be here in the morning. He got up from the bed and glanced out at the snow-blanketed backyard, before pulling the canvas curtains closed.

He walked over to the dresser, where Beverly had placed a number of toiletries, a set of forest green towels and an unused T-shirt of Paul's to sleep in. She had apologized for the 'loudness' of the shirt, which was bright red, and featured a black and white cartoon animal wearing a red sweater with a big letter 'W' on it. The shirt had been a holiday gift from Paul's employer, she had said, and it was all they had that was new. Rouzbeh looked through the selections, picking up the boxes and bottles and reviewing the brands. Unlike older generations of men in Iran who were for the most part uninterested in brands or fashion, Rouzbeh, although in his thirties, was more closely aligned with the younger generations of boys who enjoyed consumer products, especially those from the West. He recognized all of the brands, the real stuff: Crest toothpaste, Colgate toothbrush (medium), Gillette Series gel and disposable shaver, Axe deodorant, Aveda shampoo and conditioner. Rouzbeh carefully balanced the pile as he opened the door and tiptoed down the hall toward the bathroom Beverly had pointed out for him to use.

The overly long Easter service gave Rouzbeh all the more reason to watch the clock, and he could hardly contain his impatience. Once the interminable sermon was over, the congregation joined the choir in a number of hymns while the ushers began to distribute green velvet pouches with wooden handles protruding from all sides. The pouches were passed from pew to pew, and each family put in either a white envelope or money as it went by, the handles swinging, the pouch turning in perpetual motion. As it reached the Millers, Paul placed his white envelope inside. Rouzbeh grabbed a wooden handle with one hand and placed a few rial notes in before handing it off to the woman on his right. As he completed the transaction, he thought to himself mordantly: here, they are outright asking for money, and hence the patrons are provided with a seat. In the mosque, we're not asked for this kind of religious taxation, and that's why we have to sit on the floor.

The congregation read the Lord's Prayer, which was immediately followed by Communion with Our Risen Lord. The Pastor declaimed 'Welcome to the Lord's Table! Please proceed to communion at the direction of the ushers. After receiving the bread and wine, those who desire may go to the altar rail for prayer. Please return to your seat by way of the side aisles.'

Slowly, during the singing of Hymns 148, 352, 144 and 145, the congregation made its way up to the front of the church. They stood in front of the pastor, who popped a white disk into each mouth, then they moved along the line to a table of miniature glasses. Each took one and drank its contents in one gulp, placing the empty glass on the next table. Like the offering pouch, it reminded Rouzbeh of an assembly line. All of the participants knew what to do, and so the miracle was delivered efficiently and flawlessly.

Their pew's turn was nearing. Paul turned to Rouzbeh. 'I suppose you won't want to go up. Do you mind staying here with the kids while Beverly and I go?'

'Sure I will,' answered Rouzbeh with resignation.

When his parents were nearly to the Pastor, Troy leaned over to Rouzbeh and whispered, 'Thanks, we hate going up there.'

'Someday you'll think differently.'

'I don't think so.' Troy took a piece of candy from the Easter Bunny out of his pocket and started to open the wrapper, chocolate already smudged around the corners of his mouth.

'You'll find your religion.'

'I'll be what you are.' The child looked up at the Test as he stuffed the chocolate in his mouth.

'Muslim?'

'Yeah.'

'When you are older, you'll think differently.'

A moment later, Rouzbeh was relieved to suddenly feel the same sickening lurches in the stomach as when he had arrived.

Goodbye Narnia....

ABADAN: THE CARPET ANTECHAMBER

Spring song of nightingales! If I have had such a thing as a love story it has been a love story with tahdig.

When Tate arrived, the Rashidi home was a flurry of activity. Shireen and Vahraz's wedding was to be the event of the season in Abadan.

'We would be honored if you could join us at the wedding,' Mrs. Rashidi said.

'That's very kind of you, but…' His t-shirt and jeans weren't exactly a wedding outfit. 'I was just out for a casual day.'

'No matter. We can give you a suit jacket, and you can wear it over your shirt. The boys dress like that for weddings,' said Parshand.

'Leila, go get a couple of suits from my wardrobe,' Mr. Rashidi ordered his daughter. 'He is nearly my size.'

On the pretext of gauging Tate's size, Leila took the opportunity to check him out. Sandy brown wavy hair, American looks with hazel eyes—and he was tall. In turn, Tate watched Leila walk out of the room, her long turquoise lycra gown hugging her gangly body. Not an ounce of fat on her. Hair up in a bun with small curls spiraling down the back of her neck. He had noticed how much make-up she had applied to her big eyes—like the black eyes of an alien—and how thinly her eyebrows had been plucked. She wore rouge cream on her lips and had dangling diamond earrings and a matching necklace. Her face seemed stretched out like silly putty. Her out-of-proportion build was emphasized by the bun at the back of her head, which seemed to be weighing down her body. It wasn't that she was unattractive; to Tate she just looked half-human, half-extra-terrestrial.

Mrs. Rashidi suggested that Tate take a seat on the sofa. His eyes scanned the living room, which had a homey feel. On the muted TV Islamic patterns were followed by an old man with a black turban and a white beard wearing thick black glasses that covered most of his face. He would be on the screen for a few seconds, and then the patterns would fill the screen, obscuring his image. Moments later, his face would return.

Tate wasn't feeling that well. He was not fully functioning since the XYZT. Thinking that it would make sense to keep track of time, and figuring he had already been there for twenty minutes, he set the alarm on his ever-reliable Timex to go off in two hours and thirty minutes.

Sinking down onto the sofa next to him, Mrs. Rashidi held out a small packet. 'A piece of gold for you to give the bride.'

'Oh, I can give some money I have with me, would that be acceptable?'

'It's not necessary. Here in Iran, gold is given as a gift to the bride to help her start her home. It's a very small piece of gold, but it will be appreciated.'

Tate slid open the small packet, which was about the size of a business card, and a laminated piece of plastic popped out. Embedded between the layers was a dime-sized piece of gold with a winged lion embossed on it.

Leila returned with four jackets. Tate got up, and she helped him put one on that seemed too big and heavy for the warm weather.

'Let's try this one.' She picked up a lighter coat.

'It fits fine. How does it look?' Tate moved his shoulders around and checked the length of the sleeves, noticing that the exterior tag loosely sewn on the left sleeve had not been removed. As a boy he remembered getting his first suit, and how he had protested when his mother had cut off the label on the sleeve. He looked over at Mr. Rashidi and Parshand's suit sleeves, which still had the labels on as well.

'Are we are ready to go, then?' Mr. Rashidi asked.

The women put on their jackets and lightly draped veils over their heads, trying not to mess up their hair. Out in the courtyard Parshand opened the oversized metal gates while Mr. Rashidi started the engine and everyone squeezed into the grubby silver Kia sedan.

'We are off to one of the gardens in Abadan. It is arguably the most beautiful garden in the city. Our climate is scorching, so there are not that many gardens maintained here. It takes too much water to keep them green,' explained Mrs. Rashidi in her meticulous English.

'Where is Abadan located in Iran?' Tate asked.

'You don't know?' Leila was surprised.

Parshand stepped in at this point. 'We are on the west side of Iran. Our city is located at the northern tip of the Persian Gulf, and we are very close to the borders of Kuwait and Iraq.'

The passengers were tightly packed into the small car, nearly sitting on each other's laps, and the heat was unbearable. 'How do you feel about the current state of Iraq?' Tate managed to ask. Not long before he had come he had seen a news report, and he was now wondering whether he should be worried at being this close.

'The people in our family, as well as other Abadanees, are very warm-hearted people. We don't like war or fighting.' Apparently put out by the question, Mr. Rashidi paused as he turned onto a busy road, eventually continuing: 'Being so close to the border means that we know of certain things that are happening, and sometimes business related to the war trickles over to us. It reminds us of the Iran-Iraq war years ago. We will never forget what happened then. Many Abadan sons and husbands died.

We had to leave our city during the war.'

There was an uncomfortable silence. 'What do the people in New York think about it?' Leila asked.

'Me? I'm against the war. I think the United States has no business being in Iraq. I mean, what are we doing there, what good have we done? We've only made things worse, in my opinion.'

'Do a lot of your friends feel the same way?'

'Just about everyone I know. I wish we'd get out of there and let the people run their own nation. The US has enough troubles of its own. If we keep pouring huge amounts of money into the Iraq war, domestic problems will continue to get worse until the US really gets in trouble.' Tate realized he was raising his voice, stopped abruptly, and the car became quiet.

Music floated out over a cob wall, blown this way and that by gusts of wind that also stirred up the yellow-brown dirt of the parking lot, making his Vans dusty as, one by one, the family squeezed out of the cramped car. The women held their veils close to their faces and kept their coats shut as best they could.

Inside the garden, they adjusted their clothing. Turning to Tate, Parshand said, 'This wedding is a traditional one, so the men and women are separated during the party. My mother and sister will go to their section at the other side of the garden. You will come with us.'

'See you later, Tate,' Leila called out over her shoulder as she moved off, arm in arm with her mother.

The men's section consisted of an uncountable number of round tables surrounded by white plastic chairs. A male performer stood on a makeshift stage singing to pre-recorded music. A number of men were already present, spread out across various tables, talking amongst themselves. Mr. Rashidi and

Parshand headed over to where their relatives were sitting.

Tate saw a large canvas wall erected on the right side of the space, running the entire length of the garden. At its center a patterned rug hung from the top all the way to the ground.

While he was listening to the men speak, his eyes wandered. He noticed a few women walking toward the dividing wall, pulling back the patterned rug, and disappearing behind it. A kind of primordial shrieking—'IE–IE–IEIIIIIII'—filtered through mysteriously from the other side.

Tate looked at Parshand, baffled. 'What is that sound?'

'That's what the women do during weddings. Sometimes they make that sound during funerals, too.'

'What does it mean?'

'I guess it's just their way of expressing great emotion.'

'You know, I attended a funeral in Brooklyn yesterday. That's why I was in New York. I don't live there.'

'Sorry to hear that. Who died?'

'It was one of my professors from medical school. Died very young. He had a heart attack.'

'Very sorry.'

'This all has helped take my mind off it. But it made me realize that we shouldn't waste any time in life.'

Parshand nodded. 'Very true.'

The singer headed through the rug to the women's section. The bride and groom appeared and began walking from table to table greeting the men. She was decked out in an American style wedding gown, a fifties cut with no train, but with a hoop underneath that made the skirt full.

The couple was fairly young, and the slender-faced groom, with thick black sideburns and bushy eyebrows, was nearly the same height as the bride. She had on more make-up than Leila and was wearing false eyelashes as well, her hair pulled up into a giant beehive do, sculpted into a sort of cone shape that reached towards the sky. The hive was created, Tate figured, to accommodate the diamond tiara she wore, along with the numerous silk flowers and gold metallic leaves positioned around it. She was evidently very pretty, even discounting the excessive attire.

Parshand stood up and took out his gold packet and, seeing this, Tate followed suit. When the couple was introduced, he handed the bride the gold packet.

'*Motshakeram*,' she said, and passed the packet to the girl standing behind her, who dropped it into a white sack which was already bulging, reminding Tate of a pillowcase full of candy after an exceptional night of trick-or-treating.

The bride and groom disappeared as quickly as they had arrived and with the singer over on the women's side, the men's area became more laid-back. Some men smoked cigarettes, a few smoked hookahs on the edges of the garden. At this point the entertainment mainly involved watching mountains of food being delivered to the buffet tables, which were set up on the left side of the garden.

Tate couldn't believe the number of platters coming out. 'How many guests are here tonight?'

'Hard to tell because they keep coming and going. Maybe six or seven hundred,' said Parshand.

'Wow, that's a lot. Does each side have their own food?'

'Usually it's just one side. I think that the women will come over here when it is ready.'

'Doesn't that defeat the purpose of having two separate areas?'

'Yes, but that's the way it is. Separate weddings are a thing of the past. They just go through the motions, but it's not totally separate. I don't know why the families insisted on having it this way. Weddings where the men and women are together are much more fun, if you can call it fun. But as you can see, these kinds of weddings are the most boring events known to mankind!'

The food was ready. Slowly, veiled women started entering through the patterned partition, one by one pulling aside the heavy carpet to squeeze through. En masse they waited as each person took time to load food onto the oversized plates.

Tate's group headed over to one of the two lines tailing back on either side of the sprawling buffet. When they finally made it to the food, Tate followed Parshand's lead and added a heaping portion of rice with red berries onto his plate. Then they waited to add long strips of kebab meat, chicken and a glassy-looking brown substance pre-cut into square chunks.

'What is this?' Tate dropped a chunk of the hard glassy crust onto his plate.

'That's *tah-chin*. It has chicken inside. This dish is usually served at weddings. There is a simpler version called *tahdig*, bottom of the pot. Rice crust is a Persian favorite!'

They neared an animal carcass—Parshand said it was lamb—transfixed on a spit, legs spread out and head intact, eyes peering forlornly at the guests sawing at it from every angle.

Tate noticed a girl across from him in the other line. Creamy complexion, cheeks slightly flushed, possibly from the steam of the food, eyes the deepest brown, glowing and alive, hair swept up like the others', but in simple Audrey Hepburn style. She wore a black gown with a plunging V neckline and her veil was more see-through than the other women's.

Parshand smirked at Tate knowingly. 'That is Fattaneh.'

As Tate proceeded through the buffet, he kept stealing glances at Fatteneh. When he wasn't looking, he thought he felt her eyes on him too. But her line was moving faster, and she was carrying away her food and soda before he was finished. She had stopped with another woman at one of tables halfway between the buffet and the women's rug.

'Can you introduce me while she's still over here?'

'Why sure. Our families are friends.' Parshand changed direction and headed towards her.

'*Khodafez* Fattaneh!'

She turned toward them, surprised to see the foreigner in front of her clumsily holding a plate filled with food and juggling a soda and packet of silverware. '*Khodafez.*'

'This is my family's guest, Tate. He is from America.'

'Hello.' She said directly.

'You can speak English?'

'Yes, of course.'

'I saw you in line back there,' he said awkwardly.

'Well, it is hard to miss you.'

'How so?'

'You are the only foreigner here. Mrs. Mahmoudi has lived in Los Angeles for twenty years, but she's still Iranian, kind of.'

'Irangelian,' Parshand suggested, and Fattaneh laughed.

'It's too bad that this is a separate wedding, or I'd ask you to join me.'

She thought for a moment. 'We can still eat together if you like,' she said, pointing across the garden to a group of benches.

'Really? You can eat alone with me over there?'

Her eyes flashed and she gave a fierce smile. 'I can eat wherever I want!'

'Great.' Tate turned to Parshand. 'Join us?'

'Sure.'

They ate from the plates resting on their laps. Fattaneh manipulated her fork and spoon in the most graceful manner, and Tate felt awkward and clumsy.

'So you live in Abadan?'

'I do,' she said, 'but I lived in Tehran while I was going to University.'

'What did you study?'

'I have my MS in chemical engineering.'

'Really?' He suddenly noticed the exterior label on his suit sleeve again.

'Yes.'

'So you're working as a chemical engineer now?'

'Unfortunately, no. There are no jobs for me in that here, so I am at my aunt's beauty salon.'

'I guess the job market is pretty bad here.'

She nodded. 'How about you? Where do you live in America?'

'Seattle. I'm a doctor, specializing in podiatry.'

'You don't look old enough to be a doctor. Especially with your outfit,' she replied, stifling a smile. 'That's what boys around here wear.'

Now even more self-conscious, the American still managed to find the courage to say, 'Sorry for the forward question, but I feel like at any moment you're going to disappear behind that dreaded rug.' He swallowed. 'Are you married?'

'If I was, I probably wouldn't be here talking to you, would I?'

'I guess not.' Tate felt a thrill pass through his body like a wave.

'There are no guys good enough for Fattaneh in Abadan,' Parshand teased.

'That's not true. I just haven't found anyone,' Fattaneh said.

'I wish I lived in Abadan. I'd ask you out in a heartbeat.'

'That's kind,' she said softly.

'I was in New York before I came here.' Tate checked his Timex.

'How long does it take to fly here from New York?' Fattaneh asked.

'Not sure. I didn't follow regular travel routes on my way over.'

Tate glanced at Parshand to see if he was going to elaborate, but his Host said nothing and just took another bite of food.

The 'IE–IE–IEIIIIIII' chants started up again, reminding Fattaneh that she should be getting back. The three got up and started walking. 'It was really great meeting you, Fattaneh,' Tate said.

'You too. When do you leave?'

'I'll be going tonight.'

'Tonight? So soon.' She paused in front of the rug.

'I'm afraid so.'

'Goodbye,' Fattaneh said to Parshand as she leaned over to kiss him, first on his left cheek, then his right, and then his left again.

She hesitated for a moment, as if deciding whether to kiss the foreigner or not. 'Well, goodbye Tate.'

'Goodbye.'

She pulled the rug open just enough to squeeze through, and was gone.

The singer was in the men's section again, making it difficult to talk. Tate stared into space, lost in thought, while Parshand, Mr. Rashidi and the others drank Coke and shouted in Farsi. Fattaneh was the most intriguing and mysterious person he had ever met. Or was it just the intense XYZT experience—which was still affecting his mind and body—that made her seem that way? He shook his head and went back to his first thought.

Tate leaned toward Parshand. 'She's really great, isn't she?'

'I've known her all my life. She is very pretty.'

'And smart.'

'That too. Sounds like you like her.' He nudged his new friend, 'Yes...yes?'

'I do, but how could I fall for someone so quickly? I feel like I could fall in love with her. It's ridiculous.'

'Not at all, that kind of thing happens all the time here, especially at weddings. We don't get the chance to spend much time with the opposite sex. Schools are segregated and the government doesn't approve of dating.'

'Wow, but that's not my M.O.'

'Sir, you are in Iran. Anything is possible,' Parshand said with a conspiratorial grin.

Tate had been immersed in mental images of Fattaneh for some time when suddenly his Timex went off. *I didn't even get her email!* His eyes scaled the wall separating him from Fattaneh's section. The sound of music and laughter drifted through the partition. Tate leapt up and ran towards the curtain.

Parshand called after him, 'You can't go over there!'

But Tate had already made it to the rug. He stood at the divider for a moment, taking in the stale smell of carpet, which he knew he would now remember forever, and then pulled the rug open. In the darkness beyond was a small antechamber defined by hanging carpets, an in-between space nearly six feet by six where one white plastic chair sat. Tate ran to the other side and pushed through another rug into the women's section.

His eyes scanned this side of the garden, a mirror image of the space he'd come from, but with women dispersed across the garden like colorful flowers, the fabrics of their garments shifting in the wind. Clearly there were more women than men at the wedding and, to his surprise, here on the other side nearly all of them were without veils. Most were on the dance floor. The singer had now taken on the role of DJ, and the women were really letting loose to the techno he was spinning, their bodies grinding together in a mass of movement. Everything was a blur, brightly colored gowns merged with elaborate stage lighting—a full-blown discotheque. Evidently, this side was where the party was happening. Tate scanned the dance floor and the outer seating areas.

'Fattaneh, where are you?' he called out.

Some of the women, shocked by the sound of a man's voice, brought their veils back up to their heads and glared at the intruder.

The dance floor came to a halt, which in turn caused the DJ to stop the music. In a matter of seconds, hundreds of peering eyes locked onto Tate.

'Fattaneh?'

Tate stood motionless, not knowing what to do next. Then he saw Fattaneh moving through the sea of women toward him.

'*Auzubillah*! Are you insane?' she screamed.

'I guess so, but I'm leaving in five minutes, and I wanted to tell you I like you. I mean I *really* like you.'

The women within earshot gasped, some giggled and tutted, but all waited eagerly for Fattaneh's response.

'Funny, I am fond of you too.' Fattaneh was so surprised by what her lips had let pass that she lifted her hand to cover her mouth. But it was too late. She had said it and everyone had heard.

The place suddenly broke into a buzzing of repetitive wails: 'IE–IE–IEIIIIIII E–IE–IEIIIIIII IE–IE–IEIIIIIII'.

'Quick, Fattaneh, get some paper and a pen so we can exchange emails. I don't have much time,' Tate said frantically.

A woman nearby pulled out a ballpoint pen from her clutch and handed it over. No one had any paper. Tate took her hand in his, and wrote his email.

'I don't understand why you have to leave so fast. Are you going to miss your plane?'

'I'll explain everything later. Hurry!'

She took the pen and, holding his hand still with her own, inscribed her Gmail on his palm. All the while, the women were moving closer to form a semicircle around the couple, gossiping and hugging one other. Tate heard the word *American* repeated, and *doctor*. A few were even wiping tears of happiness from their eyes, and more IE–IE–IEIIIIIII E–IE–IEIIIIIII IE–IE–IEIIIIIII ensued.

'I have to go, but I'll email you tomorrow. If you don't hear from me, contact me, okay?'

'Okay!'

'We'll see each other soon,' he said, disappearing once more through the rug.

Following seconds behind Tate as he made his exit, Fattaneh, Mrs. Rashidi and Fattaneh's mother hustled into the antechamber, where they converged with Parshand and Mr. Rashidi coming in the other direction.

On the seat of the plastic chair, neatly folded, lay the borrowed suit jacket.

Estella's feet hit Persian pavement. Panic attack, full on. Her stomach lurching violently, head feeling like it was being microwaved. *Holy fuck, it actually works!* She wobbled awkwardly to keep from falling, then turned towards the noise—a road, vehicles blaring, horns, screeching. A white car, coming directly at her. Everything in slow motion. An assault on her lower body.

Amir heard the horns and noticed the traffic had come to a halt on the roadway next to where he was set up. People were out of their cars. A light-haired foreigner, maybe a Russian, had been hit. He looked over. The people attending the victim shifted. Losing track of the situation, he thought of Stell. *Poor Estella, couldn't she be more careful?* And then, trying to get a hold of himself, *I'm seeing her everywhere. This has to stop when I go back to the States.* But the longer he stared, the more convinced he became. A guy next to him said the driver was relaying how she came from the sky. 'Crazy people!' he exclaimed, and left the scene gesticulating.

The victim was awake and sitting up.

Unable to shake off his disquiet, Amir clambered over the concrete barrier and jumped into the road. He couldn't take his eyes off the woman.

As he neared, he stopped dead in his tracks. It was Estella.

'I know her,' he said, pushing his way over.

'You know the girl?' The guy closest to the woman asked.

'Amir,' she cried.

'Estella, what happened?'

'It happened so fast.' She looked around, confused.

'Are you okay?'

'My leg's hurt. I have to tell you...'

The taxi driver eyed Amir uneasily. 'She came out of nowhere, from the sky.'

Amir had to defuse the situation. 'She was with me. She must have jumped from the barrier. I'm terribly sorry, she shouldn't have gone into the road.'

'Yes, she jumped. I slowed down and only tapped her.' The taxi driver scratched his palms and shifted his eyes from concrete barrier to road to taxi.

'Can you walk?' Amir asked Estella.

'I can try.'

The taxi driver helped her up slowly. Limping, with Amir for support, she was able to make it to the barrier, where a few bystanders helped lift her up and over and placed her down on the fabric Amir had set out on the sidewalk.

Amir gave her some water. He had already tried to call Kade to tell him the location readings from the Tests were coming back garbled. On top of that, the experiment was attracting too much attention. There were too many people interested and he feared the police were going to shut him down before he could bring the Tests back—or worse, arrest him. Now Estella was causing even more commotion around the trial site. The man closest to them, dressed in an oversized blue shirt untucked over his loose grey chinos, looked worryingly like a *Basiji*. 'The police might come, Estella.'

'Amir, listen to me. Do you know why Kade got into this with you? Do you know what he's getting out of it? I don't think his vision for XYZT is the same as yours.'

Amir reeled at the mention of the four letters and, when he had regained his composure, pressed her urgently, 'How do you know X-Y-Z-T? How is it you are here, Stell?'

'The black box,' she blurted out. 'The hard drive.'

'Stell, you shouldn't have come. The plan has been brought

forward, Kade found the right contacts to make the technology viable. We met with Gary, our backer here in Iran. We refined the test procedure....'

'Listen to me.' Estella interrupted, impatiently. 'Kade is going to cut you out of the project. He'll just sell to the highest bidder, and who knows who that will be.'

Most of the crowd had dispersed. 'No, Stell, we planned this whole thing together. This will be truly revolutionary, for you... and for us.' He lowered his eyes as he removed her ill-fitting head covering, pretending it needed to be readjusted, but actually checking for blood. 'Kade found the money we needed to develop it. The gentleman has good intentions, he has a place in Iran.'

'I've seen the agreements he signed and your name isn't on any of them. Once this test run is successful, he's going to leave you in the dust.'

A nondescript couple came into view, picking their way through the thick traffic, the man lugging in his right hand a *chamedan* made of tanned animal hide and decorated with rough copper pins. The elderly woman took even paces on the other side of the suitcase as they moved closer.

Amir held Estella by the shoulders and looked her steadily in the eye. 'Stell, I'm sorry you had to get involved in this.'

The man with the chamedan barged forward like a locomotive, and the heavy case sideswiped Amir's hand as he passed.

'*Movaazeb baach*,' Amir called out.

'*Motasefam*,' the man responded apologetically and then moved away quickly.

Amir nodded, but remained confused by the incident. Maybe the guy didn't like that he was talking to a foreign woman.

'Give me the phone, I want to call Kade,' Estella said.

'That's not necessary.'

'It is!'

'Why did he send you here?'

'To make sure the trial is a success, so he gets what he wants. I'm telling you!'

Amir's hand felt hot where it had been scratched by the man's case. His mind flooded with all the suppressed suspicions of the last year. Defeated, he gave way and let Estella continue.

'This thing is already taking on a life of its own. The FBI's involved, and god knows who else. I've been followed. Do you think you'll be allowed to just do what you want with this thing, help your friends over here to take a vacation?'

Amir was sweating. It was difficult to concentrate on what Stell was saying. His mind shifted haphazardly. Regardless of his motives, Kade was right. The experiment had to continue. He had to get the rest of the voluntccrs to the US before time ran out. But when Tests started returning, would they hit the center of the road just like Estella did? He couldn't focus.

'Would you please calm down? People are looking,' Amir pleaded, as he ran his finger over the burning cut on his hand. With difficulty, he stood up and returned to his station.

Estella took a deep breath and silenced herself. As she watched Amir set off another Test on their way, she came to the conclusion that there was no more she could do. The two of them were hopeless idealists, each in their own way. Her presence would make no difference. She was just digging herself in deeper.

With a manufactured weakness in her voice, she said, 'Amir, I want to go back, I'm not feeling well. We can talk about it when you return to Boston.'

'Why don't you stay? After this I will take you to the bazaar. It is the most glorious time of the year to see it.'

'Sure, that sounds nice, but I don't think now is a good time. I should come later on a real visit.'

Amir wiped sweat from his forehead. For him, suggesting she should come to the bazaar was more daring than asking her out on a date. More than anything, he wanted to show her Tehran, but she was right. 'Iran is not a good place for you right now.'

She nodded, holding out her hand. 'It's for the best.'

He reset the bracelet and then, his impulsiveness overcoming his shyness, flung his arms around Estella.

Amir looked so pale and his body felt so weak that she returned his embrace, her head spinning. For a moment she allowed her eyes to close, her mind to empty, allowed herself to pretend that the simple warmth of his earnest fondness was all there was.

Amir's body dropped to one side, unbalanced, heavy. She opened her eyes and took his hands in hers to steady him. He was gasping, his face contorted as if frozen, a crimson thread trickling from the scratch on his hand. He struggled, barely able to form words.

'Amir, what happened?'

'...did this to me. Poison,' he said faintly.

'No.'

'Quiller memo...'

Amir was becoming delusional. He lurched back and forth as if about to fall.

'Who would do this? Iran or FBI?'

'Not Revolutionary Guard. Not Basiji. FBI...aren't in Iran. Get...out. You have all of XYZT. Do the right thing with it, bring us together.'

Poor Amir, naive to his last breath. He was going to die. Estella froze. Her perception shifted so that it seemed she was experiencing the whole scene from above. *Get the fuck out now.* With effort, she was able to force herself into motion, leaving Amir's body to slump to the ground as she sprinted for the underpass.

NAQSH-E JAHAN: PAYTEN

I already knew that Iran was separated off from the world. Most Americans don't go there—I'm not sure who does go there. And of course, I hadn't really believed that it would work.

But as soon as the bracelet tightens, I know what will happen. It all comes back to me as if it's a distant memory—not my own, but more like a scene that's been waiting for me to step into it.

When I arrive, she'll be ten feet away, coming at me fast, so tall and statuesque, the clear visor covering her face, a thin plastic band running around her head. As she turns I'll see where it tangles with her long curly auburn hair, at odds with her dark complexion. Her body will be fully covered in some kind of androgynous uniform in spite of the heat, which is already overwhelming me.

As soon as she is within reach, the towering figure will produce another shield from somewhere. 'Put this on flash-speed,' she'll urge me, passing me the lightweight plastic visor. I will notice the biohazard symbol carved into it at the bottom, smooth and frosted as Lalique. I'll fumble with the thing as I try to put it on over the headscarf the guy in New York gave me. *I'm meant to be having a meal with the Zadeh family.*

'Hurry please, you can't breathe the air here.' I'll see her shoot a glance down through the square.

My eyes will focus, but not on the task at hand. An abandoned plaza, massive in size, aged, sandy, and yet not totally decrepit. Signs of vegetation absent, but I'll be able to make out a mosque, or something like a mosque, on the other side. And then, above us, maybe a hundred feet up, I'll see it, stretching out in all directions—a translucent plane running parallel to the ground, one hundred feet above us. Constructions built up on top of it, as if its elevated surface were actually the ground, another ground, up above. A city in the air.

Once the mask is on, she'll cup the back of my head and the apparatus will suddenly contract, shrink-wrapping my cranium. A stream of air will rush into the space between the shield and my face.

No one else down here apart from the two of us. Far above, in the other place, I'll see the large structures slowly shifting above us, every one made from the same clear material. Plexiglass escalators will drop from the sky, leading off in all directions, a vision that would put Escher and Piranesi to shame, the movements of the buildings causing the reflections to cycle regularly, following their programmatic shifts. I'll see how the area where we stand is overshadowed, as if the city in the air is more important than the ground wc stand on.

With the mask on my face, I'll finally let my arms down, and breathe.

Moving closer, she'll address me. 'I didn't have time to introduce myself, I'm Tempel.'

'I'm...'

'Payten.' She'll say it for me, as if she, also, had already known I was coming. 'You still aren't safe. Nesf-e Jahan is contaminated. We need to get out of here before...come along.' She'll take my sleeve and I'll let her pull me to the outer edges of the square, then she will pass over a bracelet, not like the plastic one, reflective silver this time, sleeker and more high-tech. 'Put it on.'

Not exactly a warm welcome. Without having had time to react to the assault on my senses—the humidity, the strange visions around me, and Tempel herself—sensing that the situation must be urgent, I'll put on the bracelet as instructed, lining it up next to the other on my wrist. She'll pull out a black device and shine it at the bracelet, and I'll feel the band vibrate on my skin and contract to fit.

'Come along,' she'll repeat, and then drag me down an escalator entrance alongside an old brick wall. We'll move down, and in a matter of seconds I will feel those same sensations. For years after this, traveling this way will still give me the shivers. Chicken skin on my arms as the hair below my shirt's three-quarter sleeves stands up, row upon row of skin-bubbles.

We'll arrive in another place. 'You'll get used to existing,' Tempel will reassure me as she massages my shoulders, and then, registering my confusion, she'll spell it out: 'X-Y-Z-T-ing, Xing, moving through the continuum.'

Standing before me, she will remove her mask to reveal a strong-featured face. Maybe in her forties, still wearing thick black eyeliner around her eyes—Elizabeth Taylor in *Cleopatra,* but more exotic still.

'Can I take mine off too?' She'll nod, so I'll pull it off, longing to breathe some fresh air. Wrong—more like a plastics factory, a harsh chemical atmosphere. The headscarf will pull off with the mask and I'll try to unknot the bottom to put it back on.

She will gaze down at me. 'You don't need to wear a veil here, unless you want to.' She'll reach out to take the mask and scarf from me.

And only then will I realize: we are in the air city.

The place will be humming with activity, with many people out walking around. The plastic floor, while still transparent in many parts, will feel more solid up here. Like brutalist architecture but with concrete drab replaced by translucent sheen. The same material everywhere, the chemical aroma overpowering.

After letting me take everything in, Tempel will then say, 'We can't stop here. Some might not welcome your visit.'

'Who?'

'The remaining Hizbullahi and others.'

I won't understand. 'Stop,' I'll plead, desperate to get some hold on the situation.

She'll look at me, shaking her head. 'I'll explain when I can.'

She will keep a tight grip on my arm. As we walk, I'll notice how most of the people around me are hefty, bigger than I am, like my Host. Some look as if they are wearing a boxer's mouth-guard over their teeth, the skin above the mouth protruding.

I will notice one woman who passes us, her skin bulging above her lip as if from a bee sting.

'Why do they have that?'

'It's beautiful,' Tempel will say, simply.

'You don't have it.'

'Me, oh no.' She'll look embarrassed.

Still disoriented, I will ask 'Where are we...were we?'

'I told you, we were in Nesf-e Jahan, the place you were sup-posed to XYZT to, the old part of Isfahan that's no longer liv-able. You were displaced, just as we were told. We're in Naqsh-e Jahan now.'

We'll pick up the pace and turn down a street with a number of fast food shops: Spudulike, McDonald's, KFC, and others unfamiliar to me, Al Tazaj, Teremok, Sukiya. All with the same size three-foot sign above the door, the interiors through the windows sleek and anonymous. No cars, for the lanes are too narrow, but many pedestrians. Walking through this section I'll be reminded of a street market in Southeast Asia, the vendors tightly packed in, but without any goods on display or hanging around the stalls, only carts from which vendors pull items all wrapped in plain glossy white packaging. Without being able to tell what the goods are, I'll see the packages passed to custom-ers, glimmering from the constantly moving reflections thrown by the slow, majestic pivoting of the skyscrapers above. But no money will appear to change hands, and we'll pass by too speedily for me to catch any of the conversations.

'Rack rack. You've been spotted.' Tempel will dig her nails into my arm. 'Rack!'

I'll turn back and see that the plump vendor in the black jacket and hat is pressing his earpiece and yelling, his eyes locked on to us. The lane is not wide enough for us to pass together. I'll almost stumble and fall. She'll move out in front, barely breaking step, and I'll follow behind her, running for my life.

We'll turn down a side path, empty apart from the seedy vendors with their goods laid out on the ground. There will be no customers, and the men will be smoking or sipping drinks from polished bottles. We'll burst into a low-ceilinged place of business, lined with a few high-tech laptops and chairs—an internet café?—and Tempel will slam the door behind us. As the guy at the side of the room sitting under a *Singlezone* sign looks over, I'll realize that the place has been made partially private by flocked paper and hologram stickers haphazardly slapped over the walls but that, as usual, the floor below is translucent. I'll focus my eyes on the faded green-brown coloration way down below, in what must be old Isfahan.

'Have a seat.' Tempel will turn the chair around for me as if I'm going to get a haircut. She'll ask the guy, 'How grand?' and he'll mutter something in reply.

I'll look up at her. 'What are you doing?'

'Getting you a new fare.' Releasing my silver bracelet and switching it out for another, she'll type some characters into the clear plastic keyboard. 'Have to get it here so you aren't tracked. This fare is untraceable. Needs a grand payment.' Taking the scanner from the table, she'll aim and it will send another vibration through my new bracelet.

While she talks to the guy, I'll get on my hands and knees to get a better look at the earth below, peering down through the stack of icelike slabs. The guy will squint at me, wondering what I'm looking at, and then turn away towards the nearest laptop.

'Can you see the green river down there?' Tempel will ask, crouching down to join me.

What I'll see, spreading out below me, is a grid of brown land with churning green around the borders. Some cave-pits, holes blackening the ground and long-abandoned buildings, and a long strip of what looks like sand. A slew of surfaces, all hard to decipher through the plastic ice.

'Years ago the Zayanderud and other rivers dried up. You can see the Si-o-se Pol arched bridge, too...see it?' She gets down on the ground, taking her time to trace the outline of the long sandy bridge on the translucent floor with a distracted air, as if indulging in nostalgic childhood memories.

'Why is the river green?'

She will explain in hushed tones: 'The scientists and the municipality...they fucked it and messed with the natural flow of the water. Disaster.'

'What happened?'

'Just know it is one of the reasons why we are up here now, why old Isfahan is contaminated.'

'I've never read anything about this...this air city.' I'll tell her.

'You'd have no way of knowing about these things.' She'll move the overgrown bangs from my eyes, more touchy-feely than a New Yorker would be, making me uncomfortable.

'See, I was born late. I did not see America or the others fall, or the great Zagros quake. I've been fortunate to grow up in XYZT.' She pauses. 'I have seen nothing compared to many. Still, I can understand. When my grandparents escaped from Boston to come here, it was during the great acceleration. Isfahan became the technological powerhouse of the world. X was the new digital black gold. My mother was old enough to have seen many of the changes...to see what her mother had given birth to.'

Seeing that nothing she is saying makes any sense to me, she will bring her knees to her chest and lean in closer, and I will wonder whether I am correct in thinking that tears are about to form in the corners of her eyes. 'It's 8211L.L. now in Lulubian aeons. That's year 2098 by your calendar.'

I'm dreaming. Lucid dreaming again, I will think, and shift away from her, trying to suppress my anxiety.

'So you wonder how you are here. Well, let me tell you. The early XYZT was not yet reliable. The displacement ratio was high. Sometimes it was just a small change in longitude or latitude but other times it was a world of difference.'

None of this would be remotely believable if I wasn't sitting on this clear, almost invisible surface, hundreds of feet up, the vertiginous sensations multiplying the XYZT sickness.

She'll shake her head.

A tune will start to play on the guy's laptop. 'Better get out of here,' he'll say as he swings around and stares down at us.

Tempel will get up first, then help me stand.

Outside, we'll fly through the remainder of the alleyway, hitting a cross street where there is a station in sight. *Headed for another XYZT*, I'll think as she pulls me over to the entrance. Saying nothing, we will head down the curved Lucite tunnel encasing the escalator, my new bracelet vibrating as I descend.

I'll fare better this time, and will manage to focus more quickly when we arrive, further up again, in one of those glistening, swiveling skyscrapers.

'Have to keep moving you,' Tempel will say as she leads me over to the curved outer windows, and then onto the observation deck that runs around the exterior of the structure. We'll walk along the outer edge, the polymer odor intense. I'll look down again at the old city, but mostly I'll stare around me at Air City's buildings and the almost invisible floor spreading out to the horizon. She'll point out some stars in the sky, and tell me how they can be seen day and night. The lack of pollution up here allows it. I'll want to know where the cars are, and she'll tell me they don't need them anymore, and that the DMC-12s were the last to be recycled.

I'll ask if we can have a seat at the café to catch my breath, as the structure's rotation is just a little too fast, making me sick to my stomach.

'Only for a minute.' Tempel will guide me to a seat and will sit down herself, her body barely fitting on the undersized chair. I'll notice that she looks anxious and worn, even though she is still so much stronger than I am.

I'll try to focus on her face. The sun's glare will reflect from the surrounding surfaces, making her features flicker.

'You talk about up here and down there and the city's different names, I don't understand.'

'Naqsh-e Jahan replaces the old Isfahan nickname Nesf-e Jahan, which means "half the world". Isfahan was powerful. It had considerable influence over the new layout. But that is nothing new. The city had a long history of changing power structures. It swung from centralized to decentralized like a see-saw.'

'So what countries are in power today?'

'No countries as you know them, just one body called Naqsh-e Jahan worldwide.'

'So, what, the world is united and everything's fine? Doesn't seem like it.'

She will give a grim laugh. 'Correct. Democracy, cultural exchange, getting to know you—not so simple. You think there is such a thing as peaceful open communication and free exchange?'

'Just power games, then? And someone somewhere always profits from the tensions?'

'Believe me, the Iranians lived with that reality for many

decades, as did the Americans. But however much control there is, the outside calls to us too, and it causes disturbances, fevers...'

I will not understand, and she will know it.

'Perfect communication is a dream, sure, but dreams have real effects too. Amir and Kade both misunderstood this.' She won't leave me the time to ask who these people are she is talking about. 'This is something *Naneh*—my grandmother—used to say. You can't travel without creating some interference. For years we dreamt each other as enemies, but when she brought us into XYZT, it opened up new dreams.'

Even here at the center, the rotation will continue to disorient me. And I will remain dumbfounded.

'Some things are better left unsaid.' She'll bite her lip as she gazes over at me.

And I will sit trying to process this all, overcome by a sense of déjà vu.

After a long while Tempel will look toward the observation deck. The sky will turn faster, the room will darken. 'Angry skies,' she will announce, looking worried. She will get up and I will follow.

As we head over to the escalator bank, I'll see people going down, some disappearing calmly from view as if they were at the mall, others winking out instantaneously like glitches in a badly edited film. I'll wonder to myself where those ones went.

Then thunder. So loud, it will hurt my ears.

Tempel will say, 'In Naqsh-e Jahan I could show you our present day schools or hospitals, or the Leiurus-Giganto power plants, but I want to take you somewhere else.'

This time I won't feel troubled by XYZTing, it will feel as though I have been doing it my entire life, like riding a bike. We will land in another part of Air City, the floor translucent but surrounded by the sandy type of building material I saw down in old Isfahan. We'll enter an open area surrounded by old constructions including two giant statues, one on each side of a stone stairway.

She will notice me looking at the statues towering above us, which resemble bulls with the heads of bearded men, and will stop to explain to me.

'They are the old Lamassus that stood outside Persepolis as part of the Gate of All Nations. Moved here to be the protectors of the main gate of new Isfahan before Naqsh-e Jahan united under XYZT. They are regarded by many former Iranians as the main gate of the world.'

'How did they get these statues up here?'

She will laugh, shaking her head. 'You Americans never were anything but children. The Egyptians had their secrets, and so do we. For now, that's what they will remain for you. There's no time to explain.'

'There are a lot of people out. Tomorrow is Easter.'

For once Tempel's grin will be unforced. 'Holidays! If we had adopted those, there'd be one every day of the year. We've got to get across the main gate court. Can you do that?'

'What do you need me to do?'

She won't answer but will just start running. I'll follow behind as we sprint through curving paths, in a maze resembling a hall of mirrors made of layers and layers of plastic so that the doorways can't be made out easily. It will be clear she knows the way by heart as we twist around obstacles without making a single wrong turn.

Suddenly Tempel will scream, 'The Hizbullahi!'

I will glance back to see three figures all in black, not far behind. 'Do they have guns?'

'...for the museums. Keep running.'

I'll see them gaining on us and, for the second time that day, I will run for my life. They will trail us for blocks as the heat gradually eats away at what little stamina I have left. We will manage to get far enough ahead to dart down an escalator entrance and XYZT before they make it to the entrance.

'I think we lost them.' Tempel will take out a handkerchief and offer it to me. She'll tell me we are in a residential neighborhood, but all I will see is high gates blocking every building.

After a long walk, she will hold her arm up to one of the gates. It will slide open. 'Come along. We have to get you somewhere safe.'

We will walk into a residence with a small courtyard between the gate and the house. Inside, all neutral, translucent walls and icy floor. She will lead me into a storage room and block the door from inside, then motion to me to sit with her on the floor at the center of the small room.

Even with my disorientation and fear, I will feel safe for the moment. As my eyes glance from wall to wall I will realize how a trained eye can pick out a multitude of colors in what at first glance looks to be the same translucent tint.

And I'll think to myself: *Either I'm totally out of my mind, in the most vivid dream I've ever experienced—too many fantasy novels—or....* I will say to myself, *in any case, it must be three hours now.*

'How did you know I was coming? What happened to the Zadehs?'

She will survey my face in silence as if assessing my capacity to understand what she has to say. 'Buried on the outskirts of town years ago, I'm sure. Not important.'

Suddenly fear will overcome me. 'I'll get back home, right?'

She'll pause. 'They've always said so....*Naneh Bozorg* brought us into XYZT, but she needed your help—that's what we were always told...' Cutting herself off mid-sentence, Tempel will gaze at me with some impossible combination of awe and sympathy as we sit huddled on the floor. She will try to comfort me, to calm me with her eyes.

It won't work. The tears will begin to come, I'll try to make them stop but they will keep coming. She will begin to reach out to me only to shrink back, regarding me from a distance.

'Don't cry over burned rice.'

EMERGING FROM THE MSG escalator, Estella found Kade's spot, but he was gone, as if he had never been there. The area was full of passers-by, but no one took any notice of her. She headed towards the exit. A short distance from the experiment site she spotted a crimson trail on the concrete, its axis recording the direction of the wind. *Kade too. Is this what they meant by mitigated?*

Heading east in Manhattan, she tried to gather her composure, to understand what had happened and what her part in it had been. She wasn't sure whether the high of the XYZT was still affecting her, but somehow everything around her seemed to have shifted, and reality unfolded in a new way for her.

Kade and Amir had been living in entirely different worlds. Now Estella had decisions to make. She reached into her bag: the black box was there.

ACKNOWLEDGEMENTS

To the novel's first editor Kiernan Michau, you know well how you helped me put *XYZT* into a working format. Thank you to my longtime friend and editor Robin Mackay for having not only an interest in philosophy but a secret passion for 'airport novels'.

Oliver B. Harris, I am grateful for your support of *XYZT* and advice which came at a time when they were really needed. Thanks Amy Ireland, Tessa Laird, Brian Rogers and Katherine Pickard for your thoughts and suggestions. Peter Wolfendale, your vast knowledge of any subject from theory, to sci-fi, to D&D, to culinary delights made me gladly hand over the manuscript for you to pick apart. A very special thanks to China Miéville for sending all of your books snail mail to Iran. As a group they were wildly inspirational. Like all Iranians deprived of good and timely materials, we slowly savored and enjoyed these books.

To Nahid, Mohammad, Neda, Ehsan, Merhdad, Susan and Suzan for being there for me when I was living in Shiraz. If it was only as easy as putting on a bracelet....

Lastly, thank you RN for all your shadiness.

K-Pulp: New Adventures in Theory-Fiction

Also available

SIMON SELLARS
APPLIED BALLARDIANISM
MEMOIR FROM A PARALLEL UNIVERSE

A brilliantly written genre mashup ... a wonderfully original mix of cultural theory, literary exegesis, travelogue and psychopathological memoir.
The Guardian

Everything connects to Ballard...

Fleeing the excesses of '90s cyberculture, a young researcher sets out to systematically analyse the obsessively reiterated themes of a writer who prophesied our disorienting future: J.G. Ballard, voluptuary of the car crash, surgeon of the pathological virtualities pulsing beneath the reality's surface.

Defeated by obsessive fears and the stultifying tedium of academia, yet still certain that *everything connects to Ballard*, his thesis collapses into a series of delirious travelogues, deranged speculations and tormented meditations on time, memory and loss. Renouncing all scholarly distance, he finally accepts the deep assignment that has plagued him throughout his life, and embarks on a rogue fieldwork project: *Applied Ballardianism*.

Only the darkest impulses and the most apocalyptic paranoia can uncover the technological mutations of inner space....

ISBN 978-0-9